Her Duke at Midnight

Mythic Dukes
Book 3

Wendy LaCapra

A governess and her secret take an invincible duke by storm...

The Duke of Hurtheven will stop at nothing to protect those he loves. So, when a mysterious new governess captures his godchild's affection, he vows to uncover her secrets. Instead, she sets him aflame.

Miss Hera Bythesea accepted a governess position to secure the character reference she needs to reclaim her secret child. But she did not count on Hurtheven—curious, relentless, and temptation in human form.

In Hera's world, Hurtheven faces a challenge his power and wealth cannot solve. But for the love of unwed mother and child, he'll undertake any Herculean Labor.

Publisher:

Wendy LaCapra

http://www.wendylacapra.com/

Facebook * Twitter * Goodreads * Pinterest * Newsletter

Cover design by The Midnight Muse

Developmental Editing by Lindsey Faber & Copy Editing by Louisa Cornell

Ebook ISBN: 978-0-9994253-4-3

Manufactured in the United States of America

First Edition April 2024

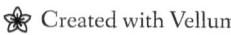 Created with Vellum

For Richard
Fight, fight, fight!

Chapter One

"Evil appears as good in the minds of those whom God leads to destruction." - Sophocles' Antigone

"Less than a mile to go, Horace," the Duke of Hurtheven gently urged his hired horse further up the path to his friend Ashbey's seat. The horse neighed in protest but then yielded to the duke's will. Most things did...*eventually*.

The duke understood the horse's reluctance. He, too, was road-weary, with quavering thighs and joints pulsing with pain, and the path he'd chosen—the more direct, but ancient entry—was less easy to navigate than Wisterley Castle's newer, Repton-designed drive. But a promised visit was a promised visit, especially to his godchildren.

He intended to deliver.

As he advanced through weeds left to wild à la the picturesque, the castle's stone tower rose menacingly from a Hawthorne hedge. Truth be told, he preferred an aspect with menace, even if the morning's bright skies rather ruined the effect. A duke going about his business in daylight tended to be noticed, what with the livery and such.

Which was why Hurtheven preferred night. And rain. And any other atmospheric condition that offered a challenge while repelling the masses.

He analyzed the trees for inverted leaves, then tested the air for the slightest breeze. *No.* Not even a hint of threatening weather. Disappointing, really. Every storm, real or metaphoric, offered yet another chance to test himself against life's vagaries. Test himself, and win.

Of course.

Two lightning strikes had, in fact, forged his life.

The first, at age nine—a literal, blinding current flashed through his father's carriage, sparing him, though not, benumbingly, his parents. The second, figurative, this time, at sixteen—the sight of a silver-blond woman stunned him to stillness before rushing onward, sending heart-pounding fervor crackling through his veins.

But his long-subdued emotions had roared back to life only to blister beneath his skin, because, in the same moment, the young lady had been equally and mutually captivated by the man standing to his right—his dear friend Cheverley.

Since then, Hurtheven dared the heavens every possible chance, never content to simply anticipate a third life-altering event.

Playing both Heracles and Eurystheus, he'd chosen "labors" that both strengthened him and sharpened the lessons he prized: Keep your friends close. Keep your secrets closer. And stay closed and coiled—always anticipating the next devastating strike.

Schooling his features, he handed off his hired horse to one of Ashbey's grooms with a curt nod of thanks. He emerged into the light, wiping the back of his gloved wrist across his sweat-damp forehead. In the distance, dozens of people milled about the gracefully sloping lawn.

Damnation. Ashbey's annual garden party. How could he have forgotten?

He spotted Ashbey in the distant clearing. Ash's wife Alicia was by his side, and, with them, the third member of Hurtheven's school-day triumvirate, Cheverley, now the Duke of Ithwick. Chev's wife Penelope, though not in view, was doubtless present. Chev hardly went anywhere without Penelope.

Not anymore.

"Now *there's* an interesting expression."

Penelope's voice trickled over his skin, sweet as summer rain.

"I'd forgotten about the party." He turned.

Silhouetted by Ashbey's Castle and looking as majestic as the mythical Queen of Ithaca whose name she bore, Pen advanced up the pathway, both hands outstretched.

"Ah." She smiled tenderly. "You know, I had the strangest feeling you were the lone rider I saw making his way up the old castle trail."

Of course she had. And, of course, she would be the one to greet him—with him smelling of horse and scowling down at Ashbey's guests, no less.

He recoiled, flexing mud-stiffened gloves. "I'm afraid I'm not in any state—"

"Never mind that." She grasped his hands through worn leather. "I may be a duchess, but I'm still a pig farmer's daughter. Besides"—she brushed a feather-light

3

kiss against his cheek—"it's been an age. How good to see you!"

"It's good to see *you*, as well," he replied. His heart spasmed.

Too good, so it seemed.

"You didn't write." She searched his eyes. "Chev has been worried about you, you know."

He *had* written. He just hadn't *sent*—a crucial part of his plan to use his time at the Congress of Vienna to finally and permanently sever the unrequited cord.

Yes, his initial attraction to Pen had been beyond his control—fate-the-trickster's play. But when Chev had been lost at sea and believed dead by everyone, himself included, *he*, not fate, had proposed marriage to Chev's wife.

Pen had forgiven him. As for forgiving himself...

He dropped her hands and took a deliberate step back.

"Well..." He cleared his throat. "My presence at the Congress was in constant demand."

"Oh, I see." Her brows rose playfully. "Heaven forbid the world turn without your by-your-leave." She leaned in. "Now, how was Vienna, *really*?"

He closed his eyes, immediately drawn back into the shadows of the old city.

What could he say that would succinctly capture the intrigue, the life-and-map-altering decisions shaped by backstabbing and ever-shifting alliances—not only in official meetings, but in bedrooms and ballrooms?

And what of the people? Each ruthlessly bargaining to retain every possible power? People like the now-disgraced prince Karl? Hurtheven had caught him secreting double-crossing letters in a doll the prince then claimed belonged to his daughter.

How selfish did a man have to be to put treason on the head of a child?

He sighed. "Vienna was war-ravaged and yet glittering. A gathering of kings and emperors likely to remain unrivaled for centuries."

"So the papers said." She tilted her head. "But that doesn't tell me much about *your* experience."

"My experience..." He echoed, resting his gaze on the horizon.

Despite the complications that arose and the rather unsavory role he'd been tasked to play behind the scenes, threatened invasion no longer menaced the blue-grey channel waters shifting lazily in the sun—*that* was something.

Great Britain was safe. His *friends* were safe.

"I'm happy for peace," he added.

"But are *you* happy?" she asked.

Happy. He sniffed.

For himself, certainly not. *Happy* was not an objective, no matter what the unhinged Americans had written in their Declaration.

"I am grateful the war ended." A hellish spring, beginning with Napoleon's escape from exile, had turned into a bloody summer. "Despite the limitations and concessions of the Congress, order has been restored and a Bourbon is once again on the throne." He forced a smile. "Though the peace, I imagine, will render any skills I have acquired about as useless as a frigate run aground."

"Useless? You? Never." She threaded her arm through his.

He braced for a surge of physical longing. Surprisingly, desire did not come.

What did this absence of feeling mean?

5

Could his initial response to her have been roused, not, as he'd assumed, by the scars of love long denied, but merely by the sight of a dear friend, deeply missed?

Had this particular "labor" been successful after all?

"Worry not." She doubled back toward the castle, pulling him along. "Soon enough, you'll be embroiled in yet another puzzle that you and you alone must solve."

He glanced askance. "Am I being mocked?"

"Of course you are," she replied.

All remaining discomfort evaporated in the warmth of her cheerful expression. He *was* content to be home. Or, at least in a place where he needn't stand on ceremony.

His friends knew his flaws, and yet they took him into their safe hands, chaff and grain together. Despite all that had passed—and perhaps because of it, as well—Ash, Alicia, Chev, and Pen were family.

Family he'd chosen.

And, of course, there were the children.

He lightened his tone. "I didn't ride a rented horse all the way from the ferry to talk about myself"—he flashed a smile—"much as you know I enjoy the topic. Tell me—how *are* my godchildren?"

"My Thaddeus grows more like his father every day." Her eyes sparkled with maternal pride. "He's taller than Chev, now, can you believe?"

"Truly? I had no idea a boy of sixteen could sprout so much in so short a time."

"Like a magic beanstalk." She thrust her free arm upward. "As for Ash and Alicia's wee ones, both seem head over heels for the woman that came to care for them after their nursemaid's abrupt departure just before Christmas last year—Mrs. Montrose."

"Ah, yes." He lifted a brow. "The *incomparable* Mrs. Montrose."

"You've heard of her?"

"The children's last letter mentioned little else." And yet Alicia's note contained nothing of true substance about the woman.

She slowed her steps. "You sound wary. Why?"

He did not relish the thought of *any* unknown person newly and closely attached to his circle—especially one who had arrived in his absence. "Children do not normally accept a stranger so quickly, do they?"

She considered. "In my experience, they do. And they tend to be good judges of character, too. Thaddeus never trusted any of my would-be suitors, the ones who overran Ithwick Castle in Chev's absence. But when Chev returned in disguise, Thaddeus liked him immediately."

He made a sound of disapproval. "Your experience with strangers should make you more concerned, not less."

"Should it?" Penelope tilted her head thoughtfully before wrinkling her nose. "*Everyone* likes Mrs. Montrose, not just the children. She's not only competent, she's also good natured and kind..." She paused, a slight crease between her brows.

"But...?"

"At times, I *have* thought I noticed a certain wistfulness about her expression." She flashed him a quelling look. "However, I could have been mistaken. Ash and Alicia consider themselves quite lucky to have found reliable help on such short notice."

"Do they, now?" He didn't believe in that sort of luck, and his suspicious nature was part of what made him successful in all his endeavors.

Anything *too* convenient should always be suspect.

Intriguing, too, this *wistfulness*. "What led to the departure of their nursemaid?"

Pen shrugged. "Her mother contracted some sort of illness, and the family requested she return home as soon as possible. Mrs. Montrose is"—she paused for emphasis—"*admittedly* more suited to the position of governess than nursemaid, but Alicia considers that an advantage. Fee will need a governess soon—she'll be six next month."

Six! "And how did they find this Mrs. Montrose?"

"I believe she and Alicia were introduced through Alicia's charity work—"

He grunted.

"—*and* Alicia is acquainted with Mrs. Montrose's family, which is good enough for me, and *should* be good enough for you, too."

When he did not immediately agree, she shook her head.

"You are the most cynical man I know. You don't trust anyone besides Chev and Ash."

"It's who I am."

"No," she replied. "It's who you choose to be."

A distinction without a difference, in his opinion. She knew him well—as did his friends—but, no matter what the game, on matter of principle, he never revealed his whole hand. Not even to those he loved the most.

Besides, why shouldn't he be wary?

Felicia and Delmare were his godchildren. If his own godfather had not regarded the role as a grave responsibility, where would he be?

Aural memory rang in his ears.

First, the sound of rain pinging against glass. Then, the squeak of an upended carriage wheel uselessly revolving in a raging wind. Finally, a voice—*his* voice—screaming out in terror and pain.

Again, he settled his gaze on the horizon, this time, just above the top of the castle tower.

The suffocating sensation would pass. It always did. He refocused on the present with a silent, but deep, inhale.

Pen was, doubtlessly, correct. He had no real reason to mistrust his friends' choice, just an instinctive sense of unease. But not having a definitive reason for concern certainly didn't preclude him from investigating the nursemaid's past on his own.

He nodded as if Pen had convinced him to let the topic go. "Alicia has a good friend in you."

"Well"—Pen arched a brow—"with you and Chev and Ash as close as you are, we ladies must stick together. In fact, when *you* fall in love and marry—which, by the by, it's high time you should consider doing—our numbers will finally be—"

"Please," he interrupted. Pen was the last person with whom he'd choose to discuss marriage. A decade and a half of denied feelings had been torture enough. "At least let me make myself presentable before you start planning my nuptials."

"Oh, very well, Spoilsport." She released his arm. "I should return to the festivities, anyway."

"Which begs the question...just what *were* you doing wandering around outside the stables?"

She sighed. "If you must know, I was interrupting a tryst."

"You're not serious!"

She nodded. "I didn't think much when Thaddeus disappeared. But then the eldest daughter of the Earl of Witford headed toward the house. I had just sent them back to the party alone, each in a different direction, when I spotted you coming up the drive."

"Thaddeus would never do anything dishonorable."

"Not intentionally, no. Consequences, however, aren't first in the mind of someone sixteen years of age."

"As you and Chev well know," Hurtheven murmured.

"Do not"—Pen cast him a warning glance—"remind me."

"Go, then. I will be down as soon as I'm presentable—but don't tell anyone I've arrived just yet. I'd like to surprise Chev and Ash."

She squeezed his arm before releasing him. "Welcome home, Hurtheven."

"Thank you, Pen," he replied sincerely.

Her enveloping scent faded as her figure swished down the lane.

Suddenly, he, too, was a youth again, watching a sleepy blacksmith in Gretna Green say the words which placed her forever beyond his reach.

Not that he would change things, even if he could. He'd made his choice all those years ago—friendship over love.

And thank God Pen had never truly given up on finding her lost husband. If she had, she might have accepted Hurtheven's proposal, and then, when Chev had miraculously returned from his ordeal, Hurtheven would have lost Chev twice—a thought too disturbing to contemplate.

He turned back onto the path and trudged onward toward the castle.

Cheverley and Pen. Ash and Alicia. Happiness all around. *So. Much. Happiness.*

But for him?

...when you fall in love and marry...

Another heart spasm.

Although fond of female company, he simply couldn't picture either. The only time he'd fallen in love had cost him only pain, embarrassment, and regret. He'd no wish to risk a second blunder. And no one besides Pen had ever tempted him to risk his heart—*if* he was even capable any longer.

As for marriage... Well, he'd been alone so long the state had become habitual. And leg-shackling himself to some innocent likely to be awed and deferential and obedient, but never able to mean more to him than Penelope, did not seem fair, although an heir was, of course, an eventual necessity.

He shifted his thoughts to a more comfortable vein—specifically, the unearthing of mysteries, the solving of conundrums...

He paused to survey the rear of the castle, sweeping his gaze across the kitchen gardens, to Alicia's rose bushes, and then, to the more distant cedar labyrinth.

All conundrums were in want of solving, were they not?

Large conundrums. Small. *Domestic*, even...

Like a mysterious new nursemaid who appeared through some loose charity connection and immediately and intimately ingratiated herself into the household of his once infamously reclusive friend.

Now *she* was a conundrum ready to be solved. And investigating her past a worthy effort...certainly less complex—and disturbing—than the contemplation of love and marriage.

* * *

"Lady Felicia!" Miss Hera Bythesea, or, as her charges knew her, Mrs. Montrose, sing-songed her youngest charge's

11

name. Then, she paused in the doorway and huffed under her breath, "*Fee!*"

Felicia-sized footprints appeared in the muddied grass just outside the castle kitchen. Hera followed them through the herb garden. *She* stopped at the freshly tilled earth's edge...the footprints, however, continued onto the more elaborate grounds.

Grounds where Felicia's ducal parents and their glittering guests mingled, enjoying the rare experience of coastal sun.

On any other day, Hera would have forced herself to look on the bright side. She might have even *celebrated* the cleverness behind Felicia's subterfuge. But for Felicia to disappear on the day of the Duke and Duchess of Ashbey's grand garden party?

Hera caught her lip between her teeth.

Disaster.

On a shaky inhale, she considered her options. If she continued into the gardens, she might happen on someone she recognized.

Or worse, someone who recognized her.

Fretting, on the other hand, would not keep Fee from harm. She forged onward, sidling toward the rose bushes. At least her frock had a greenish tint. With any luck, her white cap, if seen from a distance, would be mistaken for a cluster of roses.

"Fe-*li*-cia!"

She listened but heard only undulating peals of incoherent society gossip. As a small child, Hera had found the sound of finely dressed gentry chattering amongst themselves comforting, even pleasant.

Now she knew what they really represented—inherent threat.

She looked away from the party, scanning the hedge for any sign of her youngest charge. How, *how* had the duchess convinced her taking over the position of nursemaid in the Duke of Ashbey's household was the answer to her desperate prayers?

Well, there was her answer. *Desperate.* Nothing good ever came from a decision made in desperation, as she, of all people, should have learned by now.

She rested her forehead against her fist.

You just feel like you're going to break apart. You won't. You can't. Swelling panic was nothing more than a wave in the ocean. She breathed in deep, imagining the wave cresting, breaking, and then fizzing back into gentle swirls.

When she'd taken on Lady Felicia and her nine-year-old brother, Lord Delmare, she'd assumed she could manage them much as she had her half-brother's offspring, and, after them, the children of Prince Karl Wilhelm Albert of the Electorate of Heinenberg.

She'd seen herself taking the duchess's little lord and lady under her protective wings and lavishing on them all the unused care that had been festering inside of her like a neglected wound since the night she'd had to make the most difficult choice of her life.

A night just a few weeks prior to the duchess's appearance as her slightly tardy guardian angel.

The duchess had assured Hera she'd make every effort to assist—including providing a position and then the necessary glowing reference to prove Hera had "reformed." And she'd also promised Hera, on successful resolution of their combined efforts, a small stipend.

If all went well, by summer's end, Hera would be living in rented rooms in the village near the Wisterley estate, healed, safe, and with her prize.

Sound reasoning, that.

But what if, instead, she became the infamous nurse-maid who lost the Duke of Ashbey's beloved daughter? The duchess would withdraw her support and the board of directors would deny her petition.

Breathe in. Breathe out.

Felicia hadn't been snatched up by nefarious persons unknown, or gotten lost in the wood, or ruined the party. She'd merely escaped the schoolroom. All Hera had to do was find the termagant—a-hem—*darling child*, persuade her to come along quietly, and then sneak back into the house with no one the wiser.

While dozens of guests and an almost equal number of servants milled about.

Right.

The alternative, however, was to admit defeat. And no matter how many pernicious reversals life had already dealt her in her quarter century, the one thing she could count on was her own competence.

Keeping a watchful eye on the crowd mingling over by the pavilion, she crept along a length of the duchess's prized roses. From the edge of the bushes Fee's footprints meandered, not toward the party but the cedar maze.

She sighed.

If the guests remained in their clusters and she rushed quickly across the open space, she'd be able reach the maze with no one the wiser. She lifted her skirt to mid-calf and tucked the fabric into the ties of her apron. Then, the sound of rustling gowns grew more pronounced.

She ducked back down.

"Ah." A woman. "You were absolutely correct, Lady Adelaide. The scent *is* divine. Why, the aroma is *almost* appealing enough to cover the stench of Ashbey's past."

The woman and her companion tittered.

"Darling Elizabeth," Lady Adelaide scolded, "you mustn't say such things. In the end, our host found someone his equal...in scandal, if not in consequence."

As the ladies laughed again, Hera's heart seized.

She'd known, of course, that Ashbey's father had been tried, though not convicted, of murder. She'd also known that, for years, Ashbey had shunned society and lived as a recluse. But that was before his marriage to the war widow of a celebrated naval captain.

Before Lord Delmare and Lady Felicia.

Before Wisterley's garden parties.

He was quite respectable now.

Wasn't he?

"Oh, *my*!" Lady Adelaide exclaimed. "Could that be...? Yes! I am *sure* that is the Duke of Hurtheven!"

Hurtheven.

His name was a second blow. This one knocked her off her heels. She touched the earth—damp and clammy—to restore her balance. Although she'd never met the man, Felicia and Delmare talked about the duke incessantly. He held the same exalted rank as the children's father, but, to them, Hurtheven might as well have been a god.

Perhaps not *God* himself—the children would never be blasphemous—but of indisputable celestial origin...supremely powerful with ubiquitous cognizance.

Like Zeus, for instance. She scowled. The *last* thing *any* Hera needed was a Zeus.

"Where?" The one called Elizabeth asked breathlessly.

"Over there by the hedge. He's..." Lady Adelaide's voice lowered in disgust, "*crouching*."

Hera leaned to the right, just enough to catch sight of a man's trailing greatcoat. But the man could not possibly be

15

Hurtheven. A *duke* would not be on his knees, crawling along a hedge in the middle of a garden party, would he?

Not unless—*Oh, no.*

"That's *definitely* Hurtheven," the other woman cooed. "He's always been...unconventional."

"Unconventional? *Please.* To have survived as he did when his parents perished in such an unusual fashion *had* to have been a matter of unnatural luck. For years there have been rumors. I believe them. He is the devil incarnate."

"Adelaide!"

"Is calling a fig a fig and a trough a trough a crime? Besides his own exploits, those he chooses to keep as friends should be enough to condemn him."

"You're just angry that he hasn't called on you since—"

An unholy wail interrupted the conversation, washing Hera in a cold sweat.

"Got you, Fee!" The timbre of the duke's voice rang dissonant against a second high-pitched squeal.

Frozen in horror, Hera watched as he swept up a now-laughing little cluster of arms and legs and rose to his feet.

Heavens, he was tall. And large. Shockingly so. His gaze fixed on the ladies, his eyes so black, Hera wondered if they lacked irises. Even holding an impish child couldn't make his presence less intimidating.

You think too much of other people. She heard the words in Karl's clipped accent. *You must remember...we are all just pawns.*

She fortified herself with a deep inhale. Her perfect plan may have hit a rub or two. But she could pivot like a well-trained horse and still come out all right. She had to.

Her life wasn't the only one on the line anymore.

Hope for her deepest desire—the very reason she took

this position—flared so painfully she blinked. Immediately, she forced the feeling away—back, for now, into the same lockbox with her memories and her aspirations.

Alright, Karl. We're chess pieces—bone without flesh or spirit moving about in an endless game. What does it matter, so long as we move to our advantage?

...as I moved against you.

Hurtheven stepped between the ladies and the rose bushes.

"Be off," he said.

"Hurtheven, I—" Lady Adelaide began.

"Off, he repeated.

With twin gasps of indignation, the women scuttled back across the lawn.

Impressive. Arrogantly, *horribly* impressive.

Suspicion confirmed. Hera knew everything she ever needed to know about the duke, now...and intended to interact with him as little as possible. She lifted herself to her feet as quietly as she could and then turned away.

"I didn't mean you."

He was close enough for his breath to raise gooseflesh on her neck. Who could steal up behind a person so quickly and not make a sound? A devil incarnate, that was who.

No matter. She squared her shoulders. She'd faced devils before.

She swiveled around with as much dignity as she could muster. "There you are!" She addressed Felicia. "I'm very disappointed in you, young lady."

Felicia chewed her lip, glancing between her nursemaid and the duke. With eyes wide and innocent, she wrapped her arm more tightly around the duke's neck.

"You must be the *incomparable* new nursemaid." Hurtheven's tone suggested he found her anything but.

"Indeed." Though she dropped a quick curtsy, she made certain her tone revealed her own disdain. "I'm afraid, however, *you* have me at a loss."

"Do I?" He revealed a line of white, even teeth in neither a smile, nor a sneer, but a chilling combination of the two.

"Well"—she wet her lips—"I imagine I would remember if we'd been introduced."

"Of course you would."

Ugh. The arrogance. Her initial assessment had, of course, been correct.

Well, if he wasn't going to own up to being a duke, she needn't treat him as one. She fixed a level gaze on him and held out her arms. "If I might have my charge, Mr.—?"

He did not immediately reply. In fact, he didn't speak until the tendons on the back of her knees started to quiver. A useful silence, Karl had called that trick. But she could no longer be tricked. She kept her expression patient, pleasant.

The duke returned his attention to the child. "Hurt?"

Fee scoffed. "No."

The duke exhaled, holding her close for a significant moment.

Hera inhaled sharply. Hot embarrassment prickled in her neck as if she were witnessing something she ought not. He'd been *genuinely* frightened.

"Fee," the duke addressed the child, "you must go back inside...and stay there."

Her little fingers dug into his skin. "Can't I stay with you?"

He angled his head to meet her gaze and his expression softened. "Ah, but if you *do* stay with me, you'd have to be a proper lady and greet every one of your father's guests."

Fee dropped her jaw, widened her eyes, and then violently shook her head.

"I didn't think so." He touched her nose. "Now, you go back upstairs, and I promise I'll be up to see you when the party is finished."

Fee pouted. "You've been gone for*ever*."

He nodded. "An interminable amount of time, I agree. And I *missed* you every day—"

No. *No.* She would not reconsider her judgement of the man just because he looked into Felicia's eyes with tenderness and spoke to her as if she were the most important thing to him in the world.

"—An hour longer is all I ask. Surely the party guests will be leaving by midafternoon. And, if you go quietly, and Mrs. Montrose tells me you've been good, I promise presents tonight."

Fee considered. "*Good* presents?"

"The best, of course." Fleetingly, he met Hera's gaze over Fee's head. "They're from me, aren't they?"

Hera bit back a groan.

"You *do* give good presents." Felicia nodded. "I'll go."

"And be good?" he prompted.

"And be good." She parroted.

"That's my girl." He kissed Fee's forehead before planting her on her feet.

As Hera reached out to take Fee's hand, her arm brushed his, singeing her flesh. *Fire and brimstone.*

"I trust"—he spoke as if *she* were the errant child—"you will not to lose her again."

"Of course not. She's promised *you* to be *good*." Hera matched his authoritative baritone with her best no-nonsense nursemaid voice. "Good day."

Her still-tucked-up skirts may have belied her bravado,

19

but she turned and walk back to the house, head held high. *All will be well.*

"Mrs. Montrose?"

She stopped.

"That *is* your name?"

His voice dripped with undisguised suspicion.

She glanced back over her shoulder. *How* had he discovered her surname was false? Or—she narrowed her eyes—was he just guessing?

"Why would I lie about my name?" she asked.

"Why, indeed." He lifted a brow, not in the least cowed nor convinced by her insouciance. "I was merely making sure I remembered correctly."

She smiled, briefly and innocently. "Allow me to reassure you...your memory is sound." She tilted her head in a pitying manner. "My father had trouble remembering things in his later years, too."

Without waiting to see his reaction, she returned her gaze to the door and quickened her pace.

Obviously, all was not going to be well.

She could carefully advance across this checkered board while employing every ounce of competence and skill she possessed and *still* find herself ruthlessly knocked aside. This man wasn't a pawn. He wasn't even a rook, a knight, or a king.

This man was *the player.*

And his presence challenged everything.

Chapter Two

A resonant hum droning in Hurtheven's mind spread outward from his shoulders until even his toes prickled. He'd wanted challenge. Challenge had obligingly answered his call. He cleared his mind with a forceful headshake.

How long had he been standing there, staring at the closed door? One minute? Two?

Double damnation.

What was *wrong* with him today?

He'd bungled the dates of Ash's party. He'd ruminated on parts of his past best forgotten. He'd reacted to Pen—initially, anyway—as strongly as ever.

Excessive dread—and then anger bordering on rage—had seized him when he'd caught sight of Fee's slight form wandering alone in a hedge, reminding him of the way he'd been found after his parents' accident. And now, a single, over-the-shoulder glance from his godchildren's nursemaid —accompanied by a scathing bit of mockery—had rendered him mute.

And, if he were to be honest, electrified.

Utter madness. His journey had ended. *Breathe.* His reaction to Pen had tempered as they'd spoken. *Breathe.* Fee was safe. *Breathe.* And insubstantial memories could not harm him.

As for the nursemaid...

He frowned down at the mud bubbling up around his boots before slogging over to the kitchen steps. Which only *happened* to be in the direction *she'd* gone.

...Impertinent little minx.

Then again, *little* was hardly an apt description of the woman. She'd been tall. And, though not in the first flush of youth, far younger than he'd expected.

How young had she been?

Well, younger than himself, certainly. Which, devil take it, wasn't as uncommon as it used to be. He braced himself against the kitchen doorframe and scraped his sole across a bar fastened to the walkway. Leather rasped against metal as the damp gravel peeled away in thick, ugly clumps.

So, the nursemaid was tall, and youthful, and—*oh, very well*—comely. With a scandalously tucked up skirt and a clear, perceptive, deeply distrustful, blue gaze. And one, temptingly errant, red curl.

He sighed.

One, *molten lava* curl, spiraling out from beneath the confines of her hideous cap, left to waft lightly against her skin. Skin raised with gooseflesh and marred by a blush of heightened awareness. Awareness—was saying so self-flattery?—of him.

Anticipatory heat quickened ominously downward, exactly as it had when—

Good God, no.

He stomped his foot. His reaction to Mrs. Montrose *did not* count as lightning strike number three. He was long-journey weary, that was all. Sapped by months of intrigue in Vienna and unnerved by finding his godchild wandering in a hedge.

No wonder he'd had an instinctive, mindless reaction to an attractive, saucy lass with tucked-up skirts and uncommonly vibrant hair!

Lust born of fatigue. His shoulders relaxed. *Yes.*

A perfectly reasonable explanation. In his weariness, his body had merely confused *interest* with *arousal*. He'd been *interested* in the nursemaid before they'd even met. *Interested* because he'd known nothing about her but for the fact she appeared in his tight, family-by-choice circle while he'd been away and quickly assumed a prominent place in his godchildren's affections.

Children may trust easily; he did not.

He'd hoped to use his first encounter with the nursemaid to read unintentional signals others might fail to notice. Instead, he'd wasted his advantage and allowed *her* to unravel *him*. Then again, he hadn't exactly *allowed* the unraveling. He'd simply come undone.

Enough.

He kicked clumps of wet gravel he'd scraped from his boots off the slate pathway.

He was a healthy, powerful, well-traveled man of three and thirty. He could not be *undone* by the sight of a calf. Or curl. Or a bloody *nursemaid*, for that matter.

A *bad* nursemaid, at that.

He did not have such thoughts about *anyone* in his own or in any friend's employ. And he especially did not have such thoughts about a woman who, judging by her reaction to his intentionally misleading question about her name, he was now certain had *something* to hide.

Mrs. Montrose, indeed.

Sly humbug, more like.

He resolved to converse with her again. Next time, he would make certain she was not able to distract him.

"You see, love?—"

Alicia, Duchess of Ashbey. Hurtheven winced—judging from the proximity of her voice, she was standing just behind him. Now, he must add *oblivious to his surroundings* to his list of this morning's blunders.

"—*My* point is proven," she continued. "It *is* Hurtheven scurrying about our kitchen gardens."

Hurtheven schooled his features and then turned. Alicia and Ash stood together, as always, a vision of darkness and light.

"I beg your pardon, Your Grace." Hurtheven said with mock offense. "I never *scurry.*"

"Perhaps not." Alicia stepped forward, took his hands into her own and kissed his cheek. She gazed up at him with a merry twinkle in her eye. "I maintain, however, that the *manner* in which you moved came perilously close to a skulk."

"When?" he demanded.

"As you were making your way over to our boot scrape."

He rolled back his shoulders and raised his chin as if affronted.

She laughed. "That look may terrify the children—"

"And a few royal advisors," Ash added.

"—but you cannot scare me," she finished. She tapped her palm against his chest. "I've seen the soft heart under all that bluster..."

Soft heart? He lifted a brow. *God forbid.*

"...Anyway, the point Ash and I were disputing was not your gait, but your location, which is—unarguably, the kitchen garden." Alicia turned to Ash with an expectant expression.

"I concede, my dear." Ashbey bowed. "I was certain the gossip couldn't be true, as my dear friend would *never* arrive without properly greeting his host."

Ouch. "Apologies. I was anxious to see the children after so long a time abroad. In my haste, I'd forgotten you'd be entertaining today."

"Ah yes," Ash commented wryly. "How unpredictable the yearly appearance of the tenth of July."

"Well," he cleared his throat, "as a witness to the happy day, I believe my duty is to wish the two of you joy. Happy Anniversary." He smiled fondly. "I can still recall the look on the vicar's face when Ash burst into the church, arms filled with you, demanding an immediate wedding."

Alicia sighed at the memory.

"Thank you, Hurtheven." Ash placed his arm around his wife's shoulders and pressed his lips to her hair.

"We're grateful for your part in bringing us together," Alicia added.

Hurtheven nodded in acknowledgement. "Truth be told, *Chev* was the one to knock sense into Ash—"

Reflexively, Ash stretched his jaw.

"—I merely pointed out the painfully obvious—my infamously reclusive friend had finally fallen in love." Hurtheven winked at Alicia. "Has he been behaving?"

"Of course not." Alicia smiled up at her husband. "But he's magnificently mine and that's all that matters to me."

Hurtheven shifted his gaze toward the house, lending them privacy while they kissed. Someone standing in a window adjacent to the tower—*the nursery?*—hastily dropped a curtain.

Someone who had *not* been the height of a child.

A small smile played about his lips. So, *his* curiosity wasn't the only one piqued. Maybe he hadn't completely lost his advantage after all.

Ash cleared his throat. "What brought you back to the kitchen gardens, then?"

"An errand." Hurtheven turned back to his friends. "I had to return Lady Felicia to her nursemaid...*after* extracting her from the hedge."

"She escaped again?" Alicia exchanged an exasperated glance with her husband.

Hurtheven frowned. "If successful escapes have become a regular occurrence, perhaps you should find a new nursemaid?"

"Please don't suggest that *Mrs. Montrose* was to blame." Alicia appeared affronted.

"Be gentle, love," Ash interrupted. "Hurtheven doesn't know Mrs. Montrose walks on water around here."

"Fee *did* disappear on her watch," Hurtheven pointed out.

Alicia glanced heavenward. "Fee could escape the Tower of London's most secure cell, if given the opportunity to try. You can't take your eyes off that one for a minute. I can hardly blame Mrs. Montrose for something that's been true all of Fee's life."

"Hardly," Hurtheven repeated. *He'd* never lost track of Fee when she was in his care.

"Join us on the lawn, then?" Ash changed the subject. "After you've—*a-hem*—washed?"

Hurtheven read Ash's expression and silently agreed to drop the matter. *For now.* "Of course."

"And stay for a day or two?" Alicia added. "Chev and Penelope plan to remain at least a fortnight. You *must* stay.

You, Chev, and Ash haven't been together for such a long time."

Ash grasped Hurtheven's shoulder. "We're long past due for a meeting of the council, wouldn't you say?"

"How about tonight?" Alicia suggested. "After all the preparations, I would welcome an early evening."

Hurtheven glanced up to the nursery window and then back to Ash. He'd also welcome an early night. "On your anniversary?"

"Sentiment appreciated," Ash replied. "But our practice is to celebrate on another, private date."

Alicia exchanged an intimate look with her husband before cheerfully nodding in agreement. "That's right. Today we reserve for an unapologetic, public display of our happiness. I can spare Ash this evening."

"But can't you see Hurtheven is wearied, love?" Ash asked with a grin. "He's not as young as he once was."

Hurtheven groaned. "I see I've left you and Chev alone for too long. God only knows what kind of calamitous exploits you've gotten up to without my guidance."

"Coxcomb," Ash said.

"Rogue," Hurtheven retorted.

Alicia shook her head. "Still schoolboys at heart—the lot of you."

Ash winked at his wife. "Yet you love us anyway."

"I do." Alicia took Ash's arm, and they made their way back to their guests, heads together like newlyweds.

They'd been an unlikely pair in the beginning—a widowed duke from a twice-disgraced line and the widow of a naval hero who'd publicly scorned his wife—but they brought out the best in one another.

Like Chev, who, for Penelope's sake, had set aside vengeance for the wrongs committed against him in the years they'd thought him dead, Ash had pulled himself out of his self-imposed isolation for Alicia's love.

Could love have something transformative in store for him, too?

He snorted.

Thank you, no.

At three-and-thirty, he was satisfyingly set in his ways.

Besides, unlike Chev and Ash, he had no need of rescue. Long ago, he'd neatly wrapped his life's experiences into three lessons that now served as infallible guides—friends close, secrets closer, coiled and closed in constant vigilance.

And there were, of course, his labors—the tasks that tested his courage, strength and fortitude while keeping the demons at bay.

He didn't need a thing he did not already possess.

Movement in the window caught his attention again.

Had he just stumbled on his next labor? *Protect his godchildren...find out what the nursemaid is hiding.*

Given Ash's silencing glance and his own disquieting response to the woman, uncovering the truth could prove more of a challenge than he'd expected. *Good.* Anticipation simmered in his blood as he turned on his heel.

He *loved* a challenge.

Hera rested her head against the nursery's rocking chair. The chair's movement fanned a light breeze over her face as shapes danced against the backdrop of her closed lids. Without direct thought, all her suppressed emotions coalesced. Fear, uncertainty, and a fading but ever-present, painful hope solidified into one sentiment...fury.

Fury pointing directly at the Duke of Hurtheven.

Unfair, perhaps. He was not the cause of her current predicament. Still, she was certain the arrogant popinjay intended to ruin her refuge. Or, at least, what little refuge she'd been able to find in a medieval castle with—if rumors were to be believed—a dubious history of madness and murder.

Maybe *refuge* wasn't the proper word.

Refuge implied quiet and solitude, both of which had been in short supply of late. And if her most cherished plans came to fruition, moments of quiet and solitude would become rarer still.

Rocking in the silent shadows, Hera could almost feel the weight of a small child in her arms. She placed her palm against her cheek, remembering the soft tickle of baby hair against her skin and the overwhelming sense of protectiveness and purpose. *Annis*.

Tiny. Pure. Perfect.

Sometimes, she ached with loss.

But she'd done what she had to do.

And she refused—absolutely refused—to dwell on uncertainties. She had a plan. The plan was in motion. And there was no sense in fretting, dreaming, or worrying away her precious moments of solitude.

She adjusted her position, curling protectively within.

She supposed she should feel grateful Fee had behaved for the rest of the party and had *finally* agreed to take a nap. Grateful, too, that Delmare had been a model little gentleman and was now studiously working on his sums.

And yet, how could she dwell in gratitude when, somewhere below, one man's presence had charged the atmosphere like a pending storm charges the air?

He was only one of many guests, and yet she could *feel*

him as if he were a ghostly presence skulking through the house. The sensation made even the thin hairs on her forearms stand on end.

He was a walking, talking threat. She could handle him, of course—such was the only benefit of her experiences—but she mustn't let down her guard.

"*Mrs*. Mont. *Rose*."

She opened her eyes to Delmare's indistinct features.

"I'm sorry, Delmare." Gently, she pushed him back from his scrutiny. "Were you trying to get my attention?"

"Not me. *Him*." He gestured toward the door. "Uncle Heven."

She swiveled toward the entrance. Hurtheven was, indeed, lounging against the door, though his feline gaze was anything *but* relaxed.

He'd been intimidating in a muddied greatcoat. He was *devastating* in brushed-to-a-sheen afternoon dress. She hoped she would not be expected to take dinner with the family as usual. In tailed-and-fitted eveningwear, he just might be deadly.

"You see?" Delmare spoke to the duke. "I told you she was resting, not ill."

Had Delmare and the duke been speaking? *How* hadn't she noticed? Her gaze flew to the duke, fully expecting to see an echo of his earlier condemnation, but his attention was focused on the child.

"If you thought she was ill," the duke asked. "What would you do?"

Delmare chewed on the side of his lip. Then, he brightened. "Ask her if she felt faint. Test her skin. Get help."

"Well?"

Delmare placed the back of his hand against Hera's forehead.

"Thank you." Hera plucked away the boy's fingers. "I am quite hale."

Delmare glanced to Hurtheven for further direction.

"You have discharged your duties," he said. "You may go."

Ugh. Arrogant nob.

Delmare shifted his gaze to Hera. At least *someone* remembered who was responsible for the schoolroom.

"You may finish your sums later." Picking a fight now would not do her any favors. "At present, you may play."

Delmare grinned before shuffling off to the opposite corner and its shelves of books and toys. She tucked her hair back into her cap before rising to her feet.

"I had plans for Delmare's lessons," she said smoothly, even though she hadn't been giving Delmare her attention.

"I apologize. My purpose was not to disrupt his studies."

His apology only increased her pique. "It is your right, I suppose."

"My right?" he echoed.

"You have a great many rights, I'm sure." *Curse her tongue.*

Unexpectedly, his ghost-smile returned.

Gone was his impatience, his anger. He'd altered his demeanor, but to what purpose? This time, she supposed, he intended to unsettle her with his charm.

No matter.

She was as impervious to his charm as she was to his dark, searching eyes, his thick, midnight-black hair, and the raffish, loose-limbed way he was leaning against the door jam, arms crossed over an impressively muscled chest.

The man positively radiated virility.

And, unfortunately, her dry throat and her suddenly

damp, clammy palms suggested she was not quite as impervious as she'd like to be.

She pursed her lips. "Is your disruption at an end, then?"

"If you recall, I promised Fee I would come see her after the party."

"Lady Felicia is sleeping."

"Pity." He strode over to the small table and glanced down at Delmare's slate. "The duchess tells me she's quite pleased with your work."

She folded her hands. "I am honored, Your Grace."

"I didn't think anyone could rival Mrs. Chatten in the duchess's opinion. I'm surprised someone else could so quickly take her place."

"I shouldn't dream of trying to *take her place*. The children continue to feel her absence deeply. And, I believe, she hopes to return by the end of the month."

He employed the useful silence technique once again, holding her gaze with a gleam in his own that challenged her to look away first.

She should have. She *would* have. But how could she allow him to win?

When he finally spoke, his voice remained light and conversational. "I understand you were formerly a governess. For whom did you work?"

"A family of consequence." She chose, at random, a lie that she hoped would end his inquiries. "I'd *happily* reveal more, however, they requested, I'm sure you understand, my discretion."

"Odd." He shrugged. "But fair enough." He lifted Delmare's slate and inspected the numbers. "Very well done, Del." His gaze returned to her. "This position—nursemaid, really—is beneath your qualifications, is it not?"

"I am here at the pleasure of the duchess, of course. I will gladly serve until Mrs. Chatten returns, or Lord Delmare leaves for school."

"And then?"

Her most cherished vision flashed before her eyes and then tingled in her empty arms. She had the dizzy feeling of skating quickly over thin ice, with a cracking boom exploding beneath her feet.

What *was* she doing?

Annis.

Bating this man was a risk she could not afford.

She lowered her eyes to shutter her thoughts. "Where else but another position?"

His questions ceased. Had he noted her unease? She doubted he missed a thing. Those penetrating eyes were reading things about her person she had no intention of revealing. Perhaps even things she didn't yet know.

His gaze settled somewhere to the right of her neck...and did not move.

She became aware of a sensation she hadn't noticed. A slight tickle just beneath her ear. Blushing again—curse her pale skin—she folded another escaped tendril into her chignon.

"Why are you so curious?" she forced herself to ask. "Have you children in need of tending?"

"As yet, no." His voice cracked as he spoke.

She'd caught him off guard. *Good.*

He cleared his throat. "My godchildren mean the world to me, however. You must forgive me if I seem overly inquisitive."

No, she mustn't. And inquisitive put it mildly enough. Although she did, in fact, have a secret. A secret that, in the opinion of most, made her entirely unsuitable for her position.

"I assure you that I give the children my utmost care." That much she could truthfully say.

"And attention?" he asked with a too-innocent lift of his brows.

"I have their best interests at heart—"

His gaze lingered on hers.

"—although I should not have acquiesced to Felicia's sudden insistence on a sweet biscuit. Nor should I have turned my back when she 'accidently' tipped the tray."

He cocked his head. Eyes gleaming, his slow, crooked smile dimpled his left cheek. He was *proud* of the little fiend.

She had been, too, actually. Lady Felicia was subject to a great many rules, and occasional subterfuge was her only freedom. Hera very nearly returned the duke's grin.

She did not. She would acknowledge nothing in common with the arrogant duke.

He swaggered over to the window. "We all have our days, I suppose." His profile lit with the orangish glow of the long summer evening. "I'd like to take a short ride with Delmare before the darkness sets in. Could his studies be resumed later?"

Delmare glanced up hopefully. *Of course,* he'd been listening.

"Yes," she sighed.

"I'm grateful for your indulgence." He inclined his head. "I've left the promised present for Fee on the table."

"May she open it when she wakes, or would you have her wait for your return?"

"I am not such an ogre as that." Another smile. "Besides,

more will arrive with my luggage—and my man—tomorrow."

How long did he intend on staying? "I'll be sure she receives this one, Your Grace."

"Then I shall thank you for your accommodation and leave you to your rest."

He exchanged a low conversation with Delmare.

Delmare thanked her for her consideration in the courtliest of manners. She restrained herself from rolling her eyes at Hurtheven's self-satisfied expression. Then, Hurtheven and his skipping shadow were gone.

She fell back against the wall, realizing she hadn't taken a full breath the whole time she'd been under examination. For that was exactly what Hurtheven had been doing. Examining.

Probing.

This time, with a sheen of charm, but still...

The man was going to be relentless until either he left, or she gave up her secrets. She wrapped her arms around her waist. She would never give up her secrets. And he would be gone soon. Surely, he was not at leisure to break his journey for more than a few days.

She could rein in her tongue and her temper and her attraction to him such a short time.

She hadn't a choice, had she?

Her future depended on it.

* * *

Now, Hurtheven admitted, he was skulking.

Alicia had sent him back upstairs to escort Felicia and Mrs. Montrose down to an al fresco supper in the candlelit garden. His progress, however, had stalled a few feet away from their shadowed shapes.

Listening from doorways was beyond the pale and yet, he could not bring himself to disturb the scene. Fee snuggled in the nursemaid's lap, and, though her legs dangled almost all the way to the floor, the blanket-creased cheek resting against the nursemaid's shoulder made her look younger than her years.

In much the same way Fee was held by the nursemaid, she cradled his first gift—the doll he'd taken from a prince of a former Bavarian electorate, a doll too exquisitely made to relinquish to a trash heap once Hurtheven removed the incriminating letters hidden within.

He'd known Fee would be enchanted with the doll. Clearly, he'd been correct. But her happiness wasn't the cause of his inertia. The reason he'd melted into stillness was the obvious tenderness between nursemaid and child.

A tenderness so palpable, he ached.

Fee had, indeed, taken to Mrs. Montrose completely. And, in this moment, the woman gently humming as she stroked the hair of the unpredictable hurricane that was his godchild, did not appear to be a villain. Nor could he assign her melancholy, pensive expression nefarious intent.

Was the nursemaid completely alone in the world?

Could she be in want of protection, not excoriation?

A tight, almost ticklish sensation closed his throat.

Fee fluffed the doll's apron. "I love her."

"I can see that," Mrs. Montrose murmured.

"She's pretty," Fee continued, "but her clothes are strange."

"You mustn't think the way we dress in England is the *only* way..."

Fee snorted in disbelief.

"...Her manner of dress may be strange to you but is common where she is from."

"Where *is* she from?"

Mrs. Montrose hesitated. "The duke, I believe, has just returned from Austria."

"Not *the duke*. Uncle Heven."

Mrs. Montrose made a sound between a sigh and a groan. "I'm afraid Uncle *Heven* would not approve of my using your name for him."

"He would," Fee replied with confidence. "If *I* ask him."

"No, thank you, Lady Felicia. It would not be appropriate—"

"If he says so, yes, it would be a....ah..."

"Ah-pro-pree-aite."

Fee repeated the word in an accent sharp as cut crystal.

"Very good." Mrs. Montrose smiled. "It means proper. And there are rules of propriety even your "Uncle" cannot break."

"Yes, he can!" Fee insisted. "Uncle Heven can break any rule he wishes. Only sometimes it's better if no one finds out."

Mrs. Montrose *harrumph*ed. "Did *he* tell you so?"

"Yes," Fee confidently replied.

"I'm not surprised," Mrs. Montrose said under her breath.

Hurtheven winced. From the nursemaid's tone, he gathered she not only rightly disapproved, but she also held him in contempt...which was to be expected, he supposed. That conversation with Fee *had* been somewhat unwise. And he'd treated the nursemaid as an adversary from the start.

But was she?

Or had his inherent distrust of strangers, augmented by

both his weary return and his discovery of Felicia wandering in the hedge, led him to judge her unfairly?

"Look here." She distracted Fee. "See those little flowers stitched into the bodice? They are called edelweiss. They grow high up in the mountains."

Hurtheven frowned. Was that common knowledge? He'd no idea.

"Uncle Heven *owns* a mountain," Fee replied. "Delmare went there without Mama and Papa last year, but I have to wait until I am older."

"I'm sorry, Fee. You must have been very sad."

"Not sad—*fur-i-ous*," Fee corrected. "Maybe this year he'll take me, too."

An odd tingle spidered across Hurtheven's skin. Delmare, Fee, and Mrs. Montrose...What an interesting idea.

"But we've planned so many fun things here!"

Fee hummed. "I'd rather go and find these flowers."

"Oh, I'm afraid you won't find any edelweiss on your uncle's mountain."

"Why?"

"I-I believe they only grow in big mountains on the continent."

"Where she's from...Aus-tree-a?"

"Yes. What a good memory you have!"

"Do *all* ladies dress like this there?"

"No," she said. "But the dress—a dirndl—is frequently worn—"

Hurtheven cocked his head.

"—And not just in Austria, but in other parts of the Alps. Bavaria, too." Mrs. Montrose fingered the skirt. "In fact, I think I once saw a similar doll from—" She abruptly ended her sentence. "Fee, may I see your present for a moment?"

Fee nodded, and then Mrs. Montrose examined the doll more closely. She inhaled sharply and stopped rocking.

Hurtheven's focus narrowed. Where would she have seen a doll made in the likeness of an exiled princess of Heinenberg, a small electorate that, between Napoleon's conquest and the negotiations in Vienna, no longer existed on a map?

For that matter, why did she know so much about the region's clothes and flora? Even if she had come across the place in merely a book or conversation, why would her hand be shaking as she placed the doll back into Fee's arms?

"Where is she from?" Fee asked again.

The nursemaid blinked. "Austria, I believe."

Fee settled back against her chest with a huff. "You already said that."

"Did I?" She hugged Fee close and rested her lips against the child's head, eyes squeezed tightly closed. "Just a coincidence."

"What did you say?"

"Oh!" She took a deep breath. "Nothing important, darling."

There. Right there.

Any number of explanations could account for her knowledge, but only one justified the involuntary spasm in her features. She'd recognized that, specific doll.

And she was not happy about the recognition.

Now, he was certain she could not have been completely forthcoming with Ash and Alicia. He felt no triumph...just a tug somewhere beneath his ribs, a sharp yank demanding he *do something*. But what? Force her to reveal her secrets? Offer her his aid? Given the impression he'd made, she'd hardly be willing to take him into her confidence.

"Can you braid my hair like hers?" Fee asked.

"They're a little more complicated than your usual braids." Mrs. Montrose settled back into the chair. She turned Fee's face away and ran her hand over Fee's hair. "We can certainly—"

"Uncle Heven!"

The nursemaid whipped around.

Caught. "Good evening, Lady Felicia. Mrs. Montrose."

Fee scrambled down from Mrs. Montrose's lap. "I love my doll. Where is she from?"

He met Mrs. Montrose's gaze. "My travels."

She flushed but did not look away. If only he could read the emotion behind her eyes.

"Austria?" Fee asked.

"In the vicinity," he answered. He could be vague, too.

His mind wandered, seeking possible answers. She couldn't have had anything to do with the events that transpired in Vienna—she'd been here at the time. However, he knew that Prince Karl had resided in London prior to being called to the Congress. Had the nursemaid some connection to him when he was there?

Hurtheven didn't like the idea in the least. Karl had been manipulative, peevish, and vindictive, abusive to those beneath him while toad eating those above. In short, not anyone a young woman alone in the world should know.

"Is there something we can do for you, Your Grace?" she prompted.

Tell me the truth.

If anything, her gaze completely shuttered.

He inclined his head. "The duchess sent me to escort Lady Felicia, and you, Mrs. Montrose, down to dinner."

"Then we shouldn't keep your parents waiting, should we, Fee?"

Hurtheven lifted Fee into his arms and then settled her to one side. In another year or so, he was not going to be able to do that anymore. But for the time being, he savored the feel of her head against his shoulder.

"Escort." Fee pointed to Mrs. Montrose. "Means you give Mrs. Montrose your arm."

"Who am I to break a rule of propriety?" He winked at Fee before he presented Mrs. Montrose with his arm. "Mrs. Montrose?"

She gazed down as if touching him would leave her scalded. Then, she placed her fingers gently against his sleeve.

Fee chattered away as, together, they walked through the adjoining rooms towards the stairs.

In-between Fee's breathless accounts of her exploits, Hurtheven's mind wandered, marveling at certain contradictions...such as how the scent of a woman could feel like a pleasant memory. How a feather-light touch could produce a curious sense of connection. And how a state of vigilant wariness could be shifted in opposite directions by one, tiny preposition.

But which preposition should he use concerning Mrs. Montrose?

Wary *of* or wary *for*?
Or both?

Chapter Three

Following dinner, Hurtheven lingered in the garden as, Mrs. Montrose, Alicia, Pen, and the children, swept back up the terrace steps and then into the house. Mrs. Montrose tilted her head toward Pen, continuing the deep, low-toned conversation they'd started just after they'd risen from the table.

Whatever fears Mrs. Montrose had experienced when she examined the doll, she'd completely set aside. Impressive, really. The actions of a master deceiver? Someone who hid oceans of experience behind a polished exterior...rather like himself?

Or something else?

And why was he so consumed by the woman in the first place? Her presence disturbed *something* long buried. But *what* and *why*, he could not answer.

He tore his gaze away before heading toward a separate set of external doors that led to Ash's study.

"Ah, Hurtheven." Ash cast him a sardonic glance from his large, overstuffed leather chair. He did not rise. "You deigned to join us."

"Was I keeping you from something?" he queried.

"Nothing but our wives," Chev answered.

Hurtheven glanced heavenward. "Must you both constantly remind me of your states of wedded bliss?"

Ash set aside his pipe. "Bliss that could be yours with a simple parson's visit."

"Ah, but, first, I must find a woman," Hurtheven pointed out.

"There's the rub," quoted Chev.

"Not *everyone* can be Alicia and Pen." Hurtheven took a seat and stretched out his legs. "Anyway, I've no intention to marry at present. I'm afraid you'll just have to put up with me as I am."

"An unmitigated ass?" Chev suggested.

Hurtheven folded his arms behind his head and grinned. "I do my best."

Ash chuckled. "It is good to have you back, Hurtheven." He poured three whiskies from the decanter set beside him. "Shall we officially call the council to order?"

"That's why we're here." Chev's old injury—the loss of his right hand just past his elbow—obliged him to accept his drink with his left.

Hurtheven toasted Ash. "To you, Hades."

"To you, Poseidon," Ash gestured toward Chev.

"And to you, our dear, wandering Zeus." Chev clinked his glass Hurtheven.

Amber liquid burned a line of fiery comfort down Hurtheven's throat. All the strange sensations engendered by the nursemaid receded. Thought-soothing warmth tided through his veins.

This is what he needed. The restorative company of men.

"Eta, Rho, Zeta." Chev snorted.

"What mad boys we were." Ash leaned back, hooked a knee over the arm of his chair and swung his foot. "Coming up with a society. Tattooing our combined crests on our ankles."

"Prescient, that." Hurtheven pointed at Chev's leg. "Chev's tattoo is the sole reason I was called to identify him when he washed ashore."

"A good thing, too." Chev replied. "Else those scoundrels who found me might have thrown me back."

Hurtheven recalled the show he'd put on that evening several years past—all confidence and command when, inside, he'd been shocked and reeling to find Chev alive but emaciated, weather-worn, and scarred. Hurtheven had taken charge, of course, improvising a plan that untangled Chev from a possible court martial and, eventually, reunited him with Penelope.

"To a better future." Ash jiggled his glass.

"Hear, Hear." Chev drank. "And to bonds born of the distant past."

"How long since we came up with the idea for a secret society?" Ash asked.

"Twenty-five years." Hurtheven answered.

Not that he'd tallied. He'd never be so maudlin.

"A *lifetime* ago." Chev shifted toward Hurtheven. "I believe the idea for a lettered brotherhood came from your uncle, yes?"

"The idea was mine...though inspired by a fraternity he'd started at a university in Virginia." He snorted. "If you can call a place in that backwater a university."

"You never liked him much," Ash mused. "Did you?"

Hurtheven lifted a brow. "One tends to distance oneself from the traitors in the family." Not-to-mention guardians who didn't return in a child's time of need.

He blinked down into his cup.

Ash and Chev knew he'd copied the idea from his uncle. They did not know his uncle's abandonment had been the genesis of his desire for a brotherly bond in the first place. *Friends close. Secrets closer.*

Unlike Chev, who'd had an older brother at the time and hadn't expected to inherit, Hurtheven had come into his title scant years past leading strings. And, like Ash, he'd been an only child. He'd desperately wanted brothers he could trust.

So, he'd chosen them.

Chev with his bravado and imagination. Ash with his intelligence and brooding insight. Unto this day, nothing meant more to him. He blinked back a suspicious sting.

Where had *that* come from?

Chev swirled the remaining liquid in his glass. "You were unusually quiet this evening, Hurtheven—especially given your recent return."

"Indeed," Ash agreed. "I'd expected stories of grand and triumphant adventures, putting us all to shame."

He'd intended to regale them all, but... "Just tired, I suppose." And distracted.

Disturbingly so.

He closed his eyes, rested his head on the back of his chair, and exhaled.

"Perhaps," Ash spoke to Chev, "it is time to persuade Hurtheven to end his solo adventures?"

Hurtheven eyes flew open. "Not you, too."

"Too?" Ash prompted.

"Pen mentioned marriage this afternoon."

"Intelligent woman, my wife," Chev replied. "One *does* get concerned. A single, titled man of three and thirty? Why it's positively sacrilege!"

Ash nodded. "UnBritish, certainly."

"Sacrilege or not, I repeat—I've no intention to marry at present."

"...because you have not found the right woman." Chev added. "You should remedy that."

"I'm not about to grovel for a voucher to Almacks." Hurtheven downed the rest of his drink. "Besides, I scare debutantes."

"You scare most people," Ash observed.

"On purpose." Chev added.

"Haven't you heard?" Hurtheven glanced up. "I'm pure evil—a devil in disguise."

"Hey, now. As Hades, that's my domain." Ash hit the table. "And I say you're a demon, at best."

Chev snorted. "A goblin at the very least."

Hurtheven grunted. He'd been astonished to hear Lady Adelaide revive the old rumors. *No one* insulted him anymore. No one but his closest friends.

"So"—Ash rubbed his chin—"debutantes are unacceptable. That *does* make things difficult. Perhaps we should form a search of our own. Enlist the wives...?"

Hurtheven cast Ash his fiercest scowl, which Ash met with a widened grin.

"Believe it or not, I do know my duty. I *have* considered the matter. *When* I choose a bride, *I'll* proceed rationally. Unlike the two of you."

"Oh, this should be entertaining." Chev crossed his feet at the ankles. "Especially from a man who has—on frequent occasions—gone outside in the middle of an electrical storm and turned his face to the sky."

"He's always had a strange fascination with storms," Ash said dismissively. "And lightning. That's why we call him Zeus, remember? Now, Hurtheven, elaborate on your *rational* plan, please."

Hurtheven exhaled, glad for Ash's unintentional rescue. He adopted a careless manner. "First, I will define the qualities necessary for a harmonious household, and then, I'll set about finding someone who matches my criteria."

Chev and Ash exchanged a glance and then laughed out loud.

Ingrates.

Ash shook his head, his expression looked suspiciously like pity. "That doesn't make *any* sense."

"I believe he's telling us," Chev supplied, "that he's going to make up a list."

"Lists," he gritted, "are useful."

"And, what, exactly, would be on said list?" Ash asked.

"As I said...qualities."

"Qualities necessary for a *harmonious* household," Chev repeated, his emphasis making the idea sound frivolous.

Easy for Chev. Chev and Pen had simply recognized one another, as if they'd been the best of friends in another lifetime. For Hurtheven, however, holding out for love would be as mad as waiting for another lightning strike. He would not be made weak. Vulnerable.

When he was ready, he'd take charge.

As usual.

Chev leaned toward Ash. "I don't recall *you* having a list, Ash."

"To be fair, I had no intention of marrying Alicia."

"That's right." Chev set down his drink and clapped Ash's knee. "You rogue."

"I *maintain*," Ash said with a smile, "That Alicia and I

made a perfectly respectful, carnal agreement between equals."

Hurtheven rolled his eyes. "*You* practically kidnapped Alicia."

Ash smiled at a private memory. "Very well. Perhaps a dash of seduction was involved."

"And an accidental pregnancy," added Chev.

"My wife is not complaining, now, is she?" His lips turned up in a cat-with-cream smile. "Did *you* have a list, Chev?"

"He'd barely laid eyes on Pen when he decided to marry her!" Hurtheven exclaimed.

Chev observed him with a hooded gaze. "A list, my friend, does not appear to be a necessity."

"What *is* a necessity is an heir," Ash added.

"I am well-aware," Hurtheven replied.

Three and thirty. When had that happened? Truth be told, carrying Fee down the stairs this afternoon hadn't been as easy as it had been when he'd carried Delmare as a child. And carrying Delmare hadn't been as easy as carrying Thaddeus when Thaddeus had been a boy. Thaddeus, who was now on the verge of manhood. Why, Thaddeus would be shopping the marriage mart himself soon.

Hideous thought. Competing for a woman's hand with *Thaddeus.*

"We can't expect Hurtheven to enter 'the parson's trap' willingly, Ash," Chev remarked. "This is the man who said every problem comes down to a woman."

"I say a lot of things," he replied with a wave of his hand.

But then, remembered the moment. Ash had been forlorn. Despairing, even. Mired in an excess of sentiment brought on by abandoning Alicia. Alarming and *completely* unnecessary sentiment. The kind of sentiment that broke his third rule.

Closed and coiled, always ready to strike.

"Every problem comes down to a woman." Ash repeated as he rubbed his chin. His gaze settled on Hurtheven. "Would that be an explanation for subjecting my nursemaid to an interrogation this afternoon?"

After a jolt, he forced himself to swallow—and not spit —the drink he'd just taken.

"She complained, did she?" he asked as lightly as he could.

Ash cocked his head as if he'd heard more than Hurtheven had expressed. "She wouldn't, of course. *Delmare* repeated the conversation."

Hurtheven could not recall the exact nature of his questions.

All he could distinctly remember was the moment after she'd told him how Fee had executed her escape. The fleeting, thrilling moment of mutual understanding. She'd nearly returned his smile...and then he'd needed to leave the room. *Immediately.*

"It wasn't an *interrogation,* per se." Hurtheven shifted in his seat. "Just a few, simple questions."

"And"—Ash's brow rose—"were you satisfied with her answers?"

"Quite frankly, no." Hurtheven sensed Ash's annoyance spike. Still, he couldn't let the matter rest. He *had* to know, to understand. "I do not believe she is who she says she is. That gives me pause."

"Hurtheven"—Ash leaned forward—"do you doubt our commitment to our children—?"

"Of course not."

"—Believe we'd place them in harm's way?" Ash's facial muscles tightened in an ominous fashion.

Hurtheven answered in a calming tone, "Admittedly, she seems to genuinely care for the children—"

"That, I assure you, she does." Ash settled back into his chair.

Ash observed Hurtheven silently, jaw still clenched, though less so. Then, he sighed deeply as he rubbed his brow. "You know I'd trust you with my life..."

"And?" Hurtheven prompted.

"*However*," Ash clarified, "Mrs. Montrose is not your concern. She is Alicia's *particular* choice. A scheme, if you will. A cause..."

Hurtheven's curiosity further piqued, though he wiped all trace of his interest from his features.

"...For that reason, and this—she is in *my* employ and therefore *my* responsibility—I'll ask you not to trouble her further."

"I understand."

Ash held his gaze over the rim of his glass as he sipped. "Good."

Ash's rebuke stung. Still, Hurtheven intended to continue his inquiry, of course. Only with more subtly. He couldn't dismiss his interest in Mrs. Montrose now even if the *real* Hades—the devil himself—had issued the same warning.

"Now, having settled the matter of the mysterious nursemaid"—Chev's tone lightened the mood—"might I suggest we return to the matter of Hurtheven's list?"

Ash downed the rest of his drink. "What an interesting idea." He sat down his glass. Rising swiftly, he then disappeared behind his desk. "Let's see what we have here... Ah!

Just the thing—graphite and..." He shuffled articles around inside the drawer. "...sheets of paper."

"Marvelous!" Chev's smile spread with wicked glee. "You transcribe, Ash."

Ash arranged the paper on the small table beside his chair and poised the graphite holder as if ready to write.

Chev cleared his throat. "Whereas the Duke of Hurtheven requires an heir, and to procure said heir, he requires a wife—"

"Whereas," Ash scribbled as he spoke, "all women cannot be Alicia or Pen..."

"Whereas," Chev added, "Hurtheven scares debutantes..."

Hurtheven sighed roughly.

"...The membership of Eta, Rho, Zeta commits to setting down a list of qualities required to obtain Zeus's desired result of a harmonious household."

Ash and Chev shared a chuckle. Hurtheven considered thrashing them both...but better this sort of ribbing than Ash's ire.

"I've *so* many required attributes," he drawled. "I am at a loss where to begin."

"Height?" Chev suggested. "Some people hold proportion *fundamental* to harmony."

"He's uncommonly tall, so..." Ash scrawled *Tall* onto the top sheet.

In his mind's eye, Hurtheven pictured sparring with the nursemaid in the garden.

Her shoulders had been back, her gaze fierce...and very nearly level with his own. In fact, if he had taken one step closer, she would only have needed to slightly turn up her face for him to—

Lust born of fatigue.

He halted the progression of his thoughts. Once he'd rested, he'd be cured. And once he'd uncovered whatever the nursemaid was hiding—whatever had made her afraid— his curiosity would be satisfied, and he could let the matter go, knowing his godchildren were safe.

"Scratch tall." He kicked off his shoes and then propped his feet atop Ash's table. "I've always preferred petite..."

Hera stared down at the handle of the duchess's door, not yet willing to make her presence known. The Duke of Hurtheven had disturbed her peace. Her early morning excursion to the village, on the other hand, had left her in possession of information heralding an even greater disaster. A Bow Street Runner had been in town.

A Bow Street Runner seeking a Miss Hera Bythesea.

Bythesea not *Montrose.* She could think of only one person who would pay someone to hunt her down—and even the possibility made her stomach churn.

She did not wish to further burden her kind employer, but where else was she to turn? She couldn't help but feel she'd already imposed too much.

On the other hand, the longer she waited, the more likely she'd be found, placing herself and—she closed her eyes—her sweet, innocent Annis, in grave danger.

That she could not allow.

She had to go inside. Time was of the essence in deciding what she should do next. Why should she hesitate? Her Grace's maid had told Hera the duchess was ready to receive her.

Feminine laughter—distinctly at odds with Hera's

agitated state—sounded from beyond the closed door to the sitting room.

"She must be mild-mannered!" The Duchess of Ithwick's voice was muted, but clear.

"*And* gracious," the Duchess of Ashbey added.

"Educated, but without the pretention to become a bluestocking."

"Pleasing to the eye."

"*Blond*!" The Duchess of Ithwick exclaimed. "Appalling! He's always been eccentric, but this...*this* is *mad*."

"If this list weren't so funny," the Duchess of Ashbey offered, "it would be terribly sad."

"Sad? Your pity is wasted on him! I'd rather seek out a woman who fits this description, encourage her to set her cap at him, and then watch the rapscallion suffer."

"You wouldn't! Even if you could find this...this..."

"Figment?"

"...*paragon*, such a plan would be too unfair to the woman. Besides, such mischief would reveal we've seen the list."

"If our husbands are going to drink to the point one of them drops a *secret society* document in the stairwell before crawling into bed half dead at first light, *we're* certainly not to blame."

"True," Alicia agreed.

Hera took advantage of the subsequent lull to announce herself. She responded to the duchess's bid to enter and then closed the door.

"I do not wish to disturb you, Your Grace."

"Not at all," the Duchess of Ashbey replied, discreetly wiping her eyes.

The Duchess of Ithwick set down her cup of morning

chocolate. "We were just discussing our dear, deluded friend Hurtheven's list of requirements for a wife."

The attributes they'd been reading were Hurtheven's wifely qualifications? He'd actually written down a list?

For a fleeting second, astonishment overtook her concerns.

"We are as horrified as you appear." The Duchess of Ithwick shook her head. "Amused, yes. But equally horrified."

Casting a significant glance at her friend, the Duchess of Ashbey folded the list and then tucked the paper into her desk drawer. "Tansy said you'd wanted to see me on a matter of urgency?"

"Yes, your Grace. I—I would appreciate your council," Hera said to her employer even as her gaze remained fixed on the Duchess of Ithwick.

"Ah, then," the Duchess of Ithwick touched a napkin to her lips, "I believe that is my cue to graciously take my leave."

Hera studied the duchess as the duchess adjusted her fichu and then slid her dainty feet into slippers she'd retrieved from the side of the settee.

Could she, like the Duchess of Ashbey, be trusted?

Hera liked her easy, open manner—doubtless due to the fact she hadn't been born an aristocrat. In their short acquaintance, the duchess had extended that confidence, as well as several others—the story of her youthful elopement, the quick addition to her marriage of a child, and the trials she'd faced while attempting to protect her son during the seven years her husband had been lost at sea.

Anyone who'd survived such experiences with grace and humor intact had to have untold resources of strength.

Who could better understand the concerns of a mother trying to survive without a husband's protection?

She could be an ally.

Right now, Hera needed all the allies she could find. But would she be *willing* to offer counsel?

"I will not insist you leave, Your Grace," Hera said quietly. "...Although I would request your full discretion concerning any matters we might discuss."

The duchess held her gaze for a long moment. Then, she nodded. "You may trust me. I promise to treat any confidence of yours with the same gravity I would treat a confidence of Alicia's and, of course, offer any assistance I am able. Please"—the duchess slid over on the settee—"sit with me."

The concern in her voice pricked the corner of Hera's suddenly dampened eyes. The Duchess of Ithwick and Duchess of Ashbey were good people. Kind mothers. Devoted friends. Women of understanding and tenderness.

In other words, creatures entirely beyond Hera's experience.

How different her life might've been if she'd known women like them when she'd found herself alone, unwanted, and vulnerable following her father's death! Instead, she'd been surrounded by people who'd seen her only for what she could give to them.

"In case you haven't noticed," the duchess ventured, "we do not stand on ceremony amongst ourselves. You must call me Penelope—Pen, if you are so inclined."

She sat down by Penelope's side, feeling slightly faint...and grateful. "Very well...Penelope." *Pen* would not do at all.

The Duchess of Ashbey smiled. "Well done, Pen. I've been unable to convince Mrs. Montrose to use my name."

"Because calling you Alicia would not be a good example to the children," Hera replied.

The duchess nodded. "So, you've argued, and so I have conceded. Now, will you tell us why you look as pale as blancmange?"

Hera dropped her gaze and folded her hands.

"Earlier this morning, I went down to the village. The baker's wife pulled me in from the street, all aflutter. A stranger—a Bow Street Runner—had just been in asking questions. The Runner was looking for me."

"But who would send someone to find you?" the Duchess of Ashbey asked.

Hera met her gaze. "He *must* have been sent by Karl."

The duchess sucked in a sharp breath.

"And who is Karl?" Penelope asked.

Hera exchanged a glance with the other duchess. "My former employer. And" —she lowered her voice—"the father of my illegitimate child."

She braced for Penelope to express shock. However, Penelope's clear blue eyes remained steady and sympathetic.

"I see," she said softly.

For Penelope's sake, she recounted facts already known to the other duchess, starting with the five years she'd served as an unpaid governess in the household of her half-brother —a brother who'd been long-estranged from their father at the time of his death. A brother who had been forced to take her in due to her father's will, but who had always reviled her because she was the product of their father's scandalous second marriage.

"I was unwanted but for my labor. By the time I met the prince, I was exhausted, lonely, and despairing of my future." How vividly she remembered that misty London morning on the banks of the Serpentine! "Karl, who'd been out walking with his secretary, lingered by our little party and then engaged me in conversation. He said he was impressed by the way I was keeping my half-brother's four boys in hand."

"Four!" Penelope exclaimed.

"Four," Hera smiled wryly. "Karl showed up again the next day, and the one after, and, then he offered me employment on generous terms as governess to his own children."

She passed a hand over her face before continuing, "I was thrilled, at first, to have been offered a proper, paid position. I should have known that aristocratic diplomats don't hire their own staff—nor would they ever dream of engaging the services of a woman they met *in a park*."

She shook her head at her own naiveté and then sighed. "After I was under his roof, he became...*ardent*. Although the very idea of becoming his mistress shocked me, I must admit I was flattered. He is an attractive man, and he pleaded the loneliness of a widower. In truth, I *felt* for him."

Remembering him as she'd believed him to be then— lost and wistful beneath his elegant sophistication—was difficult. Remembering herself as she'd been then—trusting and innocent and desperately longing to be wanted—was mortifying.

"Did he force you into an arrangement?"

Hera closed her eyes. "He told me the decision was mine. He said he was not at liberty to wed in the traditional sense, but he mentioned the possibility of something called a morganatic marriage once he was able to return to his homeland. And he promised to care for me until then. So I...I..."

Her voice faded.

"And so, you, like many women before you, made a

choice among poor options in order to survive," Penelope offered for her, her gaze nothing but understanding.

Was that what she had done?

She'd since convinced herself she'd made the choice because she was *weak*, not because circumstance had left her *weakened*. Tears threatened again, hovering in a bubble at the base of her throat. Hera pushed them down.

"I did not love him, of course. Although he was"—she blushed—"quite dazzling. Urbane. Nothing seemed beyond his power...something that should have made me wary but did not."

"Yes," Alicia sighed. "Some men possess the ability to dazzle when they wish to...and turn cold when they do not. In my opinion, you are too generous with him. He took advantage of your position."

"I could have said no," Hera argued.

"Karl saying you had a choice," Penelope ventured gently, "does not completely absolve him of suggesting an affair in the first place..."

Hera frowned. Could that be true?

"...What terms did he offer you?"

"Terms?"

"Contractual terms—what was expected of both parties, how children of the relationship will be provided for, and what would constitute a parting gift—that sort of thing."

Hera blinked.

"Contracts are often drawn up when this sort of relationship is established," Penelope explained.

"He didn't offer a contract," she said faintly, "and I hadn't the experience to ask. Even if I had known enough about the law to seek its protection, I trusted him. He seemed...deeply in earnest. And he was kind...to *me* at least. And at first."

The Duchess of Ashbey reached out and covered her hand. "Again, you are too generous—especially considering what followed."

Hera felt her heartbeat spike. "That, of course, I can never forgive him for."

Pen touched her shoulder. "What happened?"

"Everything changed when I told him I was increasing. '*I will conceal you,*' he said..." She took a halting breath. "'*And when the time comes, I will make sure we are well-rid of the problem. Babies die all the time. No one asks any questions, especially of people like me.*'"

She shuddered with the same chill his words had unleashed, a chill as cold and as terrifying as Karl's resolute and coolly calculating gaze.

She'd seen, with sudden horror, that, while he'd acted the part of a gentle lover, the prince was wholly disconnected, not just from decency, but from humanity.

"Little things I'd noticed about him but long denied, took on a new, sinister meaning. The brisque, distant and sometimes demeaning way the treated his own children, for instance, which he'd falsely explained away as a manifestation of his grief."

He'd hated the wife his father had chosen for him, she later learned.

"I was scared for the potential life growing inside of me. So, when Karl went away to attend an event at the Royal Pavilion, I gathered up what I could carry, and I cast myself on my sister-in-law's mercy. She was, of course, disinclined to shame my brother or their household by taking me in, but she agreed to arrange for me to be admitted to a lying-in hospital under a false name, as if I had, indeed, been her servant."

Penelope *tsk*ed. "Your brother was content with his plan?"

Hera shook her head. "Since my brother barely tolerated me when I was respectable—blood will show, he always said—my sister-in-law decided against telling him the whole. When my father married my mother—his second wife—she was already carrying me. She was more than thirty years my father's junior and not of his class. My half-brother was appalled, and my mother, disowned by her own family—who were, I believe, London merchants, although I never knew them."

"Then you were quite alone," Penelope said.

Hera nodded. "But luckier than most, in some ways. The matron of the lying-in hospital helped me petition the Foundling Hospital to take my daughter, which she needn't have done. And the steward at the Foundling Hospital, in turn, found me a position with the duchess."

"Last year, as you know, I became a patron of the Foundling Hospital," the Duchess of Ashbey reminded Penelope. "We needed a nursemaid, and I asked the steward if he knew of any unfortunate woman he could recommend."

Unfortunate woman.

Hera hated the expression. Circumstance had rendered her without external resource, but she had fortitude and resilience. She'd outwitted a prince and saved her daughter's life, had she not?

She may have found herself with few good options, but she did not, and never would, think of herself as *unfortunate*.

No.

She'd had a choice. Perhaps, as Penelope had suggested, a choice between bad options, but a choice, nonetheless.

"When I went to speak privately with Mrs. Montrose," the duchess continued, "she trusted me with the details of her story—and her deep desire to be reunited with her daughter if she had the means. Given my own history, I found myself quite moved. But since she'd already given over the child, a strict process had to be followed."

"I must prove to the board of directors I have *reformed*," Hera explained. "And I must prove I can care for Annis."

"I've done everything in my power to help," the duchess added. "But the application process is lengthy, and even I could not persuade the directors to make an exception. But they agreed that eight months in my employ should be enough for me to truthfully speak to Hera's character—which I intend to do. The vote will take place soon—a few weeks hence, I'm told."

"I am so close, but now...I just do not know what to do."

"What makes you think Karl is the one looking for you?" Penelope asked.

"The Runner in the village is looking for Hera Bythesea. No one else but my brother knows me by that name—and *he* certainly wouldn't have *paid* someone to look for me."

"Hera..." Penelope repeated with an odd little shake of her head.

"Don't you see?" Hera injected. "He *must* have been sent by Karl. What if he's looking for me to make sure—as he intended—our child did not survive?" She spoke aloud her worst fear. "The war is over. The agreements between nations have been settled. I should have anticipated that he might try to find me...*us.*" *Annis.*

Hera swallowed what felt like her whole, jaggedly beating heart.

61

"Even if there is only a small chance the Runner was hired by Karl, I cannot be discovered."

"Did Karl try and seek you out at the lying-in hospital?"

"I don't know," Hera replied. "But even if he did not, I cannot be sure he wouldn't have if he'd had more time. His father called him to Vienna that very week. He had to leave immediately."

"I can see why you'd be concerned," Penelope agreed.

Hera's voice quivered on the surface of her swelling upset. "Karl's years of diplomatic service to his country connected him to powerful people. And now, he is free to return to England." Hera bit her lip. "I've changed my name. I've attempted to conceal my appearance. But I'm still a governess. If there's a Runner asking questions in the village, he's only too likely to see the similarities between 'Mrs. Montrose' and myself. What if he locates me...or Annis?"

"Remember, my dear," the Duchess of Ashbey soothed, "the Runner was only asking questions about you—not a child. And the hospital has no record of Hera Bythesea. Given the laws around bastardy, even if the Runner located Annis, Karl would have no claim."

"There are any number of ways he might interfere. He could, for instance, do everything in his power to ruin *my* character—and so prevent me from claiming Annis. If he's the one seeking me out, I'm convinced that both of us are in danger."

"Maybe someone else hired the Runner?" Penelope asked.

"Possibly," the Duchess of Ashbey replied. "Although, it's clear Hera will not rest easy until we can find out what's going on."

"But how can we do so without revealing I'm here?" Hera asked.

"He'll seek an audience, I'm sure," the Duchess of Ashbey said. "Instead of refusing, we'll delay. You'll just need to hide somewhere until we can find out the truth."

"With due respect, duchess," Hera replied, "don't you think the disappearance of your nursemaid will raise suspicion—not to mention place my petition at risk?"

"Your departure wouldn't raise questions if you were accompanying our children on a journey. Pen, could you take them back with you to Ithwick this evening?"

Pen considered. "Soldiers and seamen come and go freely from Pensteague. If the Runner were to somehow follow her there, he could easily insinuate himself into our community under a false name before we'd identified any risk."

"As Chev did," the Duchess of Ashbey replied.

"As Chev did," Pen repeated. "What about Hevenhyll?"

"Hevenhyll *is* remote." The duchess agreed.

"Hevenhyll?" Hera questioned.

"Hurtheven's estate..." the duchess paused.

Hera opened her mouth, but a response failed to materialize.

"...Hurtheven *has* taken Delmare to his home on his own before. And there are few I'd equally trust to keep both you and the children safe."

"*I* do not trust him," Hera said.

Both duchesses turned to her with twin expressions of consternation.

"Has he done something he ought not?" the Duchess of Ashbey asked.

"No." *Not exactly*. "He questioned me as if he knew I

was hiding something." And then there was the matter of the doll...

Penelope nodded. "He's very good at sensing when someone isn't fully forthcoming. Still, I, too, can vouch he is trustworthy. In the years my husband was missing, Thaddeus and I depended on him."

"For all his flaws," Alicia added, "he's a good and loyal friend."

"Karl appeared to be charm itself, too." At least he had been charming in the beginning. Although there had been signs of his true nature.

There were always signs.

For instance, the prince's inability to suffer being the subject of a jest while, at other times, publicly mocking those who refused to politely endure the sting of his own derision. Fastidiousness with his person bordering on compulsion. Impatience and anger manifested in one, perpetually balled fist. And the fact the prince hadn't a single close friend for any length of time. Acquaintances, yes. Servile followers by the dozen. But friends who'd challenge him? Never.

Unlike Hurtheven, who clearly held the devotion of these two women as well as the children.

Fine crystal clinked as the duchess poured a glass of thick, brownish-red liquid. "Take this."

Hera sipped. *Sherry.* She rolled the heavy sweetness over her tongue.

"I know that if I asked him to do so, Hurtheven would protect both you and the children," the duchess said. "However, as to his character, all the reassurances Pen and I can offer you stem from *our* experiences with him. I can understand why you'd be unwilling to go with a strange man."

Hera thought of the careful way Hurtheven had held

Fee. She thought of the indulgence in his expression when he was talking to Delmare. She thought of the moment of unintentional understanding they'd shared when she'd explained how Fee had orchestrated her escape.

Perhaps, given her immediate need, she could trust his aid...

Then, she remembered the doll.

How had the doll come to be in his possession? Could the duke be in league with the prince?

Engage only with those you can master—she heard Karl's voice.

The prince avoided men he could not control, men more powerful than himself. She could not imagine *anyone* holding sway over the Duke of Hurtheven, least of all a man like Karl.

She sighed. There was one thing of which she could be sure. "I know the Duke of Hurtheven would never place the children in harm's way.

"Hera," the duchess began, "the reason I sponsor the Foundling Hospital is that *I* was unwed when Delmare was conceived. When I wasn't sure I wanted to raise my child with Ash, Hurtheven convinced Ash to rebuild Wisterley to prove his sincere desire for a family. He and Chev were present at Wisterley when I arrived and were willing to pledge their support whether I chose to marry Ash or raise my child on my own. I chose Ash, but their steadfast friendship in my time of need is part of the inspiration for my decision to help you."

The duchess had been carrying Delmare *before* she wed the duke? And, knowing this, Hurtheven had offered her his help?

Perhaps she had misjudged him.

Hera was so, so close to being reunited with her daughter. She'd had her eyes on the singular prize and hadn't considered any complication beyond convincing the board of the Foundling Hospital she had reformed.

"What would happen if I cannot return before the board of directors meets?" she asked.

"We have a few weeks," the Duchess of Ashbey replied. "By then—hopefully—we will know who hired the Runner and, whether he or she poses a threat to you or to Annis. If he does, we will do what we can to protect you. If not, we can proceed as planned. Either way, I will make sure you attend that meeting."

A few weeks. Then she would be reunited with her child. But what would happen thereafter? If Karl had tracked her as far as Wisterley, she could not settle in the village near the estate as she hoped.

She'd simply have to come up with another solution.

One problem at a time.

She nodded to Alicia. "If you can convince the duke to take the children without giving away my plight, I will go, too."

Yet again, she'd been compelled to make a choice among poor options. She only hoped that this one would not prove as life-altering as the last.

* * *

Shortly thereafter, Hurtheven followed a visibly irate Ash through the massive doors that led to Ash's study. The doors ominously clicked closed.

"*How* did you contrive to make this happen?" Ash demanded.

"Really, Ash. I might, on occasion, imply I've God-like qualities, but *Alicia* requested that I take the children back with me to my estate. I don't see why you're looking at me as if *I'd* concocted the plan."

That he'd been on the verge of putting forth a similar suggestion when Alicia asked was beside the point.

"*Alicia* requested—which is the *only* reason I agreed." Ash narrowed his eyes. "I cannot express this strongly enough; I expect you to behave."

"You *expect* me to *behave*? I'm not an errant child."

"You have been known to act like one on occasion," Ash said harshly.

"You're out of line," Hurtheven warned.

"You cannot lie to me. *Me!* I've been watching you, and it's clear to me that you have been preoccupied with Mrs. Montrose from first sight."

Hurtheven bit back a retort and wet his lips. Damn Ash's powers of perception. He looked away. "My main concern was and is the safety of the children."

"I believe you. But I also believe that Mrs. Montrose is more than just a secondary concern. Are you certain your interest there is just as honorable?"

"Good God, Ash!" The insult landed with the force of pugilist Jackson's famed bunch of fives.

"Spare me your offense." Ash gripped his shoulder. "As your friend, I must be honest with you—especially when you are not being honest with yourself."

Hurtheven pulled away before he gave into impulse and planted an actual facer against Ash's cheek. "I admit I find the woman attractive." He held his palm to the throb in his temple. "But you *know* I would not insult her person."

At least not without her full consent.

Ash frowned. "In any other case, I would trust your honor, but, in this case, I want more."

"What more can I offer than my honor?"

"I want your word as my oldest friend." Ash lowered his voice. "I want your word as a member of the council, as the *Zeta* in *Eta, Rho, Zeta,* I want your word *as my brother,* that you will not endanger, compromise, or seduce Mrs. Montrose."

"I don't *seduce* women!"

"Oh?" Ash raised his brows. "A few scant years ago, didn't a bullet graze your arm as you were sneaking out some poor woman's window?"

He scowled. "I believed the lady and I had an exclusive, mutually agreed upon arrangement. Obviously, I was not her only lover at the time. And Lady Adelaide is a widow."

Ash hesitated. "As is Mrs. Montrose."

Was she? Housekeepers, he knew, often used *Mrs.* whether they'd ever married or not. His experience with nursemaids was, however, admittedly limited.

So, she'd been married. He didn't care for the idea at all. His discomfort alone was telling, was it not?

Ash might have a point.

"Well?" Ash prodded. "Will you give me your word?"

Hurtheven's face heated. "Don't you find this *pledge* you're demanding slightly hypocritical, given your history with Alicia?"

Ash narrowed his eyes. "So, you *do* have an interest in my nursemaid."

Damnation. "I didn't say I did."

Ash threw out his arms. "You didn't have to."

Hurtheven exhaled harshly. "I only admitted that I find her uncommonly attractive." He'd left out compelling, intriguingly feminine, and disarmingly tender with the children, among other things.

She'd become a tug beneath his ribs, a labyrinth he felt compelled to map.

"Despite your *high* opinion of me," he continued, "I do not endanger, compromise, and seduce every woman I find attractive. That would make me a right rogue."

"Instead of just a devil."

A hot flush shot up his neck. Now, he was angry. "You're testing my patience. Not to mention my good will. You'd place our friendship on the line over your children's *nursemaid*?"

Ash paced to the window and then grasped the sash. "Mrs. Montrose is, I understand from Alicia, very much alone, and she is now a valued part of my household. Need I remind you that, in the past, I failed to protect those in my care?"

As Hurtheven studied his friend, noting his pale-knuckled grip on the window frame. His fury drained. Ash hadn't been able to save his mother or his first wife, both of whom suffered at the hands of Ash's murderous father.

Of course he understood.

"You're speaking of the *distant* past," Hurtheven said.

"I have many faults, but I *do not* repeat my mistakes." Ash turned around and then propped himself, knee bent, up against the wall. "I cannot allow her to come to harm— and not just from you."

"Mrs. Montrose *is* in trouble, isn't she?" A cold, pointy-footed sensation tripped up Hurtheven's spine. "This impromptu visit is a means for her to conceal herself from someone."

Ash held his breath for an extended moment. He exhaled in a rush. "Her confidences would not be mine to extend even if I knew them in their entirety, which I do not."

"But you know enough to tell me if my assumptions are correct."

Ash grimaced. "They often are."

"Are the children at risk?"

"No. At least, I don't believe the threat extends to them—"

Hurtheven gripped the back of a chair in front of him, nearly lightheaded with relief.

"—The risk is only to Mrs. Montrose."

A darker, primal feeling flared within him. What could she be facing that would cause her to use a false name, hide herself away at Wisterley, and then need to flee in haste?

"Has she committed a crime?"

"To my knowledge, no. The pursuit is...of a personal nature. And that is my final word on the matter. For more, you will have to apply directly to Mrs. Montrose."

An unwanted paramour, then. Someone who thought to take advantage of her vulnerable state. He frowned. "You may trust me...*as you always have.* She will not come to harm while in my care."

Ash's cheek twitched. "I *am* being hypocritical, aren't I?"

"I'd hardly accuse you if you weren't," Hurtheven replied pointedly.

"And yet I cannot commend her to your care without *some* assurance." Ash sighed, clearly thinking. "Give me your word you will not seduce Mrs. Montrose. But if a...carnal entanglement should arise—"

"Ash—" he said warningly.

"*If,*" Ash repeated over his objection. "Then, you will do everything in your power to restore her respectability."

He blinked, not at all as surprised by the demand as he should have been. "Are you telling me you'd force me to wed the woman?"

He was not as adverse to the idea as he would have expected, either.

"I cannot force you to do anything," Ash replied. "I am *asking* that you keep in mind her honor, as well as your own."

He searched Ash's expression. Never in all the years they'd known one another, had Ash asked anything of him such as this. *He'd* become the hypocrite if he did not acknowledge the current situation was unique.

And volatile.

"Very well," he said finally. "I give you my word..."

"On your honor—"

"On my honor...and"—his eyes flashed—"*everything* else I hold dear, as that is the price you feel compelled to demand."

Ash visibly relaxed. "Shall we plan the route, then? You must avoid the more heavily traveled roads; else you, or she, be recognized along the way."

"And you'd rather we not be recognized?"

"Indeed, anonymity would be for the best."

Hurtheven followed him over to his desk.

Lines on the map spread out in an incoherent web. He knew almost nothing about this woman—not her age, not her origin, not even her family. And yet, he'd been intrigued —no, *spellbound*—from the moment he'd laid eyes on that stray curl.

What trouble lay head he couldn't fathom. But instinct told him protecting Mrs. Montrose from her foes, and from himself, just might prove to be his greatest labor yet.

Chapter Four

The Duke of Ashbey's well-sprung carriage was as comfortable as Hera could have possibly wished. The coachman's skill, above reproach. The roads they traveled...dry and reasonably maintained. Most importantly, the life-choking tension gripping Hera's heart eased as each new mile stretched between herself and Karl's Bow Street Runner.

In short, Hera had no reason for grievance.

Indeed, so long as she kept her gaze *inside* the carriage, she was fine. Given the oversized bonnet the Duchess of Ashbey had given her to better conceal her appearance, she had to crane her neck to see outside, anyway.

But even unseen, she couldn't deny her physical awareness of the duke.

Hurtheven clip-clopped along the side of the carriage, deep voice rumbling above the sounds of creaking springs and rattling wood. In quieter moments, she caught fragments of his discussion with Delmare, centering mostly on sights of historic, architectural, or agricultural significance.

She'd thought she'd accurately taken his measure—a

simple, arrogant, uncomfortably attractive bully, not unlike Karl. But his actions kept failing to meet her expectation.

Except on the *uncomfortably attractive* part, of course.

This morning, he'd accepted this dramatic change to his plans without complaint or question—at least to the duchess. He'd retreated into Ash's study and charted a route. Within an hour, a crestless carriage had been prepared, and they were on the road with a coachman, a groom, a footman, and a sparse collection of luggage. A cart with the bulk of the children's luggage would follow once Hurtheven's things from the Continent had been delivered.

He'd taken charge, yes, but less with arrogance than efficiency. Since then, he'd been considerate of the children's needs, patient with their whims, and courteous to the staff, herself included.

But *must* he also be—she turned her head—a fine horseman as well?

His body swayed in unison with the horse's canter. His posture was erect, his arms, loose. He was the picture of strong, athletic stamina combined with confident, relaxed control. Taken together, those attributes made his rhythmic movement, in her appraisal, almost overtly sensual.

Again, she felt the warm prickle of pins and needles in places she ought not.

She snapped straight and then placed her hand over Fee's closed parasol to stop her from bouncing the tip against the floor.

"*Ugh*. There's nothing to do inside!" Fee slumped against the bench. "Why didn't you let me keep my doll with me?"

"You decided you wanted your doll safely packed in the luggage—where she will not be ruined by dust or accidently lost, remember?"

She pursed up her lips in an expression that said she did recall but felt better assigning the blame to Hera. Then, her face brightened. "Next stop, Delmare and I will switch places, and then *I* can sit with the coachman."

"It isn't done for a young lady to sit on the box."

"But Delmare can?"

She patted Fee's knee. "I'm afraid so, love."

Fee dropped the whalebone contraption. She hissed through her teeth and then folded her arms. "*Not* fair."

Hera sighed. "I know, darling." Nothing about being held to standards of propriety was *fair*. And yet, following society's rules was the price women paid for survival. Be one type of woman, and men cast themselves in the role of your champion. Be another, and you became a flower for plucking, a creature for their sport.

In fact, Hera suspected fairness between the sexes wasn't a concept that would ever even occur to a man.

She sent Fee a sideways, sympathetic glance. "You'll understand these things better when you're older."

Felicia squeezed her eyes closed, her face a mask of mutiny.

Hera felt for Fee. Her own heart had never quite reconciled the disparity between men and women.

She'd been blamed for her provoking attractiveness (Karl), blamed for the expense of her "upkeep" (her brother), and, most recently, she'd been questioned as if she were a criminal simply because a man had decided she'd not been adequately forthcoming (Hurtheven). Like all women, she'd been rule-shackled from birth, confined to dependency, and then shamed for not having the means to fend for—or defend—herself.

"When we get to the castle," Fee announced, "Uncle

Heven will take me on his curricle before he takes Delmare. *That* will make things fair."

"Good thought." She brushed back Felicia's hair.

Fee was already demonstrating one of the more useful feminine skills—how to preserve her sense of dignity by cutting her losses and insisting on an acceptable alternative. The necessity of such machinations left a bitter taste on Hera's tongue.

She leaned back into the soft, velvet cushion, absently stroking Fee's arm...and studiously avoiding the window.

But Fee refused to be comforted.

And within the quarter hour, she'd resumed murmuring about her frustrations beneath her breath and clunking her feet against the bench. In another half hour, she was grimacing and holding her stomach.

"I can't stay inside one more minute!" she groaned.

"Do you feel as if you're going to be sick?" Hera placed her hand against Fee's forehead.

Fee nodded. "Please ask the coachman to stop the carriage?"

"Your uncle told you he'd planned hourly stops. We must not be that far from the next one."

"*Please*," Fee repeated. Her cheeks pinked. "I *need* to get out. Need. Need. *Need.*"

Hera propped Fee's parasol against the opposing seat so she could reach up and knock against the roof.

The carriage slowed as the wheels turned onto the grass beside the road. She held fast to the strap and glanced in either direction. On one side was a wooded area. On the other, a collection of neat stone houses with tidy thatched roofs. Hurtheven appeared in the window on the side with the stone houses.

Her breath knotted as he opened the door. She'd

expected him to be annoyed with the delay. *Wrong again.* Instead, a lock of thick, ebony hair fell across a brow wrinkled only with concern. One, quick stroke would tuck his wayward mane back into place. She could almost feel the luxuriant texture between her fingers.

She folded her hands together.

"Lady Felicia is not well." She exchanged a significant glance with the duke. "Are we close to a place we might make a"—she side-eyed Fee—"prolonged stop?"

"Worn out, are you?" he asked the child.

Fee nodded, looking pitiful.

"A moment, if you please." Hurtheven leaned back. In soothingly low tones, he conferred with the coachman. Then, he dipped his head, once again filling the open doorway. "You're in luck, Dumpling. There's an inn at the crossroads about a quarter mile up and a pathway parallel to the road that runs through that wood."

Hera turned to ask how Fee felt about a walk but only managed an *oof* as Fee was already scrambling over her lap.

"Oh, thank you!" Fee launched herself into Hurtheven's arms.

"Don't forget your coat and parasol," Hera reminded.

"You don't need your coat, do you, Fee?" he asked.

"No," she replied. "I'm not a ninny. I don't get cold."

"Stout as they come," Hurtheven agreed.

Hera sent him a look of disapproval, which he pretended not to see. So, she stepped outside the carriage to judge the weather for herself. The day had warmed, but she hooked the parasol over her arm just in case Fee changed her mind.

They stood back along a short stone wall as the carriage pulled away. As they waited for the halo of dust to clear, she marveled.

What a strange little group they must have seemed. Right now, anyone looking out one of the cottages' windows might assume they were a family.

Her fantastical thought produced an unwelcome stab of longing.

She glanced surreptitiously at the duke. Karl never would have held his own daughter as the duke held Fee. Nor would Karl have taken the time to converse with his son the way Hurtheven conversed with Delmare.

The duke respected the children as the tiny people they were, and would, she thought, make an excellent father.

Delmare's shout and Fee's simultaneous squeal refocused her attention on the road as a glossy, black cart fashioned with a cage full of screaming primates jostled past them at a considerable clip.

She lifted her scarf across her face and squinted after the tiny, travelling prison. Her heart panged with sympathy for the poor creatures, taken from their natural homes and habitats, only to be carted off to who-knew-where with absolutely no control over their fate.

"New additions for Lord Chandon's famous menagerie, no doubt," Hurtheven explained. "His estate isn't too much farther to the northwest."

Hera frowned. Why collect and cage living beings? To quell a lordship's boredom, naturally!

"Frankly," Hurtheven murmured, "I don't approve, either."

She glanced at him suspiciously. She hadn't said a word. Had she?

He slanted her a smile. "Your features are more expressive than you are aware, Mrs. Montrose."

"I'll have to be more careful."

"Now"—he winked—"that would be a shame."

His teasing wink generated a second sensation as equally unwelcome as her longing had been.

"Maybe the cart will also stop at the inn?" Fee asked hopefully.

"Maybe," Hurtheven answered.

"Let's go, then!" Fee bounced as if he were a pony she could urge into a trot.

Delmare skipped ahead toward the embankment. "The path is here!" he called over his shoulder. "Just like the coachman said."

"Jones is very experienced. Which is why..." He raised his brows expectantly.

"...We consult him before making final decisions about the route," Delmare answered.

"Very good." Hurtheven made his way down to the path without a single unsteady step.

Hera lifted her skirts and searched for a solid place to place her foot, finding none. Suddenly he was there, free hand outstretched, the courtly embodiment of manners and breeding and masculine charm. If that weren't enough to remind her to take care, a faint, heavenly scent clung to his person. She would have refused to touch him, but she couldn't be rude.

Not in front of Fee. The child was hard enough to manage as she was!

She placed her hand in his. Contact threaded the now familiar, though no less unsettling, warmth though her veins.

"Thank you." She stepped onto the pathway and immediately tugged back her hand, instinctively holding her fist against her chest as if she'd been singed.

Which she had been.

"Down," Fee commanded.

"I'd like to be set down, now, *please*," Hera corrected.

"Down, *please*," Felica revised.

Hurtheven set her on the ground. Almost immediately, her brother jumped out from behind a bush with a roar. Felicia squealed and threw her arms around Hurtheven's legs.

"Delmare—" the duke scolded.

"He *scared* me," Fee cried.

"—Apologize."

Delmare placed his hands on his hips. "I'm sorry I have a frightened chicken for a sister."

"I'm not a chicken!"

"Are!" Delmare tapped his sister's shoulder and then ran.

"Not." Felicia chased him.

"Are!" Delmare called back.

Hurtheven bit back a snort.

"It doesn't help when you laugh," Hera said under her breath.

"Likely not. They're just high-spirited."

"Please don't make excuses I will later have to defend." Hera called down the lane, insisting the children end their "discussion." "Now," she said after she caught up to them, "give each other a *proper* apology."

Once satisfied with their efforts, she gave them permission to continue onward. When she turned back, Hurtheven was there. Just behind her. Yet again, he'd moved quickly and without sound.

He inclined his head; his twinkling gaze held hers. "I'm sorry, Mrs. Montrose. I should not have encouraged them by laughing. Will you accept my proper apology, too?"

"Very well." She cursed the tug within her heart and

refused this burgeoning affection for the duke. Any affinity would be exceedingly unwise...and dangerous.

He resumed walking. Reluctantly, she followed.

"Are you enjoying the walk?" he asked.

"I am."

"You might as well walk *with* me, then."

"I thought I was."

"A step behind, if you must know." He caught up her hand and then placed her fingers against his arm, forcing her to fall into step beside him.

She turned her face so she could see him past the bonnet. "Does it matter?"

"It does, actually," he replied.

"I'm not your equal."

"No, but, in their eyes"—he gestured ahead to the children—"there is a greater parity between us than my title would suggest."

"I compel them to listen. I put them to bed. I teach them letters and sums. I make sure they are fed. All very good reasons to mind me—"

"Certainly."

"—*You*, on the other hand, dazzle their little minds." She glanced askance. "And you make them happy."

"Happy," he repeated thoughtfully.

When the children stopped to inspect the chiseled words on a marker, Hera and the duke stopped as well.

"Why, Mrs. Montrose"—he cocked his head—"did you just compliment me?"

"Were you always so good with children?" She skirted his query—as well as the school of fish leaping and twisting inside her stomach.

"Interesting question." He smiled slightly, just enough to show he'd noted her conversational detour. "I spent a great deal of time with Thaddeus when he was young. Thaddeus is my godchild as well, you know."

"Kind of you to take on the care of so many children."

"No. Not kind." He shook his head at some internal thought and then fixed his gaze in the distance. "It's important to me that the children..." He paused. "...experience childhood."

"You left part of that sentence out."

His lids hooded his eyes. "Perceptive."

Hera could think of only two reasons a duke could have such a concern—one, he'd had an idyllic childhood and wanted the same for the children he loved. Or two...

She recalled an overlooked portion of the conversation she'd heard the day of the garden party. What had that awful woman said? Something about the duke having survived an accident that had taken the lives his parents?

She searched his gaze.

There was something lurking behind the polish, wasn't there? Something deep and sad and deliberately hidden.

A different kind of internal tug yanked her from her safe mental pool into a place she could find no footing. She felt him, then...experienced his presence as if he were not a duke, but a man with whom she was in sympathy. She sensed his fearsome will and power, but also something old, dim, and murky.

Lost—the word came unbidden.

"What are you reading, Mrs. Montrose?"

She flushed deeply. "I wouldn't presume."

"Wouldn't you?" He reached into his pocket and pulled out a coin. He rolled the shiny bit of metal between his fingers. "Yours, if your assumption is correct."

She looked at him incredulously. "A literal penny for your thoughts?"

81

"A wager, not a levy." He stepped closer. "I'm quite serious."

"Why?" She couldn't properly breathe under his gaze.

"Insatiable curiosity?" He lifted her gloved hand with his own and placed the penny in the center of her palm. "Come, Mrs. Montrose. Accept the challenge."

Hera kept her gaze on their joined palms while every nerve stretched toward him.

She was hot. And cold. And dizzy. *Breathe.* She willed a light, nonsensical answer, but not a single thought entered her mind to counter the truth she'd just seen. Every falsehood scattered to the wind with each stroke of his thumb.

Finally, she sighed. "You've known great pain, Your Grace—"

He stopped caressing her wrist.

"—That's what I read."

Carefully, he closed her fingers over the coin. "Yours." He dropped her hand. "Delmare!" he called as he strode away. "Fee! Not so far ahead."

Oh, heavens! She stared down at the penny in her palm. He was, at present, her best hope of survival. And, she wagered, she'd just made him mad as the dickens.

* * *

Again. *Electrified.*

Every tendon in his extremities had gone taught. A distinct vibration buzzed through his veins. Dampness sprouted beneath his collar and in his palms.

He trod purposefully onward.

He should not have touched her. Held her palm in his own. Breathed in her light, seductive scent as he caressed her wrist with the pad of his thumb.

A night's rest had not cured him of his lust after all.

To preserve his sanity—and his promise to Ash—he'd ridden outside the carriage. And yet, at first opportunity, he'd taken any excuse to touch her. And each, successive touch had amplified parts of himself he'd thought he'd silenced.

Her direct, clear gaze had sparked lightness and hope, as if he was nearing the end of a long and difficult journey and all he need do to reach a glorious destination was quicken his pace. The reeling feeling had caused him to drop his guard.

No wonder she'd *seen* him, then.

His boots crunched in the gravel.

What had possessed him to place that wager? *An actual penny for your thoughts.*

He'd guessed that she'd heard his hesitation. Guessed that she'd seen and felt his devotion to the children. He'd assumed that's what she'd tell him. And, so, a little wager. Nothing, really. A penny for prolonged contact. He hadn't expected her to bare his soul.

Friends close. Secrets Closer. Stay closed, coiled, and ready to strike.

"Your Grace," she called. "I apologize—"

The uncharacteristic panic in her voice stopped him.

Damnation.

He was at fault, not she. She, who had so much to lose and who—somewhat involuntarily—had placed her safekeeping in his hands. Which was what she'd done, he was certain. Nothing else but her jeopardy would have caused Alicia to make such an abrupt suggestion and Ash to issue his dire warning, as Ash had all but confirmed.

He'd been unfair. And to leave her thinking he was

angry with *her* was unjust. He stretched his lips into a brittle smile and then turned around.

"You've no need to apologize." Measure by measure, his control returned. "I asked. You answered. It's a rare person capable of honesty to a duke."

"...Or a foolish one." Her exertions had prettily flushed her cheeks.

"I see no fool."

He gazed down into her eyes. Not deep green, but a shining peridot—light and wide and entirely focused on his own. Time suspended between what had been and what was to come. That they would know one another more deeply than either was prepared to admit seemed self-evident, an accomplished fact.

His heartbeat ratcheted up.

She lifted her still closed fist. "Take it back."

Was she still breathless from the walk? Or was the same, internal tide that had so fully engulfed his spirit also dragging her, waterlogged and resisting?

"What I gave"—his words bubbled up—"I gave freely."

"You didn't." She wet her lips. "I should know how to keep my thoughts to myself by now. I'm ashamed—"

"You are angry with yourself?" he asked, surprised.

Her expression grew incredulous. "Of course."

"Then you understand my own feelings."

Her brows knit. "You're not angry with *me*?"

He placed both his hands around her fisted fingers. Such a thin, small hand. Delicate and yet so capable. A contradiction, like its owner. "You see, Mrs. Montrose, I never, intentionally or otherwise, reveal a secret...especially not one of my own. Yet," he exhaled softly, "somehow, you managed to see it in spite of me."

Her pinked skin rosed into mauve. Her hand was tightly

fisted. Trembling. Ghastly of him to have frightened her so much. He brushed his lips lightly against her dark leather glove.

"Keep what you've fairly won. Please."

She lifted her face to his.

Had he been talking about the penny? Not entirely. But he couldn't quite fathom the deeper meaning while his whole being was wick to an internal flame. Her face haloed. His focus dropped to her lips. If he kissed her now, he was certain that kiss would forever alter the trajectory of his life.

If he kissed her, her breath would be warm, her lips, pliant and smooth.

When—he bent his head—he kissed her...

"A fine day to be out with the family."

She leapt backwards with spider-like speed.

He swiveled to face the stranger, shielding her with his body. "Forgive our private moment. Still like newlyweds, we are."

"Don't you pay any mind to me." The elderly stranger chuckled as he waved his hand, summarily dismissing his concern. "I'm heading to see the animals. They've been coming through all day on their way north to some toff's menagerie. Whole village is agog."

Fee peeked out from behind Hera's skirts. "We saw the monkeys."

"Rumor has it, there's a lion, too!" the man said to Fee.

"A lion?!" Delmare popped out from the other side. "Just like in the story you told me!" He tugged on Hurtheven's fawn leather breeches. "The one about Heracles. Can we see the menagerie? Can we?"

"I'm afraid the menagerie is not in the direction we are headed," Hurtheven replied.

"But *monkeys*," Felicia whined.

The stranger chuckled. "Didn't mean to rile the wee ones." He inclined his head. "Good day, then...to you, and the missus."

The stranger barely turned the bend ahead when the chorus of *pleases* resumed.

"We haven't the time." Hurtheven silenced the groans with a raised hand. "However, if the cart with the monkeys has stopped at the inn, and Mrs. Montrose has no objection, you may observe them there while I arrange for a light repast."

Groans transformed into cheers.

Hurtheven turned toward the nursemaid. Her head remained bowed, as if she wasn't certain the stranger had actually departed.

"Have you any objection?" he murmured.

"No." Her voice had gone small and brittle. "Of course not."

He'd been feeling guilty for touching her before. Now, he felt positively damned. "Since I subjected you to potential gossip, I was compelled to offer an explanation."

"We are not in a London ballroom, Your Grace."

Clearly, she'd been more upset by being caught than he'd anticipated, but he couldn't tell the depth without seeing her face. Short of demanding she look at him, however, or crooking his knuckle beneath her chin and raising her face...

"Just like newlyweds," she gritted under her breath.

"Spontaneous self-preservation." Although he was not sure he'd given the correct reason. To claim they were wed, in fact, had felt natural. He crouched down. "Children, while we're at the inn, we're going to play a game."

"What kind of game?" Delmare asked.

"When we get to the inn, we're going to pretend that we're a family."

"Isn't that lying?" Fee demanded.

"No," Delmare answered. "It's *acting*, just like in the theater. Right, Uncle Heven?"

"Acting, yes," he said. "Do you think you can pretend, just while we're at the inn?"

"But the coachman—" Mrs. Montrose interrupted.

"Has been instructed not to reveal anything about his passengers," he finished her sentence. "I find flaunting one's wealth and station when traveling a long distance unwise."

"Do we have to do acting because you kissed Mrs. Montrose?" Fee asked.

"*Hand*," Mrs. Montrose added sharply. "He kissed my *hand*. And you can just say 'act'—not 'do acting'."

"Do we have to act because you kissed Mrs. Montrose's *hand*?" Fee's sly glance said she knew that the kissing would have progressed if the stranger hadn't appeared.

"Yes," Hurtheven admitted. Fee wouldn't settle for anything less than strict veracity, anyway. "By my means of...thanking Mrs. Montrose, I subjected us all to gossip. Better to have the strangers we meet here believe we are what we appear—a family traveling together."

"I can act," Delmare bounced as he spoke.

"Me, as well!" shouted Fee. "Better than him."

"We'll see whose acting is best." He pressed down his knees as he rose to his feet. "Now, you may run ahead—just don't get too far."

They skipped down the lane.

"Do you think this is wise?" she asked.

"I think the issue is adequately resolved." *For now.* "You may trust me."

She eyed him, wary. Then, she nodded as she took his proffered arm.

Truth was, nothing he'd done since he'd first laid eyes on her had been wise. And, given the heat still sizzling beneath his collar and the profound pleasure he took from her touch, he wasn't at all certain she *should* accept his invitation to trust him.

Because more likely than not, he thought grimly, he was going to continue to be unwise where she was concerned.

Very unwise.

* * *

No matter how lightly she laid her hand against Hurtheven's muscled bicep, she could not deaden the effect of his nearness. Nor could she deny the heady, thick-lipped feeling she'd had when she'd thought they were about to kiss.

Good Lord, what a simpleton she was!

You may trust me, indeed! She'd trusted a man with a similar, pyretic lust in his eyes before. She would not make the same mistake again.

And yet, here she was with the duke's penny in her pocket, her hand on his arm, pretending to be his wife, and wishing they hadn't been interrupted before she'd tasted the honeyed temptation of his kiss.

But they *had* been interrupted. And the stranger had witnessed her reckless behavior, too. Then again, if said stranger hadn't happened along the road, where would she have been?

Giving Delmare and Fee quite the tale to take home to their parents, that's where she would have been! And— *heavens*, how would she answer the question of her *reformation* then? She'd never, ever forgotten herself like that with Karl.

With Hurtheven, however, she was not just responding to *his* express interest.

She wanted *him*, too.

She wanted him with the fever of a gambler begging just one, last card. Her deep blush throbbed in her cheeks. Her urgent sense of need left her alert and breathless. Her flesh still tingled in the spot where his mouth had touched the back of her hand. Not enough to purposely risk her future, but certainly enough to temporarily lose her mind.

What had he said? *Keep what you've fairly won.*

She hadn't felt like he'd been telling her to keep the penny. Instead, she felt as if he'd been telling her to keep the part of himself, he'd unintentionally revealed. What was more, she *wanted* him to voluntarily place every one of his secrets into her safekeeping.

More fool, her—especially when she could never reveal her own.

She had to put distance between them. Her priority was Annis. This experience was nothing more than a curious idyll that, if everything went as planned, would soon come to an end.

But for now... She glanced askance at the man who was, for the next few hours, to be her "husband."

"You did not mention our name," she said.

"Pardon?" He jerked as if her question had snapped him out of a reverie of his own.

"Well, you cannot introduce me as your duchess, can you?"

His muscle flexed beneath her hand.

"Might I suggest something...not at all memorable?" She

continued. "Smith, for instance? *If* your consequence can handle being so lowered."

He surprised her with a chuckle and then a darkly sardonic glance. "Smith it is. I will nurse my wounded pride later."

She *humph*ed.

"A fine day to find oneself wed, wouldn't you say, Mrs. Smith?"

Her gaze slid to his profile. She imagined his future bride would feel very fine, indeed, no matter what the weather on their wedding day. Peevishly, she was glad the woman would have to put up with his exceptionally high opinion of himself in perpetuity.

She recalled his list. *Intelligent without the pretention of being a bluestocking?*

That *could* describe her...

Ugh. She forced herself to remember his other petty requirements. *Mild mannered! Blonde!*

And, as to his implicit criticism of bluestockings, that was abhorrent. She hated to think herself the kind of a person who joined in derision for approval's sake. Even the most pretentious of women were her sisters in womanhood, were they not?

Of course, she planned to teach Annis to read and write and love the written word as soon as Annis was old enough to learn. She resolved right there that, somewhere, someday, she'd also host reading salons in a pair of robin's egg blue stockings.

Up ahead, the children began a repeated chorus of "the inn!" Then, a collection of white-walled buildings came into sight.

Between the largest building and the smallest—a chicken coop, most likely—sat a pile of broken furniture.

The bleached grey wood suggested the pieces had been waiting to be repaired for quite some time. A few chickens popped their heads out of an opening in the lean-to shack, and just as quickly disappeared back inside their pen. Delicious smells emanated from a doorway Hera assumed led to the kitchen.

"It appears we've come in from the rear," Hurtheven said. "I will go inside and see what I can arrange. Would you like to come with me, or would you like to go find our carriage?"

"I want to go find our carriage and see if there are any monkeys are in the courtyard! May I?" Delmare begged.

"Please," Fee added, fingers folded and eyes pleading.

She glanced to Hurtheven. "Looks like it's the carriage for us."

Hurtheven chuckled. "Probably best."

"Goodbye...*Papa,*" Fee said with a giggle.

He folded his hands behind his back and bowed. Then, he turned on his heel and strode off toward a door. Even if he was not recognized, that walk, that arrogant, self-assured stride, even in unfamiliar surroundings...

Well, few would mistake him for a man not used to having his way.

She would simply have to make sure he did not *have his way* where she was concerned.

Collecting a child in each hand, she turned toward the courtyard. As they rounded the side of the building, they came upon their carriage—but no coachman. She frowned, craning her neck, looking for someone.

Anyone.

Where was everyone? Usually, a place like this would be bustling, but not at present. Everyone had simply vanished. Even the horses were missing from the carriage.

There had been more signs of life at the back of the building.

"Look!" Delmare called. "There's a cart like the monkey cart, only it's empty."

Indeed, a cage had been left open. Then she noticed that the courtyard wasn't just empty but littered with hastily dropped objects.

A groom's brush. A broom. A basket of food, tossed on its side...

She followed a trail of food across the courtyard. There, beneath the tree near the stables were the fresh remains of a sheep—a sheep viciously torn to pieces.

"Children," she said. "Get into the carriage and close the door."

Blessedly, they did not argue. As they clattered unto the carriage behind her, the animal she'd been seeking sauntered out from behind the tree. She'd only seen such a creature in drawings, and the artistry had failed to capture the animal's awful beauty.

A sound like thunder came from the beast's throat—a terrible, threatening noise that portended destruction. A noise that was everywhere at once.

She froze in place. Completely unable to function.

"Mrs. Montrose!"

Blood rushed to her head. "Stay down!" she called back without turning. "Be quiet!"

The beast threw back its head. A long, pink tongue darted out and flicked over its teeth. She checked over her shoulder just to make sure Delmare had closed the door. She kicked aside the steps. The animal's gaze followed the clattering wooden stairs.

Yes. "That's it," she cooed. "You're not interested in a carriage, are you?"

The lion paced, eyes moving between the carriage and herself. Oh God! Where was everyone? She took a few slow, backward steps away from the wheels.

"Beast! Me!" She patted down her coat for something to catch his attention and then remembered Fee's parasol. "Over here. Come here." She used the contraption to bang the dust. "Hey!"

The lion continued to watch the carriage.

Pink fabric gave a whining stretch as she opened Fee's parasol.

The beast made another awful noise—a growl that almost brought her to her knees. *Breathe.* If she could remain calm, she could master the situation. Or, at the very least, lead the thing away from the children.

Behind the cover of the parasol, she tossed a rock toward what appeared to be a blacksmith's shop. The beast's head whipped in the direction she'd thrown.

Somewhere in the inn, something clattered. For a terrifying moment, she thought the animal would decide to stalk the carriage.

"No!" she shouted. "Me! Follow me!"

Chapter Five

The inn's rear door opened into a deserted kitchen —recently deserted, judging by the bubbling pot on the stove, the haphazard placement of utensils strewn across a long trestle table, and the hunk of bloody meat left atop a grinder.

With a growing sense of dismay, Hurtheven followed the sound of hushed voices through a pantry, and then a taproom, before finally finding a small crowd gathered at the front-facing windows of the coffee room.

His eyes took a moment to adjust to the dimmer surroundings. "To whom do I apply for assistance?" he asked.

No one answered.

He scanned the faces of a dozen or more people. But if Ash's coachman, his groom, and his footman had reached the inn, they were not present now. His gaze settled on the most likely proprietors—a tall, matronly woman with a blood-stained apron and a portly fellow with his hand atop her shoulder.

"Oh!" the woman held a towel to her mouth. "I cannot

stand it! Death in my courtyard! We'll be cursed for certain!"

"There, now." The man's grip tightened. "The wee ones made it into the carriage! There's hope yet—she's leading the beast away."

"She'll be killed for sure," the woman replied.

"Not a chance. The lion's just eaten—"

Hurtheven glanced sharply at the man who'd spoken last—a tall, thin fellow in a billowing cloak.

"—There's that in her favor."

For a fraction of a moment, he did not fully grasp what he'd heard, though a strengthening fury within him went from a simmer to a fully rolling boil.

"Do you think we should go back out there, Jem?" This from a smaller man in a black cap. "Give it another go? Ain't right leaving her out there alone."

In three, swift strides, Hurtheven inserted himself between the two men. In the courtyard beyond, Mrs. Montrose held Fee's parasol aloft. She was backing away from the carriage. The object of her focus was beyond his view.

"Heavens," the woman with the towel breathed. "Just look at that awful thing."

A large cat with a tawny coat prowled into the window's frame. *Lion.* The word finally embodied meaning.

A *lion* was loose in a courtyard with Mrs. Montrose and his godchildren.

He jostled the window's inner shutter, capturing the beast's attention and temporarily arresting its stalk. "What the devil is everyone doing just standing around? Who here"—he spoke over the banging shutter—"is responsible for that animal?"

The man in the cloak eyed him up and down. "Who is asking?"

He abandoned the shutter and grasped the man by the collar. "That is my coach. Those children are in my care. And," he added without hesitating, "that woman is my wife."

"He-he won't hurt her," the man stammered. "He's just eaten a lamb."

The beast lost interest in the window and glanced behind him. Hurtheven followed his gaze to the remains of a sheep, belly up, neck extended, eyes shocked and sightless. His fury burned hotter still.

Meanwhile, Mrs. Montrose scrambled up the woodpile stacked against the smithy. Immediately, she started chucking pieces of wood at the tree above the lion.

Hurtheven shoved the man against the shutter and pulled out a pistol. "If you won't take care of that thing, I intend to do so."

"Now just hold on a minute!" The smaller, black-capped fellow cut in. "The lion belongs to Lord Chandon. If we lose him, we'll have to pay."

Hurtheven kept one eye on the lion, ready to shoot through the glass, if needed, and the other on Montvale's driver. "You had best come up with a plan. If he moves toward her, or the children, he's dead."

"Let me just think!" the cloaked man insisted.

"You'd better think fast."

"We'd need ten people—or more—to lure him back toward the cage. And chairs. Multiple moving points will mesmerize the animal. If distracted, he won't attack."

"There's a stack of broken furniture out back." Hurtheven said. "Where is my coachman? Footman? Groom? For that matter, where are the inn's postillions?"

"In the stable, I should think," the innkeeper replied.

He'd barely been aware of the movement in the crowd behind him, but four wiry young men had already retrieved the damaged chairs.

"Got 'em, gov!"

"We'll help."

"Bless me." The aproned woman clasped her hands as if in prayer. "What can I do?"

"Wouldn't have another lamb you'd be willing to sacrifice?" the capped man asked.

"There's raw meat in the kitchen," Hurtheven replied.

"Ready meat could help get him back in the cage, though how we're to get between—"

"You—" He pointed to the smallest of the boys standing ready. "You have good aim?"

The boy puffed up his chest. "The best."

"Give him the meat—have him toss it from the roof into the cage."

"Right away," the aproned woman answered.

Hurtheven hustled the lion's keepers to the doorway. "The two of you advance. The rest of us will block his retreat." He threw open the door. The lion's attention focused on him. "Any sign he's about to attack, I'll shoot. Go!"

The lion's deadly gaze followed each successive man as they fanned out through the courtyard. Then, the beast focused on the closest person.

"There's a nice cat," Hurtheven crooned, locking gazes with the animal. The other men fanned out in a wide semicircle around the beast brandishing chairs—someone rolled one in Hurtheven's direction. He picked it up. Four points, the man had said. Keep them moving.

He couldn't do this if he had to think. Not of the children. Not of himself. "Nice, calm kitty."

The boy tossed a bag of meat from the roof into the open cage. An excellent shot—the child hadn't been boasting.

"Inside the cage, now," the cloaked man urged. "You've had your run about."

Somewhere in the distance a young sheep bayed. Saliva dripped from the lion's mouth. As the semi-circle closed in, he backed toward the open cage.

Hurtheven passed Mrs. Montrose, still balanced atop the pile of wood. His heartbeat slowed. She was safe, now. The children were safe. To attack them, the beast would have to get through him, first. And there was no way he'd allow that to happen.

The men closed in, backing the lion up the ramp and into his cage.

The click of the cage door sent a rush of blood through his veins. He slipped the pistol into his pocket, set down the chair, and then gripped the chair's warped toprail.

Breathe. Sweat beaded at his brow. *Breathe.*

He felt a hand against the small of his back. Her hand. He knew. What he did not know was how she'd managed to stay so calm through the experience.

"Are you well?" He turned. "Unharmed?"

She blinked at him, dazed. Her arm hovered in the air. The still-open parasol dangled off her wrist. A deep-rooted, fernlike emotion unfurled within; he tingled as if its fronds were lightly prodding even his utmost extremities. In bravery, she was unequaled. To say he was deeply moved was understatement.

She'd utterly stupefied him.

For a moment, he could comprehend nothing but her

face. If he could have, he would have remained ensconced in that moment, fully enthralled. But she closed her eyes and swayed.

"Mrs—" He stopped himself. *His wife.* To the curious onlookers, she was his wife. He took her by the arm. "Ma'am."

"The children..." she murmured.

"The children," he repeated, "are safe."

He kept a comforting hand over her own as, together, they approached the carriage. Delmare's low voice emanated through the door.

"You'll see, Fee. Heracles vanquished a lion. Daniel went right into the den!"

Hurtheven opened the door.

"There aren't any lions in England, Del. Except *maybe* in Exeter exchange—Uncle—Papa!" Fee corrected as she scrambled up. "Did you van—van—"

"Vanquish," Mrs. Montrose's voice was calm, but her gaze remained hazed and distant. "We did."

"Is he dead?" Fee squeaked.

"Safely back in its cage," Hurtheven replied.

"Oh, Mrs—Mama!" Fee launched herself at the nurse-maid. "I was scared! *So* Scared! I'm sorry I ever wanted to see the animals. Are you hurt?"

"I'm fine." Mrs. Montrose took the child into her arms and held her tightly. "You're fine. I'm fine. He's fine. Even the lion is fine. Oh, heavens." She closed her eyes. "We are fine, aren't we? We're fine."

She was trying to convince herself as much as the child. He understood. She'd used every ounce of her courage to tie herself together, but the ropes were wearing thin.

"I was scared." Fee repeated. "I thought—"

"I know, darling." She stroked Fee's back. "Me, too."

"*You* were scared?"

"Yes. *Oh,* yes."

"I didn't know where Unc—Papa was!" Fee shuddered as she inhaled. "But you came, didn't you? You came!"

Hurtheven's lips hardened in self-recrimination. She shouldn't have been out there alone with the children. If he hadn't been so wrapped up in what had almost happened in the lane...

"I came," Hurtheven placed a hand on Fee's head. "If in my power, I will always be here for you."

Delmare leaned against his leg. Likely wanting the same comfort, but too proud to accept reassurance in public.

He gripped the boy's shoulder with his other hand. "You did a very good job of listening to Mrs. Montrose. And keeping Fee calm."

Delmare stilled his trembling lip. "Thank you, ah, Papa."

"Come in," the woman with the apron motioned to them from the doorway of the inn. "Come in and have a sit down."

"Well?" Hurtheven raised his brows.

"You're asking me what we should do next?" Mrs. Montrose replied with a question.

"You are my wife," he reminded her of their deception.

"Ah, yes." Mrs. Montrose adjusted Fee's clothing—twisting her stocking back into place and then retying a bow. She wobbled a bit as she stood. "Your wife." She cupped her forehead. "Yes." She gazed down at the children. "I think—" She glanced back at the beast pacing inside the cage. "I think... We should..." She closed her eyes. "I must beg your pardon. I—I cannot seem to..."

Her skin paled. Her eyes unfocused. He caught her as she crumpled.

"She's dead!" Fee waled.

"Just fainted," Delmare took his sister's hand.

He lifted her up. Despite her height, she wasn't heavy at all. He brought her head against his shoulder. Her disarrayed hair tickled beneath his chin. The shame he'd felt transformed into a calling.

He'd protect her, now. She'd not know fear like this again.

"It appears," he said with determination, "my wife and I are in need of lodging."

* * *

A light breeze cooled Hera's face. She turned her head into pillowy softness and breathed in a scent—spiced, rich, and with a lightly floral undertone. She'd inhaled the scent before but could not remember where.

She'd no recollection of climbing abed, either. Nor of removing her coat and bonnet. Although she'd had some hazy awareness of having opened her eyes to a woman clucking with the command that she rest. However, the last thing she *clearly* remembered...

She sat up straight. "The children!"

The bedlinens that had been tucked up around her neck fell away. She blinked into near-darkness from a bed opposite a window and vaguely haloed in moonlight. A figure beside the mattress set aside the book in his hand—the one he'd been using to fan her face.

"The children are asleep. *Finally*." His deep baritone whisper came from the shadows. "If you make too much fuss, they'll wake."

Hurtheven.

She glanced down. She was still in her clothes, thank

goodness. She gathered the bedlinens back up beneath her chin anyway. She may be hot, beaded with sweat and disoriented—but *he* need not know the extent to which she was disheveled.

"Where are they?" she asked.

His inky form leaned to one side. A coal fire glow beyond revealed two bundles in a tiny trundle. *Safe*. And, apparently, sleeping in the same bed.

Despite her unease, an involuntary, quiet laugh bubbled up. "*That* couldn't have been easy."

"Vienna negotiations were less of a challenge." His voice held an unseen smile. "We must've gone ten rounds before finally settling on head to feet."

"With no face-kicking?"

"I should have known you'd tried the scheme before. Fee did complain of Delmare's odiferous stockings, but, on threat of dire consequences—unnamed, of course, to increase their hideousness—they eventually settled into a mutually agreeable position."

Well, at least not *everything* came easily to him.

She frowned—*uncharitable thought*—and herself uniquely indebted to him, too. He'd been the one to organize their rescue, she was certain. No one else had come to her aid until he burst out of the door.

How had he persuaded the people who finally mounted the rescue to risk their lives for strangers?

"Did you tell the men who helped you that you're a duke?" she asked.

"Still plain old Mr. Smith, traveling with my family." He snorted derisively. "Although Fee's penchant for calling me *Uncle Papa* has raised a few brows."

She blinked into the darkness, still focused on the fact

he had convinced the men to face the lion entirely by the force of his character.

"I imagine," he continued, "the story will be spread over half the county by morning. To avoid awkward questions—and the inevitable crowds—we'll have to leave at first light. As it is, the characters gathered below have demanded reports on your health hourly until the innkeeper closed the taproom just after the midnight bell."

She gasped. "That late already?"

"I'm afraid it's only you, me, and the moonlight." He cleared his throat. "Do you think you'll be well enough to travel in a few hours?"

"Yes, yes of course," she lied. "But the children. Have they sufficiently recovered from their ordeal?"

"They are children." He rested his elbows on his spread legs, though his face remained shrouded. "They'll retell the story until they feel beyond its reach, and they will take on the spirit of those they trust."

"Like you?"

He inclined his head. "And yourself."

"What did you tell them?"

"I told them the outcome was never in doubt. That they can trust us both to care for them and keep them safe..."

So, he'd lied. But what a beautiful lie! How long had it been since she'd felt cared for? Safe?

When she was little and her mother was alive, she'd felt the curious stares and derisive whispers whenever they'd gone out as a family with her much older father—not harmful so much as hurtful, although she'd sensed they were objects of derision. Only after her father died had she learned what it was to truly lack security.

"Perhaps I laid it on a bit thick," Hurtheven continued,

"but they needed sleep. And to sleep, they needed to set aside their fears."

"I'm glad you were able to calm them." She reached to her hair only to realize her braid had come loose and her wretched spirals had hopelessly matted. "I apologize for being...indisposed."

"There's no need to apologize. I left you alone. If anyone is at fault—"

"There was no need to escort me back to the carriage." She cut in before he could shoulder the blame. "I am not a lady." Why was she forever feeling the need to remind him?

"A fundamental wrong, in my opinion."

"Nonsense," she croaked.

He poured a glass of water. "Drink."

How had he known she was thirsty?

She, of course, was constantly anticipating—feeling her charge's feelings, apprehending her employers' desires. She'd a natural sensitivity to others she'd honed. Because her livelihood depended on being thoughtful, aware and one step ahead.

She'd never, however, had someone not only divine her yearnings but endeavor to meet them as well.

The water went down roughly through her parched throat. Their fingers brushed as she handed him back the glass. He wasn't wearing gloves. Nor was she. Contact shocked her once again.

She doubted she was in danger from him, not with the children so close by, but still, the situation was far too intimate.

"You," she said, "And I...*we* should not be... What I mean to say is..."

"I'm going down to spend the night on a bench off the taproom." He saved her from inelegance. "What's left of the night, that is. But I did not wish to leave you until you came fully to your senses."

She did not wish him to leave at all. She wished him to stay right there. To keep speaking in a low-toned, lulling cadence. To tell her the same lies he had told the children. To tell her that she was safe.

That nothing bad would happen while he kept watch.

She'd believe him.

The moment he'd come into the courtyard, brandishing a chair in one hand while a pistol glinted in the other, she'd lost all sense of danger. She'd trusted he'd do whatever needed to be done.

"You marshaled the rescue, didn't you?" she asked.

"*Marshal* is a bit overblown."

Him? Being humble? "You were magnificent."

He exhaled, harsh and uneven. "*You* were magnificent."

"I didn't think." She leaned back against the pillows. "I just acted."

"You kept the children safe—at great risk to your person. Without your quick thinking there would not have been time to 'marshal' additional forces."

"So, you *did* inspire the men to mount a rescue."

"Threatened, more like."

She half-laughed. "That, I don't doubt."

"I am only a bully—"

His accurate self-description made her smile into the darkness.

"—Whereas you embodied bravery."

An unfamiliar tone thread through his voice, a tone that made her tingle with pleasure. Was she hearing admiration?

She wasn't to be admired. What she'd done had been foolish. And, while she was fond of Delmare and Fee, what would have become of her child if she'd been seriously injured or killed? The workhouse. Or worse.

That she'd acted without thought and might not have survived to claim Annis had been her last thought before all the fear she'd kept subdued had rushed back into her veins, overwhelming her consciousness.

She set her shaking fingers to untangling her hair even as her throat thickened with unshed tears. What she wouldn't give to have family she could rely on.

Hurtheven's hand came over her own, resting lightly against her neck. He was real. And solid. His touch didn't stop her tremors, however. Instead, his tender gesture broke an inner dam. First came a stifled sob, and then those unwelcome tears flooded her cheeks.

The ropes beneath the bed squeaked in protest as, keeping hold of her head, he moved from the chair to the mattress. He cradled her with the same gentleness he showed the children. Caught up against his chest, she listened as he poured out all the soothing words her heart longed to hear.

"There, now," he crooned. "You're perfectly safe."

Her body absorbed his solace even as her mind continued loudly clamoring like a night-watchman's panicked bell. No matter what kindness he'd shown, no matter how deep his love for the children in her care, she needed to stay vigilant.

He, like the lion, was a predator at heart.

And despite having the world's best reason to remain vigilant, and knowing better than to let herself go, she had somehow ended up on a bed with him, trembling uncontrollably in his arms.

* * *

Contact had been selfish—gratification and solace he did not deserve.

He could tell himself all he wished that he was performing a chivalrous service here in a darkened room on a loudly creaking bed.

He knew better.

Embracing her had been indulgence of the most dangerous sort. He'd been holding himself back—taut and restless—ever since he'd carefully laid her down on top of the coverlet and then reluctantly released her into the ministrations of the innkeeper's wife.

And if the children hadn't been present, he wasn't sure he'd be able to let her go again.

When she'd roused a bit, his worst concerns had allayed —that she could be suffering from something serious like a heart complaint brought on by the shock. But her partial consciousness and steady pulse reassured.

Then, he'd had the children, of course, to occupy him. He'd been compelled to convince them of their own safety and their nursemaid's eventual return to complete health. He'd made them comfortable with what he'd thought was an ingenious solution to the single trundle problem. Finally, they'd fallen into exhausted slumber.

Ever since, however, his unholy meditation had been unbroken. She hadn't stirred again. Instead, she'd lain, pale and pretty and tragic in the moonlight—quite the Gothic novel heroine—while he indulged in a brood deep enough to have shocked Byron.

Attack a lion with nothing but a child's pink parasol!?

What was he to do with such an impetuous, brave, and clever creature?

While he'd count Alicia and Pen as stalwart ladies of great fortitude and was certain they'd have done the same to save their own children, her sacrifice had not been made to save any family of her own.

When she'd opened her eyes, her first thought had been the children. *Naturally.* Ash and Alicia had been right. No matter what she was hiding, no matter what trouble she faced, she took full responsibility for those in her care.

A rare quality, that kind of complete and loving commitment. He'd wanted to gather her up and hold her apart from the wild, unpredictable world.

And now, he had.

But to what purpose? He wondered as he stroked the soft, tangled spirals that crowded around her neck.

While she'd been sleeping, the colors of the setting sun mirrored against her face, setting her features aglow. Even then, she'd looked so pallid. So other-worldly. He'd been afraid she'd simply slip away. As his pulse galloped again, he sternly reminded himself she hadn't been in any danger of dying.

She'd only fainted, after all. Under normal circumstances, fainting would have barely registered as a concern. But he couldn't get the image of her throwing herself between the children and the beast out of his mind.

"Hurtheven," she wept against his shoulder. "Heavens, what a shock."

His sharp intake of breath made them sway. She'd never used his title.

Darling, he wished to respond.

Only, he would not. One did not hold a frightened rabbit too closely. And she was still frightened. She trembled, each shuddering exhale working through the mortar of his carefully constructed walls.

Walls that concealed what?

Even he did not fully remember. The walls had been set in place since...

The screeching of wheels. The torrent of rain. The darkness and the cold.

Breathe.

He rested his cheek on top of her head.

She was nothing he'd imagined in a bride—in some ways, even more unsuitable than Penelope had been at the spark of his mad infatuation. He no longer had the excuse of youthful folly, either. And she had secrets, too. Ones even Ash had not been willing to divulge.

But the reasons he wanted to know her secrets had undergone a fundamental change. Nothing in his life would ever be the same.

Lightning *had* struck again.

He'd been denying the consequence. Refusing to understand the impact of that first meeting which had set his world reeling. Now, well, after pretending they were a family all afternoon, he realized he no longer wished to pretend. But if he wanted to keep her in his life, if he wanted to make his pretend notion of a family real—not to mention keep his promise to Ash—then the only solution was marriage.

Marriage...and all its benefits.

His admission shifted the direction of his blood—complicating a moment already too fraught for comfort. He suppressed a groan.

The innkeeper's wife had given him a stern look and lectured him on not 'troubling' his lady before she went back below stairs. Not that he'd dream of doing so under these circumstances, even if they had been completely alone.

Even if she had been his own.

She was not.

Still, he reacted with a growing carnal need to her light breath against his neck, the tickle of her hair, the sweet softness of the body resting, if not trustingly, then at least in grateful fatigue against his own. His breath slowed. His grip tightened.

If the children had not been asleep but a few feet away, he'd have had a rough time mastering his natural inclinations.

Her breath caught, as if in dawning awareness of the direction of his own thoughts. She pushed him away. Even in dim light, her expression was such a mask of horror he almost checked behind him to see if the great beast had entered the room.

"You *must* forgive me, Your Grace."

"Extraordinary circumstances,"—he cooled his heated thoughts—"compel extraordinary reactions."

He let his arms fall slowly from her shoulders. He couldn't help himself from indulging in one, last caress. He wouldn't allow himself to touch her again. Not until he'd decided for certain what was to be done.

He removed himself to the chair. "Nothing improper has occurred."

"Naturally not," she hesitated, "since the children are in the room."

He searched her gaze for any sign she'd welcome his attention under other circumstances. But the dim light and her evident weariness concealed any answers he might have found.

"So, nothing improper has occurred," she repeated, adding, "yet."

Her frank response disarmed him.

"Yet," he repeated with a sigh.

"I'm tired." Her grip on the bedlinens tightened. "I don't know what I'm saying."

The wariness in her tone was enough to leave him chastened. "I apologize. I've taken advantage."

"No! I—we... We've both had an exhausting day. I'm sure you only meant to comfort me." She didn't sound sure.

And she was right to question his motives.

"Have I lost a chance at winning your good opinion?" he asked.

"You do not need *my* good opinion, Your Grace."

"Need? No. But I find myself in want of it all the same."

"Because my good opinion is not yours for the taking?"

The unexpected jab set him on his proverbial heels. "Is that fair?'

She hung her head, completely concealing any perception of her true sentiments.

"You are an excellent godfather. And—by report—an excellent friend. Anyone would be happy to have your good opinion."

"But we weren't speaking of *my* good opinion, were we?"

She shook her head *no*. "Oh, but just think for a moment and you'll see, Your Grace. You could not possibly have an interest in mine."

A neat set down. Polite. Careful not to wound his pride. He supposed he should be grateful. "You do yourself an injustice," he said quietly.

She sighed a piteous sigh.

He had transgressed. Again.

Then again, she'd no way of ascertaining his intentions, had she? For all she knew, he'd have taken advantage of her innocence without thought of reparation.

She would come to know him better. The next time

they were alone in a darkened room would be but a prelude. And she'd be fully aware of his sentiments.

He rose. "Now that I know you are well, I will take my leave. Is there anything I might order for you?"

"No," she said meekly.

He paused at the foot of the children's bed and stared down at them. "Allow me to thank you sincerely."

"And I, you."

He nodded once. "Good night, then."

"Good night."

The door snicked softly closed and he rested his head against the wooden panel. She was not well born. But she was what he wanted. Long ago, he'd had to give up the one woman he'd desired above all else. He'd not had such a reaction to another, since.

Until now. And, this time, no dear friend stood in his way.

The beauty. The bravery. The service of her trustworthy good sense. They would be his compensation, to hell with anyone who thought to question.

If he courted her at his estate, far outside the purview of those who would condemn, he was certain she could be won. All he needed was patience. She'd come to accept the inevitable.

Yes. He'd decided. She was going to be his.

And his decision, in his mind, settled the matter beyond a doubt.

Chapter Six

By Hera's third and final day on the road, Hurtheven's distant, civil behavior left her doubting the incendiary, mutual desire she could have sworn they'd both experienced. *Had* she made too much of the near kiss in the lane?

The latent possibility in the heat of their embrace?

The penny in her pocket she'd been repeatedly running through her fingers?

She must have because he made no further attempt to draw her in. Although he was as solicitous and attentive to the children as ever, to her he chose instead to be excessively and irritatingly polite.

At each stop, he arranged a guard while he procured them a private parlor and adjoining bedchambers—one for herself and the children, the other, for himself. Then, he'd return to guide them all inside, where she'd invariably find a table already laid with tea prepared in her preferred manner as well as the children's favorite foods. And every night, he spent an hour with the children recounting some tale woven to extol bravery, making the story come alive with excited tones and dramatic flair.

They'd followed him on fantastical, fictional journeys through grave depths of untold anxiety to the heights of glorious, heroic triumph. When the children's eyes were happily drooping, he'd reassure them all in his deep, ducal voice that they were perfectly safe and that none of them should worry while he kept watch.

Heady prospect.

His words never failed to work their magic—all three of them had fallen under his spell. When she'd heard one maid sigh and whisper to another that such a nonpareil she'd never seen, Hera found herself in full—if begrudging —agreement.

But when he'd taken his leave each night, he'd done so without betraying even a hint of desire for her company.

By the time they'd entered Hevenhyll Castle's extensive grounds, she was frustrated, even though the children's natural temperaments had been restored, and they had nothing to speak of but the wonders that awaited. For them, she was both happy and relieved. For herself, she was conscious of having lost a vibrancy, an exhilaration, she hadn't even been aware had taken hold, until she was bereft.

Had she imagined his interest? Or had he simply changed his mind?

Because if the duke had come to his senses, and decided he no longer wished to make her the object of his seduction (for what else could he possibly have in mind?), she *should* be thanking God for her good fortune. Never in her life did she have a better reason to avoid scandal. And she could never tell him about Annis.

A proper distance was required.

...Only she would not have minded if the distance were not so *exceedingly* proper.

She *missed* him.

Which was absurd. He was *right there*, cantering along beside the carriage not ten feet away. She turned her attention to the slack-shouldered boy sitting in the backwards facing bench.

Once they'd entered Hurtheven's grounds, Fee abandoned her first-to-ride-the-curricle plan for a better one. She cajoled the duke into allowing her to ride atop the box, arguing that she might, as they were so close to the castle and wouldn't possibly be seen by anyone who'd cause a fuss. Poor Delmare had been left to make do with Hera's company.

"Please stop kicking your heels against the box, love."

Delmare obliged without raising his head.

"Perhaps," she suggested, "you might look outside the window? I hear there are deer in the park."

He lifted his head, suddenly alert, and then begged a sheet of paper. She retrieved one from the writing box, which he promptly rolled into a tube and placed against his eye. He scooched over to the window, and, peering through his 'telescope' he swept his gaze across the land.

"What *are* you doing?"

"Keeping an eye out for lions...and such." He glanced over his shoulder. "I apologize. Wasn't the thing to just sit around coddled up like a *lady*. A man must anticipate disaster."

"Ah." So *that's* what had been bothering him. She nodded understandingly. "I appreciate your vigilance."

Graciously, he inclined his head. "Uncle Heven told me I must always be vigilant."

"I suspected as much." She slanted a gaze at

115

Hurtheven's figure, admirably situated atop his horse. "What else did he tell you?"

"That we are always perfectly safe in his care." Delmare looked over his shoulder and lowered his voice. "None but a Canterbury tale, I said. *You* led us away from the lion, even if he did help finish the matter." He grabbed the strap and set a knee on the bench beside her before adding in a whisper. "And I don't believe for a second that we were *never* in danger."

"And how did the duke reply to your challenge?"

Delmare pursed his lips. "Well, first he said, 'wasn't I just the picture of my father!'—though I don't know what my looking like Papa has anything to do with anything—and *then* he told me he would never lie to me and that I should take care with my phrasing because an insult between men was no small matter."

"Did he?!" She asked, incensed.

"Yes. But *then* he agreed that his assertion of safety could be called into question, and so, for my sake, he'd provide claridation."

"Clarification?" Hera suggested.

Delmare frowned. "That's what I said."

"Do go on."

His face twisted with suspicion before he shook his head *no*. "Not sure the rest is for a female's ears, if you'll pardon me. Men's business, you see."

She eyed him with a glint that would've adorned any female's eye who'd been subject to such a statement from a boy hardly out of short pants. "Shall I ask him myself?"

"Oh, no, ma'am!" He drew back. "That won't do."

"Well?" She raised her brows expectantly and then nearly laughed out loud at his mulish expression. "You don't *have* to tell me, I suppose." She folded her hands in her lap.

"Although clarification would doubtless, ah, reassure me, too."

Delmare sighed. "It's like this," he said. "Life has many dangers and facing them is often necessary. The only way a man can hope to be safe, and to protect those he loves, is to cultivate strength and bravery *on the inside*," he emphasized the words, "where he cannot be touched. *That's* what he meant by us being safe. We're safe as we can be, because he's constantly ready—on the inside."

"Where he cannot be touched..." She echoed in astonishment.

"He shared his rules, too. There's three." Delmare counted the rules on his fingers. "Keep your friends close. Your secrets closer. And stay closed, coiled, and ready to strike."

Instinctively, she adverted her face as if she'd peered inside a box she did not own—one she was forbidden to touch.

"Did your uncle's...ah...philosophy scare you?" she asked carefully.

"Go on," he scoffed. "Why should it have scared me? I understood well enough. I don't have secrets, anyway." He turned back to the window. "And I *can* be ready, at any time, to strike."

With that, he resumed his sweeping scour of the countryside.

She wasn't sure what to think. Part of her wanted to box the duke's ears for painting such a bleak picture for so young a child. Although "the child" would be off to school soon enough, and she knew too well the kind of views he'd encounter there.

She supposed an inner sense of stability—*if* that was what he meant by his words—couldn't hurt. And...did she

117

not approach life in a similar fashion? What did she always remind herself when she was afraid?

You just feel like you are going to break apart. You won't. You can't.

"You *are* strong and brave, Lord Delmare. And you were very good to keep yourself and your sister quietly hidden in the carriage."

He glanced back over his shoulder. "Naturally, I would have rather helped corral the lion, but my duty was to protect Fee." He shook his head with a conspiratorially knowing expression. "No telling *what* mischief she would have gotten into without me there to keep watch."

Hera's lips quirked. "How lucky she is to have such a fine, big brother." And how lucky Delmare was to have a sister that would always do her utmost to keep his tendency toward imperiousness in check.

Delmare set down his telescope, hoped back up on the bench across from her and studied her with an alarming intensity. "Do you have a brother, Mrs. Montrose?"

"No." She simplified a rather complicated reply. Not exactly a brother.

"Who is your protector, then?"

"Ah, *my protector* is not quite the phrase you're seeking..."

Knowing he did not understand the more salacious connotation of his words, she thought better of giving him a blunt scold, which would only embarrass the boy.

"...But don't worry, love. I assure you; I am strong and brave on the inside, too. I require no protection."

Delmare's frown deepened. "*I* will be your brother, then."

Her heart melted for her little knight errant. "Thank

you, Delmare. I'm *most* beholden. But I'm afraid we cannot choose our family."

"Uncle Heven chose Papa as a brother. Uncle Chev—I mean Ithwick—too. Papa told me so. If they can choose each other as brothers, I can choose you as a sister." The set of his chin proved he was not going to be moved on the point.

"Uncle Heven" had *chosen* his brothers? An odd idea. Then again, the night she'd dined with Hurtheven, Ithwick and Ashbey in the garden at Wisterley, they *had* seemed more like family than friends.

A strange tickle gathered in her throat—a heavy cloud of longing threatening to condense, precipitating tears.

Good lord, these last few days had turned her into a watering pot. *Breathe.* These people, how they related...they were none of her concern. But, oh, what an idea—that one could simply create the comfort and security of a family unit if one had none.

Or at least none one could count on.

She retrieved a handkerchief and dabbed at her eye.

"Are you ill, Mrs. Montrose?"

"No, dear. Just..." *What was she?* "...weary."

Remembering his discussion with the duke in the nursery, she let him touch her forehead. Then she attempted to assuage his distress with a bright smile.

"Thank you for your solicitude." When his frown deepened, she added, "Solicitude means concern and care."

"Solicitude..." he repeated thoughtfully before adding a solemn, "You're welcome."

He resumed his stance at the window—one knee on the backwards facing bench, one hand on the strap—as he earnestly scanned the home wood for any possible threat.

Her protector—of all things!

119

She'd have to ask the duke to explain the varied meanings of the phrase to the boy. Although how she was going to put such a request into words without mortification, she did not know.

She imagined—and discarded—several possibilities.

Leaning back, she cast her gaze out the window.

Hurtheven was not in view, as the carriage was passing beneath a stone archway. She glanced up at the sharp, pointy edges of an ancient portcullis and had the ominous sense she had tumbled back in time.

They then traveled over a large, grassy inner bailey surrounded by fully intact ramparts that disappeared only when they entered a second archway. Soon, a great commotion descended on the now-stopped conveyance.

Liveried men procured stairs and opened the door. Delmare exited first, and then dutifully offered his hand, making good on his chivalrous promise.

She accepted his assistance descending the stairs. Avoiding the amused Hurtheven, who stood to the side, Fee already in his arms, she raised her face, taking in the breathtaking, upward expanse of what she presumed to be the family and state apartments towering inside the inner courtyard.

Of course, Hevenhyll was not just any seat, but a proper medieval castle.

Narrow slits formed apertures of the first floor while wider, though equally tall windows peered down from the upper floors. From her vantage, she could barely make out the statues atop the parapets, although from the shields and swords she gathered they were warriors.

The whole affect—much like the castle's owner—was one of intimidation.

She turned back toward the man in question.

"Don't worry," he said with a half-smile. "My father had the dungeons sealed well before I was born."

"Mrs. Montrose does not ever need to worry," Delmare replied. "We've settled it between us. *I'm* going to be Mrs. Montrose's protector."

Hurtheven raised his brows.

"My *brother*," Hera corrected. "Delmare has offered to be my *brother*, and we have *not* settled the matter, although I do appreciate the sentiment."

"'Tis settled!" Delmare insisted. "She hasn't got a brother, you see. You're forever telling me I must protect Fee. I figure Mrs. Montrose could use protecting, too."

"Do you?" Hurtheven asked with a suppressed mirth as he set Fee on her feet.

Hera exchanged an exasperated glance with the duke.

"I don't need protection!" Fee exclaimed.

"Do so," Delmare retorted.

"Don't!"

Fee raced ahead—Delmare hot on her heels—and, like magic, the heavy wooden doors opened.

"Your Grace," she said under her breath. "Perhaps, at some later time, you would be so kind as to warn Lord Delmare that his words convey an impression he does not intend?"

There. That hadn't been quite as difficult as she'd anticipated. And yet, she could feel the blush creeping slowly up her neck.

"I'm at your service, of course." He inclined his head.

"Of course?" she repeated questioningly.

Her awareness of the activity around them faded as she held his gaze. The late-day sun hung low in the sky, casting his features aglow. Fine lines sketched his forehead and light creasing marred the edges of his eyes. Yes, he'd known great pain. But he'd laughed often, too.

Fleetingly, she wished he would confide in her those secrets he'd told Delmare he kept close. And then, perhaps, she could confide hers as well. Maybe he—like the duchess —was the rare sort of person who placed understanding of their fellow man's flaws over righteous condemnation.

She blushed even further when she realized she'd been studying him as if he were a still life arrangement she intended to capture in paint.

"I presume the servants are waiting in the hall to welcome you back?" she asked.

"No doubt," he replied. "But before we go in, tell me...do you like what you've seen of my home so far?"

She blinked. Then, she turned wonderingly in a circle, taking in the overwhelming majesty of the place. "Does one *like* a castle? The intended effect, I think, is one of menace."

"Menace," he echoed. His brows lifted in a hopeful manner. "You wouldn't happen to have a penchant for menace, would you?"

She widened her eyes. "Not in the least!"

"Alas." He observed her with a strange, compelling glimmer in his gaze. "...Although, on reflection, a complication rather than an impasse. Or even"—he closed one eye— "possibly even a depth as yet unfathomed?" He hummed thoughtfully. "What additional, valiant facets would a fixed, approving regard uncover, I wonder?"

She drew her brows together. "I'm afraid I don't follow."

"No?" he asked lightly. "You'll catch up eventually." He straightened his clothes, steeled his back. "I trust I am presentable?"

"You know you are," she replied dryly.

"Certainly. I just wanted to make sure *you* noticed." He

winked before turning and entering his home. The cheer that followed echoed all the way into the courtyard.

She shook her head slowly in exasperated disbelief.

While she could not fully decipher a word of what he'd just said, especially what he'd meant when he'd said *a depth unfathomed*, with him, she understood she was far, far out of *her* depth.

And, given her surroundings, the situation could only get worse.

* * *

After having had *the talk*, Hurtheven relinquished Delmare to the stables, where the boy was greeted by the head groom with great enthusiasm and promptly given a brush. He left Delmare happily tending the pony he had obtained for him the prior year, all-the-while chattering away about their journey.

Delmare had scoffed when Hurtheven told him he should not have offered to be Mrs. Montrose's protector, as that was a phrase reserved for affairs of the heart and something he would not be able to fully comprehend until he was older.

Delmare had then blushed deeply and rather belligerently inquired if kissing in the lane constituted an *affair of the heart*.

The kissing of *hands*, Hurtheven had informed him sharply, did *not* count.

Hurtheven wandered back toward the hall, wondering if the boy had developed a slight *tendre* for his nurse. If so, he sympathized.

He certainly had, after all.

He'd had to keep himself at a distance while on the

road, but now that they were settled at Hevenhyll, he fully intended to set about engaging Mrs. Montrose's affections.

Mrs. Montrose.

Was that even her name? Odd how he could feel so deeply drawn to someone whose family name could be a fiction, and whose Christian name he did not even know.

Then again, she'd seen farther into his soul than the friends who knew him best.

And, of course, she set him aflame in a way he'd not felt since he'd reached his majority. To be next to her, to inhale her light, feminine scent, gave him the same feeling he experienced when clearing a high hurdle on a sunny day on his liveliest grey. Touching her was a fast-paced reel, sending his heart racing and his mind spinning.

Nothing improper has occurred.

Yet.

How many times had he internally replayed that pithy but pregnant exchange? In fact, he'd kept his distance because he hadn't wanted things to progress too quickly.

Lightening had struck again, but this time, he wanted to harness the power.

He sighed as he ran his gaze over the parapets. He'd hoped she'd be dazzled by Hevenhyll Castle. Most people were, naturally. But she'd cast a critical eye over his abode and then shivered with dismay.

Not an auspicious start.

Then again, she hadn't been impressed with any part of his consequence so far. Why should a fortress with a long and—frankly— terrifying history be any different?

The porters opened both heavy, wooden doors at just the proper moment. And then, with a light step he bounded up the internal marble stairs with the energy of someone ten years his junior.

He spotted his housekeeper, Mrs. Whitby, hurrying off in the direction of the laundry and quickly and quietly fell into pace beside her.

"Why hello, Mrs. Whitby."

"Oh!" She placed her hand against her chest. "I see you haven't changed your sneaking ways!" Her voice scolded but her eyes twinkled.

"It's Ashbey's boy, I suppose. Brings out the Puck in me."

Her slanted glance suggested she did not believe he needed any encouragement to create mischief.

"Have I troubled you too much with my unexpected guests?"

"If course not." She sniffed. "The message you sent with a postillion allowed me a full *three hours* to prepare."

He kept his laugh to himself. *Yes.* Returning to Hevenhyll was heartening—his deepest secrets haunted the grounds, but the gothic castle had been his cradle, and its people, the source of his strength. And none more loyally serving than the efficient, ever-discreet, comfortingly over-familiar, Mrs. Whitby.

"Are my guests all settled in the nursery?

"The children are."

"You have my gratitude, as always." He paused; head cocked. "But only the children?"

Mrs. Whitby hesitated, as if torn between pressing the matter or deferring. "I thought you might invite Mrs. Small back into the household while the children are in residence. The arrangement suited the little master his last visit."

"But he hadn't his own nurse with us, then."

"And I'm certain the young woman is fine. ...Only, Mrs. Small would be disappointed if you didn't ask her to stay.

She's not had children to tend to for some time. And many hands make light work."

True. And he knew his old nurse would delight in the opportunity to spend time with Ash's children...while taking every chance to quiz him on the absence of his own.

He could put up with a bit of gentle probing, however...especially if Mrs. Montrose found herself with more time on her hands than she'd originally anticipated.

"You've convinced me, Mrs. Whitby."

"I'm sure it was your own idea," she replied innocently.

"My own idea, was it?"

"I wouldn't presume."

"Of course not," he agreed solemnly. "Please inform Mrs. Small that we would appreciate her assistance, so long as she is willing and not placed at any inconvenience."

"I did so this morning, just as soon as I received your letter. I was sure, in your haste, you'd simply neglected to inform me of your intention. But you can depend on me to understand, as you know. Mrs. Small prefers to sleep in the room next to the children's, of course. So, I've installed Mrs. Montrose in the room closest to the nursery stairs. I trust that will be satisfactory."

"Certainly." She meant, he believed, the room connected to the enclosed armory. He smiled slowly as his mind grew ripe with possibility.

"If I might say," she continued, "it is mighty fine to have you back, Your Grace. Finer still, to have children in the house. Been far too many years."

He recognized her light comment for what it was—a gentle chiding at his still-single state. He couldn't yet tell her he intended to soon alter the situation, nor could he reveal how she'd unconsciously aided his scheme.

She loved him dearly; the shock might do her real harm.

"While my godchildren are here, you may spoil them to your heart's content."

Her expression transformed. "Apple tarts?"

"As many as Cook will allow."

"And peppermints?"

He chuckled. "Make whatever adjustments to the household accounts you require."

"I'm sure I can manage without adjustment," she replied, affronted.

"I have every faith in you."

He paused resting his hand on the pineapple shaped finial atop a newel post as he glanced around the hall with a critical eye.

Hevenhyll seemed, at times, almost tomb-like, especially in the last few years. But having a wee banshee, a 9-year-old budding cavalier, and their enchantress nursemaid did enliven the place. The castle's renewed spirit seemed a harbinger of what would come once he secured her regard.

His smile widened.

Here, things now operated according to his command and expectation. Here he had full and free reign. And *miles* of halls and chambers and passageways that would certainly aid him to his end.

Mrs. Montrose may have vanquished a lion, but she had no idea she'd just walked into the true lion's den.

* * *

Hera's heavy, echoing footfalls both emphasized her smallness and amplified her annoyance. Her breath jumped high and rapid in her chest. Try as she might, she could not master her emotion.

Frankly, she did not want to, either.

She'd been deceived by Hurtheven's calm civility and consideration. By his pretty compliments. By his laughing eyes. All complete hum dudgeon—a ruse to hide his true purpose.

Which had been her humiliation all along.

She should have recognized his disposition and expected his intent. *No!* She *had* recognized him of what he was—before she'd been so distracted by...by, well, his other *qualities*. Although '*his qualities*' was, perchance, the wrong phrase.

He wasn't responsible for his height, his dark, frequently tussled hair, his speaking eyes that made mushy peas out of her stalwart resolve. Nor did he consciously generate the heat rolling off his body like a breeze from a warmer clime.

But he *was* responsible for the near kiss in the lane, the embrace at the inn, the two *days* of polite distance, and now, the deliberate insult. And since he had left her with so much time on her hands, she intended to confront him and demand an explanation.

She stopped at a fork in the corridor—which did not seem possible, as she'd *thought* she'd been walking through the inner rampart. Then again, the whole layout seemed to go in circles. She chose one direction and continued onward.

Confound this blasted gothic castle and the small army who ran the place, each attendant welcoming, friendly, and more complimentary of their beloved liege than the last! Weren't all aristocratic households supposed to be as arrogant as their head?

Not this one, apparently.

Only he, at the very pinnacle, had insufferable conceit. *Of course*, he'd return to his high-handed ways once he'd lodged her in this remote remnant of a brutal time. And, *of course*, the first thing he'd done once she was fully in his power was usurp her position.

In fact, he'd probably started planning this affront to her authority the moment she first mocked him. This time, she wasn't about to let the outrage slide. She'd show him brave and strong *on the inside*. Arrogant, beetle-brained, hornswoggling...well, *duke*!

Bitterly invoking his title as an insult mollified her for thirty straight seconds. Then, the corridor along which she'd been stomping ended abruptly.

She'd taken a wrong turn. *Again!*

Mrs. Whitby had informed her that she'd find His Grace in the library—a new (she assumed this meant less than a century) addition. She'd begged two additional sets of directions since—one from a startled chambermaid, the other from a footman...whether the second, the fourth, or the tenth footman, she'd no idea.

She'd seen too many to count. All in stunning livery.

She folded her arms and steadied her breath. She judged the iron cage on the opposite wall to have once been a receptacle for a torch. A slight chill ran through her body as she thought of the tensions this structure had seen.

A medieval castle was an *absurd* place to call a home.

A faint sound arrested her thoughts. Wind, most like. Every passageway in the blasted place whispered in singular tones. She wouldn't be surprised to discover the place was alive with spirits.

But, no—she turned slowly—not a whisper. *Whistling.*

She followed the sound in the opposite direction, and then stopped at the edge of a gallery to listen again. Had she passed this way before? If so, she'd missed the arched opening between the balustrades—a curtained opening that had, at one time, been an external door, judging by the fanciful stone beast staring down at her with evil glee.

She glanced up at the clawed feet and scaled stomach. "I don't suppose *you* can direct me to *his illustrious person?*"

A now-familiar chuckle sounded from the opposite side of the fabric. She clenched her fists as the *woosh* generated by the suddenly upswept velvet fanned her cheeks, emphasizing the results of her exertions—dotted perspiration just beneath her ears, and a burning flush that traveled from her cheeks down her neck and across her chest.

"You've met Homer, I see," Hurtheven said.

Her body responded to his voice with a puppy-like eagerness that plunged her into shame. Why, in his presence, did she always seem to be panting?

"Homer," she nodded to the creature as if the stone figure had been real. "Might I have a word, Your Grace?"

He cocked his head and his stupid black hair once again fell across his forehead. "Is something amiss?"

"You've played a cruel trick, *duke*." The words came tumbling out. "And one I should have expected." She held her hand against the gathered fabric beneath her bodice. "I thought you'd come to trust me..."

His brows darted up.

"...with the children," she hastily added, "but *no*. All along, you were simply biding time until you could deprive me of my responsibilities."

He'd gone still. Only his gaze moved, carefully searching her face. "I cannot imagine why you would, after what we've faced, doubt my faith in your competence."

"Can't you?" She challenged. "You have such faith in me that you saw fit to request additional help!"

He frowned as if she were a puzzle box, and he could not find the seam. "Is additional help *so* terrible?"

"Yes!" she spat.

He hesitated, gaze calculating. Then, he offered her his arm. "Will you walk with me while I explain?" When she did not immediately comply, he added, "I have something inside I'd like to share with you."

She hesitated, but then placed her hand into the narrow crook of his elbow and allowed him to guide her into the passage beyond.

"The fact is, my housekeeper, Mrs. Whitby, is responsible for instigating the change," he said. "The scheme was hers, although she did her best to convince me I had come up with the idea. ...As for my impression of your capability, I'll admit that you and I, ah, started out on rather the wrong foot, so to speak. However, I no longer doubt your competence in the least." He placed a large, masculine hand over her own. "In fact, for some days, I've held you in the highest regard."

His sidelong gaze briefly captured hers, his dark, eyes warm with an emotion she dared not attempt to identify. Then, he strode purposely forward.

His *highest* regard?

The air suddenly felt heavy and difficult to draw in, as if her lungs had taken on the consistency of a sodden sponge.

Did she believe him? He certainly *sounded* sincere.

Though she kept her gaze on his face, she was vaguely aware that he'd drawn her into a chamber with soaring ceilings.

"There now," He released her and then held out his right hand. "Let us be friends again?"

"Friends?!" Of all the—*friends*! With a *duke*!?

"Friends," he confirmed. "Unless, that is, you consider me beneath your touch?"

"You..." She pushed his hand away. "You're *such* a

duke!" she spoke his title with all the venom and confusion and frustration that had been building within her for days.

His left-cheek dimple briefly appeared. "Well, now, that *is* an insult. ...Which rather places us on equal footing, does it not? You feel I've insulted you, and now you've returned the favor."

She glanced heavenward. "But you *are* a duke."

"The slight was not in the word, but the tone, as you well know. Come" —again, he offered his arm—"let me show you the library. The workman only recently finished the addition—and I confess I find myself extraordinarily pleased with the result."

She'd barely given their surroundings a glance. Now, however, she took in the room. Three-stories of bookcases set neatly within tiers of balconies surrounded them in a semi-circle, all standing opposite a single wall of glass that felt, from this vantage, as if it extended to infinity.

For a moment she could not find her voice.

Three full floors of books. More books than could ever be read in a lifetime. And he'd said *recently* finished. Did that mean the room was of his design?

His nose wrinkled as he laughed. "My castle, you disdain. My library, however..."

She craned her neck toward a ceiling painted night-sky blue and set with glass that formed the constellation of Heracles. She dropped her gaze, turning wonderingly to the series of marble sculptures anchoring the room. The one nearest them depicted a rather impressively muscled man with a sword confronting a multi-headed beast.

"The hydra?"

"Yes." He indicated the next statue. "And the boar. Then there's the cattle, the hind, the stables..." He stopped next to a statue of a man and woman, both finely formed.

"And here," she said, "is the poor, unfortunate Amazon who, though willing to give up her belt, is then brutally murdered."

He frowned down at the depiction of Hippolyte handing the hero her girdle. "Not Heracles *finest* moment, I'll admit."

"Ah, but an excellent warning to women...concede nothing, else you be stripped of the whole."

Something flashed behind his eyes—something that left her feeling adrift. He drew back, brow furrowed as if he were wading through his own internal quagmire.

He pursed his lips. "You do not concede anything easily, do you?"

"Not easily, no." Or so she'd vowed.

"I understand," he replied thoughtfully. "Though, I trust that, for harmony's sake, we'll eventually learn how to negotiate to our mutual benefit."

He was babbling again.

What did he mean by *eventually*? Or *harmony*? Or, for that matter, *mutual benefit*? Had he lost his mind the moment they'd entered Hevenhyll?

"Alicia," he changed the subject, "tells me Fee could escape the tower of London, if given the chance to try. I should think you'd appreciate extra help."

Of course, he hadn't forgotten—nor, apparently, forgiven—the incident. "Felicia never goes far."

He gazed out the window, surveying the fields beyond the baily with a severe expression. "Just the same, I would hate..." His voice faded. "She's not familiar with these grounds. *You* aren't familiar with these grounds. A child could easily"—his voice cracked—"get lost."

"But..." Not one retort came to her lips. "But..." she tried again and came up empty a second time.

He softened, chuckling quietly.

She sent him a furious scowl.

"I apologize for the laugh. But the play of emotions on your face was simply priceless. Never wager at piquet, my dear."

She dropped her face embarrassed by his easy use of the endearment.

"Is allowing me a single point *that* objectionable?" he asked.

"How, pray tell, is Mrs. Small going to chase after Fee? She's 110 if she's a day."

"Unfair. She is barely in her fifth decade. She was my nurse, you know. A beloved and indispensable part of the household for years."

She mimicked his brow lift. "If she was *your* nurse, how could she be so young?"

"You *wound* me."

She *piff*ed. "Doubtful."

"Haven't I a heart? Here"—he shrugged out of his coat—"you may check for my pulse if you wish."

Her eyes rounded as he undid his cuff and inched up his sleeve. A man's hands were so different. His, in particular...

She stared at the bluish veins crisscrossing his outstretched wrist. He had a small scar on his thumb and a lightly raised callous a little lower. A smattering of hair peeked out from his forearm. Although rougher than she would have expected, his hands were strong and clean and well-manicured. She imagined them quite capable of bringing a woman to...

She halted the thought. Her gaze flew to his.

"That won't be necessary," she replied primly.

"This isn't the first time you've mocked my age." He

shook down his sleeve and refastened his cuff. "And yet, what are we..." he appraised her, "...five, maybe six years apart?"

"I turned twenty-five last month," she said.

"Right again," he grinned. "That makes two points you must concede to me."

"*Ugh.*" She rolled her eyes. "You're impossible!"

"Difficult, certainty. Impossible, no. And you do enjoy the challenge, don't you?"

She ignored the question, unwilling to concede yet a third point. "Was hiring Mrs. Small really your housekeeper's idea?"

He nodded. "And I am pained you're angry."

"*Pained?*"

His brows rose innocently. "I hire help, and then you argue *against* a decreased burden." He shrugged. "I'm at a loss how to respond."

"*You're* at a loss." She pursed her lips in disbelief. "*You* are *never* at a loss."

"Not often," he agreed. "If you wish, I will ask Mrs. Small to yield to your judgment."

She stiffened. "I can manage without your interference."

"Of that, I have no doubt. Nevertheless, I have already promised to be at your service. Have you any other complaint?"

"She's evicted me from the children's rooms."

"Is the chamber Mrs. Whitby prepared not to your liking?" His gaze appeared innocent enough, but something in his eyes raised gooseflesh on her forearms.

"You *know* I can make no complaint on that account."

"And yet..."

She silenced him with a sharp glance.

He cleared his throat. "If you will accommodate Mrs. Small, I would quite frankly be in your debt. As Mrs. Whitby pointed out, Mrs. Small would never have forgiven me if I hadn't requested her help. And you can hardly wish to damage me in the eyes of my own dear nurse."

She snorted. "Not possible, from what I've already heard." She shook her head and then turned up her palms. "Well, then. I have no occupation at present. What am I to do?"

The laughter returned to his eyes. "Don't tell me you've succumbed to ennui after a mere quarter hour?"

"It took me a quarter hour simply to find you. Although now that I have done so, I expect to succumb at any moment."

"Succumb?" he asked in a purr.

"...to *ennui*."

They locked gazes. Then, his dropped to her lips. A shout from a workman sounded from the baily beyond. Then, the workman's shadow passed across the room.

The duke bowed slightly and then folded his arms behind his back. "What would you like to do? You have an entire ducal estate at your disposal. And, at present, the *duke*."

"Entire?"

"Anything within the walls."

Fleetingly, she wondered what lay beyond the walls. She dismissed his words as a figure of speech. "Most indulgent of you." She curtsied.

"A curtsy, no less! And a prettily executed one at that."

She blinked in exaggerated innocence. "I aim to please."

"You?" His expression turned wolfish. "Never."

She recognized an echo of her own insult.

"Oh, do stop pulling that face," he laughed. "I'm sure it

stops Delmare in his tracks, but you're punching above your weight."

"About twice my weight, I'd say," she replied with excessive sweetness. "And remember Goliath? Glory does not always go to the blessed-by, ah, girth."

His laugh ripped through her as a wave of delight.

"Now there's a better expression," he said. "No, don't stop smiling. Please. You enjoy besting me. And I wish you nothing but joy."

He could not be serious, and yet nothing in his face belied his words. The lines around his mouth had softened and he was gazing down at her with something terribly like tenderness, something that warmed her all the way to her toes. She was suspended, as if she'd just been thrown from a moving carriage and was flying.

The landing was going to hurt.

"Hurtheven, I—I—"

"I" —he stepped closer—"find myself unaccountably drawn to you, too."

Her heart made an unwise leap.

"Grant me a boon, would you?" he asked.

"What *boon*?" she asked warily.

"Tell me your name—your real name."

Her throat dried. "Mrs. Montrose *is* the name I intend to use henceforth."

"Mrs. Montrose, I've assured you of my trust in you. Can't you return the favor?" Can't you, at least where your well-being is concerned, permit me the presumption of good intent?"

"And what *is* your intent?"

He hooded his gaze. "Right now, my sole intention is to keep you from harm. An intention I've maintained since our unusually rapid departure from Wisterley."

His unasked questions hung heavily in the air, and the closeness of their bodies stood in sharp contrast with the distance between what she was experiencing and what she was willing to reveal.

"I grant the urgency of our flight was unusual." She spoke slowly, as if feeling her way through a long, dark tunnel. "I assure you the children are not in danger. The Duchess of Ashbey is fully aware of my circumstance."

"Ash implied as much."

Had he?

She felt the blood drain from her cheeks. Thank goodness the duchess had promised to keep Annis's existence a secret...even from her husband.

"Ash also implied that you have no family on which to depend. I'm intrigued by your circumstance, which has led me to wonder..."

For a desperate moment, she thought he was about to guess the truth.

"...were you, perhaps, born a foundling?"

The word left her cold. Colder, even than she had been. She bristled. "Sheltering a foundling beneath your roof would offend you, I suppose."

He frowned. "Several older foundlings from Lincolnshire are, in fact, apprenticed on the estate—a circumstance due to Alicia's influence. I see no reason to hold a child's manner of concep—" He stopped abruptly, and then colored, as if just realizing how far they'd strayed from the boundaries of polite conversation. "I see no reason to shame an innocent child."

His expression—slightly confused, deeply earnest, and plainly desirous of her confidence—tugged at her heart. *Confound him.* She had to tell him *something*, before all her secrets came tumbling forth.

"I am not a foundling...but neither do I have my family's protection," she said. "I lost my mother as a child. My father, some five years past."

"It's been longer for me." A muscle twitched in his jaw. "But I understand the loss beyond what I am... easily able to convey..."

The beat of her own heart thudded in her ears.

"...Would you grant me the honor of a description? Tell me something you remember about your parents."

Ah, *this man*.

Capable. Confident. Master—at all times—of his person, was asking about her parents with the expression of an urchin with his hat clutched in his hands.

Karl had never asked, even though he frequently spoke of his own grief.

In fact, she did not think she'd ever had the opportunity to talk about her parents since her father died. She found herself wanting to recall, if only for a moment. But...

"Would you do the same for me?" she ventured.

He flinched and then gazed silently out the window for what felt like a full minute. "I will," he replied finally. "...but at a later time."

She searched his face for devious motivation and found none. Could he simply want to know her? Warning bells chimed. She ignored them, responding instead, to the phrase *beyond what I am easily able to convey*.

She understood this pain.

She turned her gaze outside the window, where a lone bird was calling out in the distance. "My mother was lovely and warm. She smelled of lavender and she always wore two bracelets that clinked when she drew me into an embrace. ...Unfortunately, that is about all I remember."

"And your father?"

"My father was...kind—when he thought to acknowledge anyone else's presence, that is. He could be obstinate." She smiled. "And arrogant—though I never doubted his love. Books were his chief solace after my mother passed."

"And yours as well?"

She nodded. "And mine."

"We share that, at least." His smile was rueful. Almost relieved. "Not menace, but, well, a place to begin." He touched her cheek. "There now, was confiding in me so terrible?"

Ironic laughter bubbled up in her throat. "This from a man who told me he never reveals a secret, least of all his own?"

"Touché. We're quite the pair, aren't we?"

The question, she decided as he was drawing her into the shadows and beyond the view of any of the workmen outside, was rhetorical.

"May I," he started uncertainly, "...that is to say...I should like to..." He made a frustrated, growling sort of noise. "Devil take it, Mrs. Montrose, may I hold you?"

Could this be her arrogant duke?

She nodded by rote. "I *am* feeling rather unsteady."

Tenderly, he gathered her into his arms. She buried her face in the crook of his neck, letting him cradle her so close she could not distinguish between his heartbeat and her own.

She did not need to use her fingertips to feel him in other ways, too—one, large hand warmed her hip, the other splayed against her back. Every tiny hair on her body lifted away from her skin as if he were a magnet and they, slivers of metal shards.

"Thank you for your confidence," he spoke against the

fabric of her cap with the reverence of someone who'd received a precious gift.

Oh, he was dangerous.

Dangerous enough for her to be dazzled into forgetting all the reasons that being this close to him was a very, very bad idea. Dangerous enough for her to be seized with the desire to lift her hand, caress his lightly stubbled cheek, hot beneath its sharp angles, and then follow the ridge of his cheekbone beneath her thumb. Dangerous enough for her to curl her fingers around his nape while she lifted her face...

She closed her eyes against the onslaught of his blurred features.

At the first brush of his lips, her heart took a downward plunge, throbbing in places she dared not define. Her breath mingled with his, and then, with vast, immeasurable gentleness, he explored her mouth.

Again and again, he softly claimed her kiss, until she liquefied in his arms.

She was moving, yes, but like a leaf on a tumbling stream—not the least in control of her destination. This wasn't the raw, hard lust she'd shared with Karl, but something deeper. A journey. A true connection.

A sensation she never wanted to end.

At the sound of footsteps, he thrust her behind him just as he had in the lane. She caught a glimpse of a liveried fellow in the archway.

"Yes?" Hurtheven queried sharply.

"If you'll pardon, Your Grace, are you at home to Mr. Barton? He said you requested his presence."

Caught between the bookcase and his back, she felt rather than heard his under -breath swear. "Please place him in the West Parlor and tell him I will join him in approximately ten minutes."

The footman bowed and then departed.

With her lips throbbing and dazed with desire, she rested her cheek against his shoulder. His chest rose and fell as he struggled to regain full control. Then, he turned.

He was darkly flushed, and his dilated eyes shone more than a little wild. "I'm afraid I must see him. There's been some trouble with a dam in the river that joins our properties. It's been affecting a field where his cattle graze. Even so, he's waited until I returned to commence any repairs."

"Please do not delay on my account," she replied.

"You'd be surprised what I would do on your account." He cradled her face and then he kissed her again, this time swiftly but gently. "Before I go, here's what I wanted to give you—what I intended to give you later today." He pulled a slim volume resting on the base of the final statue.

She glanced down at the gilt lettering. *The Castle of Wolfenbach, Volume One.*

"One of my favorites." He brushed her hands as he handed her the book. "Until later, then."

His words were heavy with promise.

She listened to his footsteps fade.

He'd brought her here to give her a book? *A book.*

With shaking hands, she opened the cover.

Minerva Press.

As she turned the title page, a slip of paper wafted to the floor. She crouched down and read his message.

My library holds untold fascinations. Should you wish to explore them, there's a convenient passage from the third floor to the top balcony, rendering a late-night ramble through the house quite unnecessary. I will leave the second volume in the upper reading alcove at midnight if you wish to retrieve it.

Her heart sank, even as her pulse galloped.

Seduction, not humiliation, had been his real purpose—the reason Mrs. Small had been hired, the reason her sleeping arrangements had been altered.

He'd held her in his arms, and, for a glorious moment, she'd forgotten everything.

Her situation. *His* strategic gifts.

Just like Karl, he'd used her sympathy to create a false intimacy. Elation transformed into murky acid that swished dangerously around in her gut, threatening to make her ill.

And, like Karl, he meant to make her his mistress.

No wonder she'd been breathless—she'd just been lifted and swept across an entire chess board. Despite her plans, despite her reservations, the player had her in check. But check*mate*?

Not yet.

She was older. Smarter. More confident of her worth. She set *him* back into his place. She simply could not lose her head.

Or, God help her, her heart.

Chapter Seven

A low fire sizzled, its faint glow joining the only other source of illumination in the library—Hurtheven's oil lamp. Together, the two light sources barely pierced the gloom. The duke stared into the darkness from his vantage on the topmost balcony. Each time the flames crackled; another fissure ran through his taut nerves.

The stolen taste of her lingered on his lips. The embodied recollection of their embrace clung to him like a tantalizing scent. Instead of having satiated his need, he was restive, fitful and on edge.

But why should he feel as nervous as a boy in the clutches of his first infatuation? Surely, he *must* have secured her regard. But what if he had not?

Bloody hell.

Uncertainty was a novel and disturbing experience—a land he did not know and dared not dwell in for long. He *never* left his fate solely in another's hands. And yet, here he was, about to offer her all that he was when he was in no way convinced of her answer.

She'd softened—he reassured himself—opening to his kiss with the innate facility of a gracefully budding floret. Of course, she'd see the advantages of a match between them, however unlikely—and unequal—their pairing might seem to others.

He hadn't meant to kiss her this afternoon—not before he'd made his intentions clear. But his infamous self-control failed when she was near.

When she was near, a current compelled him to connect to her the way magnetization forced a compass needle North, or a bolt of lightning found its inevitable way from cumulus cloud to earthly target.

Strange this impetus to tether his heart so firmly to another's. Strange and unsettling. What recourse would he have if she refused?

Was offering her marriage at this early stage presumptuous? He didn't even know her Christian name, for heaven's sake. Would she think him mad?

A subtle shift in sensation, a heightened awareness, warned him of a change in the room.

"Mrs. Montrose." He spoke without turning.

"How *do* you do that?" She sounded wary. "How do you sense me before I have made my presence known?"

"The truth is..." He stretched his arm across the back of the sofa and folded one leg over the other—a posture at odds with his inner turmoil. "...I simply *know* whenever you're near."

Her skirts rustled as she came into the faint ring of light. *Swoosh. Swoosh. Swoosh.* His male parts responded to the distinctly feminine sound, further disordering his thoughts.

She was dressed, not for the evening, but as she'd been this afternoon. Serviceable, in dark brown. She'd again hidden her mass of red curls, and her cap was, in a word, hideous.

Armor.

Not an auspicious start.

"Do join me..." he suggested.

She set down her candle, parted her lips as if to speak, and then quickly clamped her mouth closed in an oddly enticing mockery of a pout.

She did not usually resort to pouting, he'd wager...nor, for that matter, did she use any intentional means of manipulation. She would fight, if she must, honestly for anything she desired. And if she failed, she would retreat and replan. He knew. He knew because he would do the same.

Kindred understanding. A central ingredient of her allure.

He noted the book in her hand as she set her candle next to his lamp. "...Or have you simply come in search of Volume two?"

Her gaze withered. "I came, as you are aware, at your command."

His *command*? He'd carefully worded his note as a *suggestion*. He wanted her to agree to his proposal of her own free will, not because she felt compelled to comply.

"Since you've made up your mind to be obliging"—he slid to the side to make more room for her to sit—"you might as well heed my other charge."

His voice had come out harsher than he'd intended, as if unconsciously matching the martial look in her eye. Something had changed since this afternoon, and instinct urged him to take up a position of defense.

She examined him with disconcerting frankness.

"After another penny, are you?" he asked. "I'll have you

know I'm pockets to let right now. Unless I return to my rooms and retrieve my purse."

"This time," she said slowly, "*I* had better offer *you* my thoughts."

He raised a brow. "From the look on your face, I hesitate to ask."

"I did not come to be obliging. I came to put a stop to this farce before we both do something we cannot help but regret."

If he'd been in less a state of suspense, he might have seized on his fleeting thought that she, too, was simply scared, that reason had, in the intervening hours since they'd kissed, reordered her thoughts, and then, as reason often did, trampled with glee on the true desires of her heart.

But she'd said *farce.*

She'd compared the third most life-altering experience of his life to staged buffoonery.

"I'm afraid you'll have to explain."

She flashed a frown. "An age-old story. Quite unremarkable. *Trite*, really."

Each word she uttered dug deeper than the last, punctuated by her increasingly caustic expression.

"Trite." He over enunciated the word, as if considering its meaning, and then hid his growing anger beneath an insouciant tone. "You've my complete attention. Please continue."

"Well, the story beings when a prince, or the lord of the manor—"

"Or I presume, the *duke?*" he said, mimicking her derisive inflection.

"—discovers a *pressing need* to seduce and then abandon the governess."

"Seduce *and then abandon* the governess," he repeated.

"Well, it needn't be *the governess*." She either mistook, or did not perceive, his emphasis. "The nursemaid, the cook, the housekeeper—they're all equally at risk. The story's most salient elements are an imperious, powerful male on one hand, and a female who displays high competence in some feminine art on the other..."

Imperious?

"...Although," she frowned, "why possession of a vulnerable female preoccupies men already influential enough to have every whim indulged, falls to you to answer. *I* cannot."

Astonishment wholly silenced any response.

In a few moments, he would relive her words, hearing the pain she had disguised, but, at present, certain phrases grabbed his attention, rousing in him a very different emotion than anything akin to understanding.

Seduce and then abandon. Every whim indulged. She'd painted the image of a leering lordship, a libertine with neither dignity, nor respect for his fellow beings. He'd been prepared to beg her to walk through life by his side when this—*this*—is how she saw him?

A swift stab of indignation pierced his chest, sending needles of heat outwards in every direction. His gaze sharpened. His lips turned down.

"As for you, *duke*"—the word held only disgust—"I grant that I might have given you the wrong impression when suffering from a severe shock. And" —she blushed— "when responding without thought earlier today, but that does not absolve you of demanding—Well!" She stopped abruptly, her gaze fixing on his curled fist. "I see I've hit the mark."

He snorted. "Well, you've certainly achieved a hit."

"I daresay you'll recover. I trust we understand one another?"

"A moment, please," he managed.

If she'd known him better, perhaps she would have shrunk from his deceptively quiet, extraordinarily polite tone. As it was, she appeared relieved. Or, at least spent. She sunk down onto the settee, careful to keep an arm's length between them.

"Are you suggesting..." He forced open his hands and spread his fingers out on his thighs. "...that your successful management of Ash's children has bewitched me?"

"*Bewitched*? Gracious, no. I'm not so arrogant as to believe *I'm* any threat to *you*..."

She'd absolutely no idea how tormented he'd been, did she?

No idea how she'd besieged him with a single look, and then advanced on him, until every aspect of her singular character had left him utterly conquered.

"...I'm merely pointing out that you *think* you want me because I'm already subservient to you."

"Oh!" He replied as if she were making sense. "So, your subservience and your feminine arts *combined* have rendered me so demented, not only am I helplessly driven by lust, but I also no longer *know my own mind*."

"Hurtheven," she placated, "you must see I am at your mercy in every way."

"Ashbey is your employer," he snapped. "Not myself."

"That doesn't exactly bring parity to our positions. And I don't see why you should be so clearly infuriated with me when you know exactly what you invited me here to *discuss*. I'm well acquainted with your kind."

His kind.

If she'd looked closely, she would have noticed a certain

tension in the tendons of his neck and been chastened. As it was, she'd turned her face toward the fire, her back right-eously rigid.

"You've complimented me on my own high competence in managing Ash's children," he observed. "May I therefore assume you are also struggling against the overpowering allure of *my* charms?"

"Now you're being absurd!"

"Absurd, *of course*, to think you might hold me in *any* esteem."

"Oh, do stop using that wretched tone. I cannot possibly have caused *you* offense!"

"As I am entirely devoid of sensibility?"

She made a dismissive sound. "You don't see *me*, at all, *duke*. I am simply an object. Something that must be possessed to satisfy your whim. Your desire for me is little different, for instance, than Lord Chandon's desire to cage and transport that unfortunate lion."

He stood up with so much violence, her candle's flame danced. But the furious set down he intended to deliver died as he met her terrified expression.

Terrified. Of *him*.

Good God.

She really did think him a complete cad. She was the lion in her analogy, but she stared at him as if he were the one likely to pounce. He folded his arms behind his back and turned away toward the railing.

"What if," he spoke as evenly as he was able, "I told you I had honorable intentions when I *suggested* this meeting?"

"I'd say you were being *deliberately* cruel. And intentional cruelty is not, I believe, in your nature."

"No." He swiveled back. "Only reckless abandon in the face of your *feminine arts. Such* high praise."

He stopped himself from wishing her, presently, to the devil.

Still, his wounded pride had so inverted his admiration, he forged onward when he should have retreated to decipher just how and where this conversation had gone so terribly wrong.

"I admit, a *current* fascination with your..." He swept his gaze down her person with slow and open depravity. "...assets. But you are correct. I *will* recover."

"I'm glad to hear it. Your lewd interest is none of my—"

"Lewd?" He interrupted. "*Lewd!* Of course, I am lewd. Vile. Crude. Inconsiderate."

She had the grace to blush, but stammered angrily, "Am I mistaken? Or did you not just undress me with your gaze?"

He had, damn her. And he hadn't found her at all wanting. Fury and lust had him throbbing everywhere from his temple to his groin.

"Your theory appears excessively detailed, decidedly settled, and none too flattering." He took a measured breath. "It is also *wrong*. As it happens, my absorption began, not with a wild, covetous passion, nor with the vision of you as...as *comely shepherdess* to my godchildren." He'd practically spat the word shepherdess. As he ran a hand over his mouth, his gaze fell to her throat. "My absorption *began* with a whisp of an errant curl...a curl rather like the one you have been repeatedly threading through your fingers."

She shoved the curl beneath her cap. "If untidy hair is your weakness—"

"Not *anyone's* untidy hair. *Your* untidy hair. I promise you I have never taken particular note of any other lady's tussled coiffure. And that before I knew a blessed thing about you, but for the fact I was furious with you for having lost track of Lady Felicia, which is rather the opposite of what you've accused."

She eyed him sharply. "I may have given the wrong reason, but you cannot deny the whole. You want me, and you mean to have me with no thought to the consequences to me."

"No thought?" he sputtered. "How *very* wrong you are!"

"Well, then!" She waved her hand between them. "*You* define *this*."

Seized by a reckless, malignant thrill, he fixed his hands to the furniture, one on the sofa's arm, just to her right, and the other, on the backrest to her left. "Far be it from me to *dissemble*. Would you prefer a detailed, anatomical justification?"

"That won't be necessary. The snug tailoring on your trousers has made your state obvious enough."

His smile was anything but blithe. "There's no need for fright, my dear. It's but a tool, and, if skillfully handled, a useful one."

"Ah, but tools are so cumbersome." She raised her brows in an expression of sweetness. "I prefer to use my own hands."

He jerked back, only able to stare. Caught between fury, lust, and a mad urge to laugh, he slowly shook his head. She was beyond *anything* he'd ever known and this entire conversation, perfectly outrageous.

And yet...

And yet, he felt so vital, he should have been sparking. And he knew he'd deserved that counterpunch she'd so calmly and impressively delivered.

"You are beyond audacious," he said, not without a flicker of admiration.

She rearranged her skirts. "I'm nothing more to you than prey."

"I would *never* think of a lady as prey, particularly not you." Although earlier, he had compared the act of her entering his home akin to entering a lion's den, hadn't he?

If he could just catch his breath, maybe he could redirect—

"You would never think of me as a *lady* at all."

"But I *do*, heaven help me."

"You never stand when I enter—"

"Is *that* your standard?"

"—nor have you had any compunction about giving me imperious directives. And, at Wisterley, you felt free to come into my bedchamber."

"I order *everyone* about, as is my right *and* my responsibility. And you shared your Wisterley bedchamber with the children. As for the night at the inn—"

She gave him a significant look.

"Ah yes, you were simply seeking reassurance." He'd been almost certain that she'd come to hold him in *some* regard. He ran his hand through his hair. How—*how*—could he have been so wide of the mark?

Then again, *had* he been wide of the mark?

"Would you have me believe"—he eyed her carefully— "you are completely unaffected?"

She held his gaze. "Of course not." Her cheeks stained with two patches of red. "But you are bad for me, *duke*."

He sifted again through the elements of her "story," this time, feeling *her* anger and fear. Slowly, his understanding altered. "Do you really believe *I* am bad for you?"

She turned her face slightly away, although her gaze remained fixed.

"I think, perhaps, the subject of the phrase may be at fault..."

She flinched. *Ah.* He felt a sharp pang. He'd been right.

"...I gather from our exchange that you aren't completely without," he paused, "experience."

"I've experience," she answered darkly, "that would put even you to blush."

He searched her gaze and did not doubt. Then, in one, fluid movement, he draped himself by her side and stretched out his aching legs. At a complete loss to find something he could say that would set things right, he, instead, captured her hand.

A strange specter arose within his chest, an apparition newly born, flailing and blind with fumbling limbs not yet fully blooded. He held fast to her limp fingers while the thing inside him slipped and slid and tried to steady.

"If you find these," he caressed her knuckles with his thumb, "less cumbersome than a fully readied cock. I doubt you've been properly introduced to *le petite mort.*"

She expelled a puff of air. A half-chuckle?

"Doubtless," she replied lightly, "you feel you could do better."

"With you"—he side-eyed her with a rueful half smile— "I *know* I could do better."

She made a noise low in her throat. "Part of the problem is"—she dropped her head back against the cushion and closed her eyes—"I fear you could be right."

Well, then. "Bad for you..." he echoed, hearing his own voice as if in a dark canyon—a canyon that he feared was the gulf between them. Was there a way to traverse that gulf? *Perhaps*—he winced—*not.* "If you *truly* believe I am bad for you, we will end this conversation now."

She made a soft sound—part confusion, part protest,

part need. A sound that pinched down low within his gut. Then, by what felt like organic means, her formerly flaccid fingers tendrilled around his own.

The specter inside him stilled, overpowered by something stronger—the first, pale flicker of hope.

"Then again, perhaps the preposition is the rub..."

Her eyes flew open.

"...There's also bad *to* you. Which, at present, I—I..." He lost his voice.

Her breath slowed. Her brows arched at the center as if she could not believe—or did not wish to hear—what he had to say.

"...I must acknowledge I have been."

He lifted the back of her hand to his lips and closed his eyes. She was present. Right there beside him. But the flesh against his lips was cold.

He'd done that.

"...I apologize for reacting badly to your concern, for speaking coarsely, and for goading you into coarseness..."

He lowered their joined palms. He would have let her go, but her grip had tightened. "...You were correct, however. A part of me..."

The specter flailed again.

"...A part of me," he started again, "very much wishes to be bad *with* you."

He steadied his breath, holding his focus on the single point of her fingers wrapped around his own as remnants of his anger and lust flamed up around him like burning ash, threating to spread a fire he was still struggling to snuff, a fire that hadn't yet cooled.

"Even now, I am painting you in my mind—and no, my thoughts aren't at all gentlemanly."

"Hurtheven..."

She'd spoken his name like a plea wrapped in want and frustration that matched his own.

"I am about to be vulgar again." His voice cracked. "Do you want to stop? Or do you wish me to tell you what I see?"

Her throat moved as she swallowed. "I don't know."

The hope and the beast struggled. This time, the beast won out. His eyes unfocused and his breath slowed. "Your hair is spread out against a pillow. Your"—he closed his eyes —"wetness surrounds my cock..."

Her breath caught.

"...your breasts, with stiffened nipples, brush against my chest. And you're making that sound you made before—that soft, almost reluctant whimper—over and over while you quake with your release."

She made that sound again. He stopped, unable to continue and unable to open his eyes. He wet his lips.

"So, yes," he forced the words, "I want to be bad *with* you. But I vow that I will not *ever*"—the word came out as a growl—"be bad *to* you again."

"Hurtheven—"

"But," he interrupted, "I could only be bad *for* you if I bore *any* resemblance to the libertine you just described—a man who would take from you and give you nothing in return. Am I that man?"

He opened his eyes and gazed out into the darkened library. He'd posed the question, he realized, as much to himself as to her.

"No," she whispered.

He turned his head, and, with his gaze, he caressed her face—the lips he'd tasted, the cheek he'd cradled, the eyes that had seen so deeply into his soul.

Her mouth was pinched, with signs she'd been incessantly worrying her lip since last they'd met. The usually pale angles of her face were wine-dark and radiating with heat. Her gaze was troubled and her eyes, wide.

She was...scared.

Whether or not her story had been true *of him*, her story had been truth.

She'd been hurt. Badly.

Inwardly, he cursed. Winning her was not going to be easy. He might even fail.

He'd wondered, while he'd been waiting for her to arrive, what he'd do if she refused him. Now, he had his answer. Let her go, of course...if she truly did not wish to be with him.

But if she did?

He would do, he would give, he would *be* anything.

The only way to survive a storm—or a fight—was to keep your eyes on the horizon and ruthlessly navigate the waves.

* * *

She'd watched his fury grow, first with anger of her own, then with awe, and then with a growing awareness of his physical presence. He was only holding her hand, and yet the way his gaze was moving across her face was intimate—*palpably* intimate.

He'd been angry. He'd been hurt. And his pained fury, like her own, had taken him outside of himself. Now, though drained, he watched her intently, as if the key to her soul could be found in her features.

"I insulted your pride, didn't I?" she asked.

"What pride? I've none where you're concerned."

Again, he lifted her hand to his cheek. His stubble prickled against her skin. "Were you in love with him?"

"No," she replied truthfully. Nor had she'd felt anything for Karl even close to the storm that was engulfing her at present.

"Did he...hurt you?" The tightness about his mouth fascinated—a tightness fierce as the moment he'd burst from the inn to take on the lion.

"I willingly acquiesced, if that's what you mean...although someone recently suggested to me that, as our positions were unequal, his advances were inherently unfair."

"I see," he said.

Did he? "There hasn't been anyone else since." Why had she added that?

"Do you regret your choice?"

With a sharp heart spasm followed by a rush of unbearable love, she thought of Annis—her round, baby cheeks and her wide, serious eyes.

"No," she said softly. "I *cannot* regret my choice." She inhaled. "Although I was disappointed in him. He was not...the man I believed him to be."

Briefly, he closed his eyes.

"Please don't ask me who—"

"I already know."

She frowned.

"I *see* because the story you described—the story of seduction and abandonment—was not a story at all, but your lived experience. And I *know* who to blame because you recognized Fee's doll. You worked for Prince Karl when he resided in London, did you not?"

The heat was so high in her cheeks her eyes began to burn. "I begin to understand how you felt when you gave

158

me the penny. You know Karl, too—well enough that he gave you that doll."

"Yes, I know Karl..."

Something in his voice made her shiver.

"...but as an *adversary*. He is a scoundrel of the worst sort. A libertine, a seducer, and a traitor to his country. Or" —he lifted his brows—"what was his country. I am not at liberty to tell you how or why I obtained the doll, but this much I can reveal—he was driven from Vienna in disgrace."

Karl....*driven* from Vienna? Her frown deepened. "Could he have come back here to England since?"

"Would you want to see him if he did?"

She shivered again. "No!"

"Does he hold something over you?"

She felt her color drain but shook her head *no*. Hurtheven did not look convinced by her denial.

"I will not let him harm you," he said fiercely. "I swear."

He believed what he was saying. Then again, he didn't know the whole. "You can't promise to keep me safe from him."

"The devil I can't!" A muscle worked in his jaw. "There is one thing that will definitively place you beyond his reach." His throat moved beneath his hopelessly rumpled cravat. "Marry me."

Reflexively, she set her free hand against his lips.

They stared at one another, frozen in shock.

"Please," he spoke against her fingers.

Ah. Her heart melted.

She'd never seen him so disheveled, so intent, and yet so wretched. In such a state, he could not possibly know what he had just offered. She could not allow herself to believe him.

He *couldn't* be serious.

159

Karl had offered marriage, too, but he'd never followed through. And she'd seen Hurtheven's 'ideal' list, and she didn't meet a single qualification. Her hand, clasped in his, may feel secure and right, as if she could be confident of his care, but she couldn't.

"*That*," she said, "was the lust talking. You don't know me at all."

"But I do," he protested. "Yes, I want you in my bed. I also want you as my wife."

His bed. The blunt admission quickened sparks beneath her skin.

She wanted him, too.

She wanted those deeply intelligent, sharp eyes entirely focused on her own, just as they were in this moment. She wanted—her gaze dropped to his mouth—to kiss him as she had this afternoon. And—*damn him*—she wanted every detail of the scene he'd described just a few minutes ago.

She hadn't *reformed* at all—not that she had ever felt she needed to 'reform.' If she could have Hurtheven without consequence, she would do so whole-heartedly.

Oh, hell.

Could she have him without consequence?

She trembled—a long, subtle shiver of desire that started in her shoulders, pooled in her groin, and then spread all the way to her toes.

Would a brief, cultivated liaison threaten her plan to reclaim Annis? If she and the duke were the only two people ever to know...

But such a thing was impossible with a house crawling with servants.

"Can we," she asked breathlessly, "achieve the latter preposition without running afoul of the first two?"

He blinked. "Pardon?"

"Bad *for*...Bad *to*... Bad *with*..."

He shifted his position, bringing his knee up onto the settee so he could face her in full. She matched his posture, still holding tightly to his hand.

"Will you agree to marry me?"

She let go of his hand. "I—I am not yet sure."

"Then what are you suggesting, Mrs. Montrose?"

She swallowed. "Hera."

He cocked his head.

"Hera Bythesea." She wet her lips. "My legal name. You'll need it...for the contract."

"Hera," he repeated as if dumfounded. He gave his head a little shake. "Did you just say *contract*?"

"I—I have been given to understand that contracts offer protection in...affairs of the heart. Karl didn't...I mean, well, I—"

"*Marriage*," he insisted. "I offered—"

"I *know*," she interrupted him again before he could further embarrass them both. "And I also know I am not the kind of woman you'd ever wish to marry..."

Even if she were, Annis rendered the unlikely unattainable. He could not possibly agree to raise another man's bastard. And she would never again give up her child.

Not even to be a duchess.

Not even *his* duchess.

"...But neither can I enter another arrangement without protection. I will not repeat my mistake."

He rose to his feet. Then he stalked back to the balcony where, but for the snowy white lawn of his shirt, he blended in with the gloom.

She was thankful for the distance. Without him close, she could think.

She wanted him. What was more—she bit her lip—a

161

contract could leave her with something solid and reliable. And if there was even a chance Karl could be in England and had hired the Runner who tracked her to Wisterley, she could no longer depend on taking a rented room in the village near that estate.

She would never again have a better opportunity to secure a future for Annis and they needed a place to live.

He glanced over his shoulder. "Just so I understand, you are agreeing to be my mistress, but not my wife?"

Ah, but what must he think of her? "For now," she said carefully.

"*For now*," he repeated. Again, he turned away. His shirt stretched across his muscled shoulders as he folded his arms. "Eyes on the horizon."

"Pardon?" She prompted,

"Never mind." He rolled his shoulders. Then, he sighed. "Very well. You may, of course, name any terms you desire."

Oh, how she wished she could see his face. *Or perhaps not.* She named her chief concern. "We *cannot* be discovered...at least until we know one another well enough to truly consider marriage."

"The simplest issue to answer." He continued to speak into the darkness. "Your chamber is an enclosed anteroom. The paneling that runs along the wall as well as the stairway beyond the room inside conceals the former armory—windowless, quite out of the way and never attended."

Tingles of awareness ran up her arms. "You've planned well, I see."

He turned. "As I told you before, the scheme to hire Mrs. Small was wholly devised by Mrs. Whitby. I was merely responding to your concern."

She closed her eyes. "I cannot *believe* we are discussing this."

"Can't you? An age-old story. *Trite*, really...the wealthy duke and the—"

"Oh, do stop before you say something I will *not* be able to forgive! You *just* promised not to hurt me."

The tension in his body slacked. "*Hera*..."

"Can't you see that I must protect myself?" *And Annis.*

"I can," he conceded warily.

"I have a reason," her voice cracked, "a very good reason, I cannot fall victim to empty promises yet again. Before this evening, I just...well, I had not considered the possibility of accepting a lover on...terms."

"Terms." His mouth twisted ruefully. "Shall we negotiate, then?"

Her heartbeat galloped. She was really going to do this. "I should, once we part, like a place to live. Something small and out of the way, suitable for a widow."

"*If* we part," he corrected.

"If we part," she repeated.

"That can be arranged."

"And an annuity?"

"Why speak 'annuity' as if the word were a question? Unless you wish *me* to suggest a price."

"I am"—she broke their gaze—"inexperienced in these things."

He made a long, inscrutable noise. Then, he sighed. "Would, say, an annuity commensurate to the one I pay Mrs. Small suffice?"

"I trust your judgment."

"Finally," he said wryly, "she pays me a second compliment."

When had she paid him the first?

Ah, yes. In the lane behind the inn. What had she been referring to then? Suddenly, she remembered. She'd been speaking of his way with the children.

"Is there anything else?" he asked.

She ignored the note of derision in his voice and steadied her breath. She *could* ask for something more...something she *wanted*, rather than *needed*. Something that could make all the difference in the world. But did she dare?

She'd dare anything for Annis.

She raised her gaze. "You will agree—in writing—to be the guardian of my child."

Surprised flickered in his eyes. "*If* there is a child."

"*Any* child."

He raised his brows.

"I am not...in a family way." She had to be very, very careful. "And I do not intend to live my future life...in the manner we are discussing. You are an exception." She lifted a shoulder in a shrug. "But, if you do not believe me, I will withdraw from further negotiations."

He stared at her long and hard. "*All* my beliefs are, at the moment, entirely suspended." He returned to the sofa. He hesitated, and then he took her hands into his own. "Why? *Why* are you doing this?"

"Because I am certain you would protect any child in your care."

"Indeed, I would." He searched her face. "And I will."

"You accept, then?" she asked breathlessly.

"I do," he answered.

She'd taken the most shocking gamble of her life, and, in so doing, secured a home for her future and a wealthy, powerful guardian for her child. Her audacity left her dizzy.

And if the admiration in his gaze had dimmed, it was a small sacrifice.

"Now, shall we discuss *my* terms? he asked.

She nodded slowly, feeling the heat in his palms.

"You will meet me in the armory at midnight tomorrow —and every night thereafter, unless you send word that you are indisposed. And, before Ash comes to collect his children, we will once again revisit the question of marriage."

She'd wager he could not imagine a woman's rejection. Would she hurt him again when she left him to collect Annis?

But she would not dwell on his possible sorrow.

Even if bruised, he would heal. This man had the world at his feet. He could have his pick of any available lady of the *ton*.

"Agreed," she replied.

He stared down at their joined hands as if he, too, could not believe what had just passed between them. Slowly, he raised his gaze as he pressed her fingers to his lips. His warm breath and the soft touch of his mouth against her skin, ignited ripples of longing.

Longing—Lord help her—not *entirely* carnal in nature.

When he released her hands, she instinctively wrapped her arms across her chest. Protection. But from what?

"I'll ask nothing of you until the contract is drawn up and signed. But when it is"—he caressed her bottom lip with his thumb—"I promise you pleasure. My complete attention. Breathlessness. Coupling without shame...or restraint...but my price is your full surrender."

"I won't hold back." Even if she'd wanted to hold back, she couldn't.

"Well, then. We have reached accord." He rested his head against the sofa's back and closed his eyes. "Now go,

Hera. Unless you want me to change my mind about waiting for the ink to dry and further debase us both by ravishing you on my library floor."

She glanced doubtfully at the cold marble tile and shivered.

Then, she went.

* * *

The duke hadn't appeared at breakfast—he'd been, in fact, called away on estate business too early for him to have spoken with either Hera or the children, a fact which disgruntled the children.

They voiced their disappointment in the strongest of terms, prompting a disapproving frown from Mrs. Small and placing Hera in the uncomfortable position of having to list the many ways in which the duke had proved his courtesy and care to them over the past few days.

Which, of course, only heightened the feeling she'd wronged him with her assumptions about his intentions and her brash, accusatory manner. He, too, had been deliberately wounding, of course, but *she'd* been more than wounding; she'd been outrageous in her demands.

Not that she regretted the outcome. Quite the opposite, in fact.

She was, for the first time, anticipating her future. She'd arranged for Annis security she could never have provided on her own. And, between now and then, she could freely indulge in a fantastical reality.

Her dreams had been feverish—alive with an arousal as strong as a living, vining thing refusing release. Dream-vision Hurtheven caressed her throughout the night, stimulating her in the most intimate of places while she responded just as he'd suggested—*without shame*.

She sighed. Perhaps she *was* a wanton.

She spent the rest of the damp, unpleasant morning alternating between similar spasms of guilt and bursts of anticipation. And so, when the skies unexpectedly cleared, and the children expressed a desire to walk along the bridle paths outside the bailey, she readily agreed, hoping the brisk air would turn her thoughts in a more pleasant direction.

She'd not forgotten the duke's implied warning—free reign *inside* the castle—but the duke was not present, and none of the staff raised any objection to the scheme.

As she wandered a few lengths behind the children, she fixed her thoughts on a secure future for herself and Annis. How wonderful to have a place of their own—even if her means of obtaining one left a sour churn in her stomach.

Hera barely noticed when Delmare turned onto an ill-tended gravel pathway—not too different from Wisterley's old drive.

"Mrs. Mont*rose!*"

Felicia's tone brought her abruptly back to the present. "A lady doesn't shout, Fee."

"How else," Fee replied, "is she supposed to get the attention of the person with whom she wishes to speak?"

"In most cases, ladies are expected to wait until attention is bestowed on them."

Fee stopped short, even as Delmare skipped further ahead. "That's *stu*pid."

Hera sighed. "I don't fully disagree—"

Fee peeked up, incredulous. "*You* disagree with a *rule*?"

"—*Nonetheless*, you must, at least, *know* the rules before you can choose how and when to, ah, *bend* them."

"Uncle Heven says—"

"Yes, I remember," Hera interrupted. "Uncle Heven told you he can break any rule. It's different for him. He's a man. And a duke. You are a lady..."

Fee put her hands on her hips.

"...although you are also the daughter of a duke, so I suppose that does give you *some* advantage."

She squinted suspiciously. "What does *bend* the rules mean?"

"*Well...*"

She weighed her doubts about the wisdom of providing an explanation against the certainty that Fee would persist in pestering her until she explained.

"...when an intelligent person *fully* understands the reason behind a rule, they can often figure out a way to break the rule in a way that will not bring harm to themselves or anyone else. That's what's known as bending a rule. In other words, you adhere to the *spirit* of the law—the reason for its existence—without necessarily obeying the *letter*, or the exact dictate."

Fee considered. "Why didn't you ever explain rules that way *before*? I would have been far more likely to listen!"

Hera winced inwardly. And yet, perhaps, she should have approached rules in such a manner. With Fee's family history and her fiery spirit, she would, by necessity, be compelled to cut a unique pathway through the world.

"Was there a reason you shouted my name?" Hera changed the subject, hoping to distract Fee from the schemes Hera could see developing behind her eyes.

"Oh, yes," Fee replied.

"And...?"

Fee looked doubtfully off into the distance. "Before I tell you, I need to decide if we are, right now, *bending* a rule or *breaking* one. If we're just bending, then I don't have to—"

"Lady Felicia," Hera interrupted, "what do you mean *right now*?"

Fee lowered her chin and raise her eyes, looking sheepish. "I'm afraid Delmare has played a trick on you."

"A trick?"

"Last summer, when Mama, Papa and I came here to collect Delmare, we stayed on a few days. When Uncle Heven took Del and I on a walk down this path, he told us we were not allowed to come back on our own. But, since I don't know *why* Uncle Heven did not want us to come back, I suppose this counts as breaking, not bending, his rule."

"You *knew* you were not supposed to come this way when we set out?" Hera demanded.

"Not *exactly*." Fee bit her bottom lip. "Del just said the bridle paths. There are quite a few, you know. Only *this* one is forbidden."

She should have realized! "We strayed from the main path more than ten minutes ago! Why didn't you warn me then?!"

"I didn't *really* recognize where Del was headed until I saw the haunted house."

"*Pardon?*"

Fee pointed down the lane to an overgrown patch of trees and brush Hera had assumed was simply a thicket.

"Delmare!" she called ahead.

The boy promptly disappeared into the brush.

Rascal.

Hera scooped up Felicia and then doubled her pace. As she came close, she could discern earth-colored bricks through the weeds. Just as Fee had described, the plants hid a building—and she could see why Fee had called the place haunted.

The building was in the style of the castle, though clearly not as old, nor made of stone. Several of the windows, though boarded, appeared to be missing glass. And the visible beams had not only faded but cracked.

What was this place? A crofter's cottage?

She didn't think so. In fact, the structure had the look of an outbuilding rather than a house.

A dairy, perhaps?

Delmare's grunts interspersed with scraping noises. She followed the sounds, hoping he hadn't already found a way inside.

"Delmare!" Would there be rats? *Please, no rats!* "Come back at once!"

"Very well, ma'am. *After* I've had a look."

She spotted him above them and gasped. Using a tree, he'd scrambled up the side of the building and was peering into one of the windows with a loosened covering.

"Come down! Now! It doesn't look safe."

"It's not," he replied cheerfully. "Board's loose."

"You don't know how dangerous it could be."

"I know what I'm doing," he insisted. "We've been here before, haven't we, Fee?"

Fee and Delmare exchanged glances.

"Uncle Heven was with us," Delmare added.

She narrowed her eyes. "And did Uncle Heven not also forbid you from returning on your own?"

Delmare groaned. "I *knew* you'd babble."

"I didn't know about bending rules, then," Fee explained.

"Delmare!" Hera called up warningly.

Fee wrapped her arm more closely around Hera's neck

in the manner of someone about to bestow a confidence. "We aren't permitted on the lane *by ourselves*. But you're with us, aren't you? That changes everything."

"I'm not sure the duke would agree," Hera replied. "Come *down*, Delmare."

Deftly, he swung off the tree. "What could *possibly* be so bad about a carriage house?"

"Ghosts, Dunderhead!" Fee replied.

"No such thing, Goose," he answered.

"Is that what this is?" Hera directed the question to Felicia. "A carriage house?"

Fee nodded. "A *second* carriage house. There's another inside the lower bailey. But Uncle Heven's Papa had a great many carriages, so he built this one."

"Let me show you," Delmare suggested.

Before she could protest, he had rounded the building and, from the metallic squeal that rent her ears, was already tugging at the door.

Just a carriage house.

What harm could there be? Then again, why did she have such an eerie feeling? And why did she suspect the children weren't telling her the whole story?

"Wait!" She cried. "Don't go inside."

The squeaking ceased. And, when she rounded the corner, she found the door partway open and Delmare standing guard. At least he'd listened, for once.

And, she hadn't seen any rats...yet.

Perhaps he'd forbidden the children because the structure was not sound?

The gloom within protested the invasion of light. From what she could see, however, the beams were intact. The floor looked solid. Nothing screamed danger. In fact, but for a pile of black wood near the back, the building was empty.

"You see? There's nothing at all to be concerned about," Delmare pointed out. "Now, May I go in?"

She shook her head no. "We ought to leave everything as is."

"Quick, Del!" Fee exclaimed.

Delmare darted inside.

"Felicia!" Hera scolded.

"A bent rule?" she suggested hopefully.

This was what came of rule breaking. "I suggest you forget about bending any more rules. And if you cannot, remember this—a bent rule is a broken one as far as punishment is concerned."

Fee winced. "We have *always* wanted to know what was inside, but Uncle Heven wouldn't show us. It's ghosts. I'm *sure* it's ghosts. *Is* it ghosts, Del?"

"Bah! I already told you there is no such thing," Del said from within. "The only thing in here is just what's left of an old, stupid carriage. But ahhh!"

Hera's heart stopped.

"I'm not hurt! Just got my foot caught, is all."

"Fee, I'm going to put you down, and you are going to stay *right here*, do you understand?"

Fee wrinkled her nose. "*I* only wanted to see a ghost. I'm not interested in a dusty old carriage."

"I believe you," Hera replied. "But if you disobey me—if you bend or break this rule—you can expect a supper of gruel in the nursery!"

Fee shuddered. "I'll stay right here. I promise."

Hera set Fee down by the door and then edged her way inside, carefully placing her feet. The further she ventured, the thicker the damp, musty smell.

"Delmare?"

"Here," he called. "Shoestrings got tangled in a nail. Bad luck, that."

"Serves you right." She knelt. "Deceivers don't prosper, you know." Although she was one to talk, wasn't she?

"Are you going to tell Uncle Heven?"

"If I did, your uncle would be very, very disappointed in you." Not to mention how he'd feel about her! "Did you give him your word you would not come out here on your own?"

"Never. He just commanded." Delmare frowned. "And *he* went off without a by-your-leave to us this morning, and that, after he'd given his word he'd take us on a picnic."

"Which is no reason to disobey him!" She reached through what appeared to be a broken wheel to untangle Delmare's shoelaces from a broken spoke. "He had more pressing issues to attend. Besides, this morning was inclement—not at all picnic weather. He didn't break his word but was compelled to delay. Mrs. Whitby *told* you he would take you tomorrow instead."

She freed the shoe. Delmare immediately scrambled back to his feet.

"And," she continued, "You should have made me aware of his stricture. This trick was not worthy of you."

"No." Delmare hung his head. "What's worse, there's nothing exciting here at all. Nothing but a dumb, broken carriage."

Now that her eyes were fully adjusted, she again observed her surrounds. Delmare had been correct. What she'd first identified as a haphazard pile of planks had, at one time, been a traveling coach. The old-fashioned conveyance had once been grand and glossy but was now mangled almost beyond recognition.

A terrible suspicion dawned. The duke's parents had

been killed in a carriage accident, hadn't they? But this *couldn't* be the carriage.

One of the two seats showed signs of rodent-gnawed stuffing and pilling velvet, while all that remained of the other was springs. Coal-colored paint peeled from part of the door.

Much of the rest was similarly blackened, but not from paint. What had been the box was clearly charred, and the charred line seemed, almost to have split the conveyance in two.

The carriage was not just splintered but burnt.

How, *how* had he survived?

She glanced over to Delmare, who was inspecting what remained of the axel.

"That's enough. You'll be filthy."

"But I want to see!"

"This is *not* Wisterley," she said harshly. "We need express permission before we enter the buildings, and we both know the opposite, in this case, is true. What *am* I to tell the duke?"

"*Must* he know?"

"He *should* know." She rose, wiped off his hands on her petticoat and then shook out her skirts. She placed her hands on her hips. "If I decide not to tell him, I would do so not to spare you pain, but to spare him the disappointment of knowing you disregarded his directive."

She took him by the hand—something she rarely did—and led him out into the light. She instructed him to stay put and then grunted as she pushed the door back into position. *There.* She could not explain why she was so very relieved.

"Did you say you're sorry, Del?" Fee asked.

"*Yes!*" Delmare replied. The *obviously* was implied by his tone.

"I'm sorry, too," Fee added. "Don't feed us gruel, please?"

She couldn't, could she? Not without explaining to Mrs. Small and Mrs. Whitby why the children were being punished.

"If you both promise me you will behave—and be entirely truthful—for the rest of our stay, I see no reason why you cannot enjoy a proper supper. And, just this once, we will keep this adventure to ourselves."

"Oh, thank you, Mrs. Montrose," Fee threw her arms around Hera's skirts.

"That's enough, Fee. I don't wish to be thanked for perpetuating a wrong. Come, we must go."

With a child in each hand, she carefully picked her way to the lane. She didn't breathe easy until they were back on the main pathway. Even then, she continued to feel as haunted as she would have been if she actually had met a ghost.

Seeing the wreck had been like peering into the duke's private anguish.

She shivered, remembering how angry he'd been when she'd told him she thought he'd known great pain. He told her she'd been right. She did not want him to know that she now understood, in a visceral way, just *how* right she'd been.

Had his parents been killed immediately, or had they lingered? Had he been conscious? Had he been alone?

How he must have suffered! She could imagine no easy sequence of events. Any possibility would have forever altered his outlook and his character. *Yes.* He'd known great pain. She ached for that pain.

Had anyone since showed him the tenderness he

deserved? Had anyone cared enough to attempt to mend what the accident had broken? She suspected that there was a good deal more to the rules he'd shared with Delmare. What had he told the boy?

To stay strong, on the inside, where a man couldn't be touched. To keep his friends close. His secrets closer. And be ready to strike before stricken.

...Or to take furious insult when incendiary desire met cautious criticism.

She closed her eyes and swallowed roughly.

Ah, they were playing a dangerous game. And, after tonight, the stakes would only grow higher.

Even if he *had* truly meant his proposal of marriage, she could not fully regret last night's turn. What they had now —a four cornered contract—she could control. Anything more would demand an excess of what she was able to pay.

She knew this.

She knew this because, even now, however impossible, she wished she could be the woman meant to forever safeguard his heart.

Chapter Eight

Before tragedy thrust the Duke of Hurtheven into his title, *His Grace* had been an honorific reserved for—and fully embodied by—his father.

His father...a man whose quick, clipped footsteps echoed across the hall and through the corridors of Hevenhyll in a reassuring manner, whose booming laugh set all to rights, and to whom everyone in the world—or at least Hurtheven's world—petitioned with their concerns, because his father could solve any problem, no matter how large.

The young heir's sphere had been safe. His father was in charge.

Until he wasn't.

In the months of the newly minted duke's convalescence, those closest to him—mainly the people whose livelihood depended on the ducal estate—had treated him with patience and care.

Still, he'd understood, without being explicitly told, that his duty was to recover quickly and then subsume his father's role. By stepping into the prior duke's shoes, he would give *them* back the world they understood, even if his own remained irreparably shattered.

Those expectations hung off his fever-shrunken limbs in much the same manner as his father's court robes had hung off his body, even as the wind and the cold and the hard, shock of that night haunted his every hour.

His solution?

Banish base emotions—the messy, human kind of sentiments that made one prone to careless mistakes.

Mistakes like driving out into a threatening storm because *you* wanted to reach home. Because your beautiful, loving duchess would have acquiesced to anything you desired. Because neither you nor she would have paid the slightest heed under any circumstances, let alone a simple summer storm, to the concerns of a coachman, never mind your young boy.

He'd boxed up his fear and his anger and mimicked a sovereign's stride.

Stoically—and under his godfather's guidance—he'd refitted his father's mantle. And, as for the grief engendered by his sudden, inexplicable loss, he'd lowered the wick until the burn dulled to a barely discernable glow.

But in the library—he tremored—rage had reappeared as a white-hot broadsword, severing him from his dedicated control in one, stunning thwack.

She'd painted his character with what he'd perceived as casual cruelty, unknowingly making a mockery of every sacrifice he'd made in the name of his honor and his father's memory before wounding him where he was still most tender—that ephemeral landing place of the second and third strikes.

The very seat of his emotions.

Still, he'd regained his center, and made the offer he'd

decided to make that night in the inn. An offer which she'd rejected. As he tossed in his bed, he wondered anew why she'd refused to be his duchess but agreed to be his doxy.

Not just agreed—*suggested*. On extravagant terms, no less.

He'd fallen asleep bedeviled, lost in Versailles's Hall of Mirrors, unable to discern the real from the reflected. Vividly, he dreamt of smiles, soft sighs, red spiral curls, and her hand in his own. He awoke to a grey morning damp with drizzle convinced again she would soon be his wife.

Her extravagant requests *did not* reflect her nature.

He'd missed something.

He pondered the mystery as his newly arrived valet fitted him into his country clothes. He further mulled as his steward—the excellent Mr. Irving—explained to him the urgent business he must attend...not only an inspection of the drainage problem caused by the compromised dam, but other issues that had arisen in his absence.

First, he'd seen the dam and resolved to divert the river by rebuilding in a slightly different location. Next, they met with the bailiff. Then, they settled disputes among tenants which Mr. Irving had not been able to smooth over on his own. Finally, on the home farm, he'd looked over crops of potatoes and beets and beans before discussing a price for the sale of feeder lambs.

She, however, was never far from his thoughts.

By midday, his cheeks were wind-burnt, his boots muddied, and his lungs full of earthy, clean quintessence— the kind utterly unimaginable in town. He was, without knowing, gaining succor from his roots. And, as he cantered toward the village, his head was finally clear.

He was able to imagine what Mrs. Montrose might have been feeling.

Hera—he corrected—not Mrs. Montrose.

Hera to his Zeus.

Hera had entered the library wholly ignorant of his true intention. And, he now accepted, she had good reason for her suspicions.

He could not grasp, however, that a woman who could attack a lion with a pink parasol could be as vulnerable to him as she'd suggested. Nor did he suspect her of having any secret more complex than the affair she'd revealed.

And so, when he began to form an answer to the question of how he should react to the revelations of the prior evening, the answer was not one Hera would have approved. A less arrogant man would have questioned himself further. But he knew his worth. He realized his honor. He intimately understood all that was expected of him and attended to his duty without complaint.

Those robes had not fit for a good long while, but now, they were snug and intact with never a stitch out of place.

The prior night, he'd already decided her suggestion of a farce hadn't had anything to do with *him*, but Karl. Now, he went a step further. He convinced himself she'd only refused to wed him because Karl held something over her that left her frightened. And since she was, quite literally, under his protection, who better, he thought, to address the matter?

So, secure in that knowledge his anger had a proper course, and his resources a direction to apply, he'd undertaken his final task of the day and franked a letter to his godfather via the Home Office. Soon, he'd know everything possible to know about Prince Karl since he'd left Vienna—and anything knowable about the man's hold over Hera.

She would come to understand, as everyone did, he was a person on which she could rely, the one to apply to in any time of need. He would prove this by meting out just retribution to the man responsible for her distress.

Meanwhile, he intended to keep their sordid agreement.

Nights of indulgence would soften her heart. She'd see *him* again, by God—not the swine of a man her past had inspired her to create. He'd take care of Karl. And then, they'd wed.

Simple, really.

By the time he'd returned to the castle, the sun had disappeared beneath the horizon. Mrs. Whitby informed him that the children—and those who had charge of them—had taken an early dinner and had already been sent to bed.

Strange, he thought, but just as well. He had, weather permitting, a fine treat planned for them on the morrow.

He trudged up the stairs to his rooms. And, as he washed off the day's exertions, the recriminations of the wee hours of morning and the day's concerns fully transformed into anticipation of the coming night.

He prepared to bed Hera with the full and unquestioned assurance he was just the man meant to safeguard her person.

* * *

Hera waited, perched on the edge of her bed, listening for the midnight bell.

She'd hidden in her room most of the evening, staring at the same page of *The Castle of Wolfenbach* while alternatively reliving the times she'd either sparred with or connected to Hurtheven in their short, tumultuous acquaintance, or wishing she could console him for the boyhood he'd abruptly lost.

She hadn't seen the duke since the prior night, or, more

accurately, the wee hours of morning, which had been her intention.

Her charges were wily but not at all competent deceivers. So, she'd convinced the children to take an early supper—thereby avoiding the duke—and then left them with Mrs. Small for the evening.

If they'd all dined with Hurtheven, she was certain something would've slipped out, alerting him to their clandestine carriage house visit. But she hoped, by the time he'd gone up to tuck them in, they had exhausted themselves too much to unintentionally reveal the whole.

As much as her heart wished to comfort him, she knew he'd had a lifetime to build his internal walls. And, since she could not promise to protect what was behind them, she did not want him to know what she'd seen.

Or what she now understood.

The long clock on the landing peeled, loud as a cymbal at the apex of a symphony's fourth. The pulsating echo barely receded before a second, careening knell sounded.

Then again, perhaps the volume was only in her mind. A sound so offensively deafening as the one she perceived would have awoken the whole house.

No.

Only her awareness had changed. Anticipation had heightened her senses until every floorboard creak sang like a diva, and every clock strike landed with the resonant thump of a death march drum.

Midnight had come. Midnight—the delicate pinpoint on which the calendar day turned, the moment she must meet the consequences of her choice.

Choice, in fact, was the crux. The truth she must hold close.

She might tell herself she altered her position on a

liaison with the duke because she'd seen the advantage of a shrewd negotiation. She had a child to protect and no one who'd been in her circumstance could have blamed her for seizing on security.

She *might* tell herself that, and it would be true. But not the whole truth.

She had enjoyed Karl's intimate visits, but she had yielded to *his* desire, rather than her own affinity. But, last night, *she* had chosen the duke.

She could have walked away. Hurtheven would have let her go. He was not, as he'd pointed out, her employer. Even if he wished to do so, he had no power to alter Alicia's opinion, nor threaten Hera's position. But she hadn't wanted to walk away, because she did feel...oh, *something* for him.

She'd been enraged and insulted but feverishly tempted as well. And, as he'd prowled about the sofa, all lust and temper and indignation, temptation had given way to yearning, and yearning, in turn, to a thirst so strong her throat had completely dried, leaving her head light and her palms clammy.

There'd be a reckoning, of course, if only an internal one.

But she'd push that reckoning off, out and away from here and now. And she'd indulge. She placed a trembling hand on the latch and unhooked the panel, anticipating the hour to come with the breathless expectancy of a theater spectator watching the curtain lift on a thrilling and fantastical scene.

The clock's tenth chime reverberated all around. Her single candle formed a poor light as she resecured the doorway and then crept through the passage.

She opened a second door just before the last chime. She stood on the threshold, taking in the large space. The lamps within glinted off spears and broadswords hung neatly on the walls. The floor, on the other hand, was haphazardly strewn with assorted trunks, chairs, tables, and even a large, heavy oak bed—a collection of mismatched furniture that had clearly been banished from other parts of the castle.

She entered the room, pausing beside an oddly shaped, wooden contraption about a foot and a half high with brass decorations, leather straps, and a bright, red cushion.

"A camel's saddle..."

His voice gave her a start. She hadn't seen him just to her right, sprawled across a cushioned sofa with one raised side, his features aglow beneath an oil lamp atop a stand.

"...I obtained it in my travels, intending to use it as a footrest in the dark-paneled parlor downstairs. Mrs. Whitby disapproved."

"Your housekeeper dictates your decor?"

He shrugged. "She *is* present more often than I am. And she did not expressly disapprove, but whenever she glanced at the thing, she had an ill-concealed look of distaste."

"I like it," she decided.

"Really?" He smiled crookedly. "I'm glad."

She was conscious of his gaze. Conscious of his state of half-dress, much like her own. Conscious of the way his body filled the cushioned sofa.

Would they couple there?

Or in the bed at the far end of the room?

She and Karl had only ever used her bed. Her narrow, uncomfortable bed in her tiny, practically airless room. He'd showed up there one night, his bare legs visible beneath a banyan, and asked her if he might enter.

She'd said yes, but perhaps she hadn't truly been given a

choice. Perhaps she'd only convinced herself she'd had the option of saying no because the alternative was too unsettling to contemplate.

"Hurtheven, why did you ask me to meet you in the library last night, when you could have directed me to meet you here?"

"*Suggested*, not directed. And isn't that obvious?"

"No."

"I wanted to propose to you, to persuade you to be with me...not intimidate you into an agreement. The enclosed nature of this room—the weapons, the bed—I judged them slightly more intimidating a setting than I preferred for the conversation I wished to have." His brief smile was rueful. "The conversation went awry nonetheless."

Ah, duke. He'd taken her feelings into consideration in a way she hadn't understood. "I'm here with you now because I wish to be here."

"Are you sure?"

Her heart went tender. "Yes."

She fixed her gaze on a table with a quill, an ink tray, and a blotter set beside a sheet of paper. "Our contract?"

"Yes," he confirmed. "You'll find I've committed a good deal more than a penny."

She glanced askance. "My *thoughts* were never part of our agreement."

"I suppose not...though I would, of course, welcome any you might choose to share." He crossed one leg over the other. "Do you wish to review the document, or would you first like some wine?"

"I will review and sign now, thank you." She sounded brisk and efficient—ever the governess.

Her dressing gown rustled as she edged toward the table and into the ring of light. Lines neatly scrawled across the page seemed to move like an undulating flag. She placed her fingertips against the edge of the page to still them, and then she read.

The contract made no mention of midnight meetings, but granted her, for extraordinary service to his godchildren, all that she asked of him the prior night as well as a one-time settlement of a staggering amount. In fact, were she to abide merely by the letter of what he'd written down, she would not have to give him a thing in return.

A gesture of faith? Or simply one of discretion?

She glanced up. "This is far more than the amount we agreed. Why?"

"Isn't your worth apparent? It is to me." When she did not immediately respond he added, "You said you trusted my judgment."

She had, only this...was far too generous.

On the other hand—she swallowed roughly—he'd already signed. If he wished to leave her extraordinarily comfortable simply for the pleasure of her company, who was she to argue against an embarrassment of riches?

She lifted the quill, carefully dipped the tip in the ink and signed her name pithy *Hera Tyche Bythesea* next to his —Godric Henry Alan Alexander Bohen. followed by a dizzying number of titles ending, of course, with *Duke of Hurtheven.*

There.

The thing was done. The wet, black ink was already drying to darkened grey. She was, for now, his. No matter what the contract read, *she* intended to abide by the negotiated terms. She returned the quill to the holder.

He stood up and held out his hand. Hesitantly, she gave him hers.

Godric.

She wondered if anyone had ever used his name. She supposed, from birth, he'd been called the second to the last title, just has he was now only ever Hurtheven.

No, she corrected. He was also *Uncle Heven.*

And, on one, extraordinary occasion, *Mr. Smith.*

She *wished* he were Mr. Smith. Simple Mr. Smith, having no great and noble line to uphold, might, with little comment, choose to make a life with a woman and her bastard child. She could have shared this very moment with Mr. Smith as his bride.

She breathed through a sudden, dangerous tingle at the bridge of her nose until the danger of tears had passed.

"Do I have your leave to call you Hurtheven?" The question seemed like something she should ask...and she hadn't any idea what else to say.

"You already do." He grinned. "When you're not angry with me, that is."

"But Godric is your given name, yes?"

Briefly, his face blanked. So briefly, she'd wondered if her eyes had deceived.

"Alan, Henry, and Alexander are also among my given names," he said lightly. "You may call me what you wish, as long as you don't call me *duke.*" Again, he mimicked her derisive inflection.

He was smiling again—a dear, dimpled expression. So, she smiled, too.

"I'd like to call you Hera."

"You may, of course."

"An unusual name..."

"Yes. I believe I've already told you my father loved all things ancient Greece."

"We'd have had that in common, then, if I had met him."

He spoke as if he truly wished he'd known her father.

She had to be careful. She had to remind herself she would soon have to leave. Because as she watched his hair fall over his forehead yet again, she realized she was very much in danger of forming an attachment.

"Wine?"

She nodded.

He sauntered over to the table at the opposite end and poured two glasses from a full decanter. "Such a deep and satisfying red." His eyes fell to her lips as he handed her a cup. "Shall we toast to your future as a woman of means?"

"Or to my present, as your—"

"Lover," he interjected. "I'll not permit aspersions."

How imperious...and kind. She touched her glass to his. "To my lover, then."

"And to mine." His gaze gleamed as he drank.

They sat down together on the cushioned sofa—she, nearer the high, curved edge.

"Your rigid posture won't do at all...the sole purpose of a méridienne is feminine repose."

"Feminine repose?" She lifted a brow. "Shall I create a tableau?"

"Certainly."

"What famous painted pose would you prefer?"

"Something Italian, I think. 17th century, perhaps?"

"Are you familiar with the works of Artemisia Gentileschi?" She blinked innocently.

His smile widened. "If you've murder on your mind, we've come to the right room." He unwound his already loosened cravat and tossed the crumbled silk aside. "Perhaps I should offer you my neck and plead for mercy."

"Mercy," she repeated. She downed the rest of her glass,

barely tasting the earthy richness. "I wonder...*would* you ever place yourself entirely in my hands?"

As I have in yours, she left unsaid.

"I already have."

She saw no mocking light in his gaze. *Had* he placed himself in her hands?

How could he, when he was so much stronger physically, and more powerful socially and had every possible advant—

Suddenly she remembered the penny...and the haunted, lost look that had won her the wager and then she thought of the wreck. Her heart spasmed.

What was he? *Who* was he?

He drew her close. The heat of his body seeped into her person; she cared less and less for answers. He was a man. And she was, quite frankly, drawn by the contrasts between them.

His chin's rough stubble. The hard muscles of his shoulders and chest.

What made the basic differences between them erotic and exciting?

"Feeling reticent, my love?" He cupped her cheek. "So many thoughts flickering across your features. Are there none you wish to share?"

"None," she replied. "At present."

As he searched her gaze his mouth softened with sympathy. "I'm not being very lover-like, am I?" He crouched down. "Allow me to see to your comfort?"

"As the *duke* wishes."

"The *duke*"—he reached for a pillow—"*expressly* wishes."

He arranged the pillow behind her back. His closeness compelled her to lean and filled her lungs with his scent.

"Now, I think, your feet."

He moved the camel saddle so he could sit down opposite. He cupped the back of her calf as he slid off her slippers. Then, he propped one foot on his knee as he kneaded her muscle. A low groan escaped her lips.

"Shockingly tense," he murmured.

"Imagine." She closed her eyes as his delightful fingers soothed her wine heavy body. She sank into the support of the curved arm. "More, please."

"Of my ministrations? Or of the wine?"

She opened one eye. "Your ministrations will do."

He appeared pleased with her answer as he turned his attention to her other foot.

"You," his voice had gone melodic and low, "have *nothing* to fear from *me*."

"Mmmm," she replied. How could he be right about so much and still be so very, very wrong? She stretched one arm up over her head. And then when his hands began traveling up her leg she exclaimed. "Oh—*oh*."

"Don't dissemble already," he murmured. "I've only just begun to touch you."

She peered down through her lashes. "Ah, but I am a wanton, or so I've been told."

"A wanton? I'd expect nothing less from a woman named for both a Titan and an Olympian."

She held out her hand. When he took it, she urged him nearer.

"Midnight," he continued roughly, "is the time for unmasking. Unmask yourself. Let me see you in all your goddess glory."

His words, assisted by want and wine, warmed her prickling flesh.

Holding his gaze, she removed the pins in her hair, one

by one. The weight of her curls drifted down over her shoulders, and she reveled in his arrested expression. He buried his fingers in her tresses and then pulled her close.

His light but lingering kiss tightened her inner muscles. *Mercy* was her final, coherent thought.

And then she could not think at all.

* * *

She melted by measures like a sculpture of ice. Her edges gradually smoothed beneath the heat in his hands. He'd been near mad with frustration for days, but strangely, he preferred this gentle thaw to a frenzied satiation.

She was everything—*everything* he'd known she'd be and more.

Leaving her dressing gown fastened at the throat, he parted the bottom and slipped his fingers inside. Slowly, he slid his hands over her shift, caressing the body beneath.

He learned her shape, first, from her hips to the inward curve of her waist, then climbing inch by inch to where her rapid breath expanded and contracted within her chest. When he ran his palm over her already hardened nipple, hot desire knifed through him.

She wanted him, however rocky the path they'd taken.

He teased the proof of that desire with the pad of his thumb. All female breasts were a marvel. Hers were pure gratification, their soft sensitivity, relief he hadn't known he'd been seeking.

"Duke," she breathed.

The lust-infused version of his title had a curious effect on him—part pique, part passion. He repeated the caress and her whole body shuddered. She was exquisitely sensitive. He returned her heavy sigh—a moan, really—with a low hum of approval.

"Godric," she said in softer, sweeter tone.

This time, the shock of the syllables didn't rock him.

Since his parents died, he'd rarely heard his name spoken aloud. He'd left the syllables behind, carefully pressed like an autumn leaf between the pages of a heavy book—preserved, but fragile, libel to break apart with the merest breath.

She had—he kissed them both—gentle hands.

If his name were ever to be safe again, it would be safe in her keeping.

But he'd paused too long. And now, she was watching him with her too perceptive gaze. Once more, he feared he'd revealed more than he'd intended.

Devil take it, she was his now, by legal agreement. Just as he was hers. Why should he hold back at all?

"Say my name again," he said.

She leaned forward and kissed him. "Godric," she repeated against his mouth. "Would you like me to call you Godric when we are alone?"

Yes. "Flick your tongue against my lip that way, and I will answer to anything you call me."

She repeated the action. He cupped her neck and held her still as he plundered. He couldn't get enough. Her heat. Her sweetness. The way she matched each thrust of his tongue. They weren't so much kissing as hungrily devouring one another.

She pulled back, panting—staring at him with flushed cheeks and wild eyes.

"Snuff the lamp, would you?" she asked.

"Why? I like to look at you."

"I prefer to feel."

She stretched the single syllable *feel* into a long, breathy caress against his skin. Darkness, he decided, had advantages, too.

"For tonight, then." They'd have others. But never, he thought, enough.

Languidly, she lifted herself from the couch and then lowered the wick. She did not completely quench the light but dimmed the glow enough to cast them both in shadow— a shadow that charmingly outlined her shape. Soon enough, he'd learn that same curve with his mouth.

"Now," she stretched out her arms, "you may undress me."

He pulled the string at her throat and slid her dressing gown down over her shoulders. A dowdy thing. Too dowdy for such a prize. He'd buy her something better. Some frothy concoction of laced lawn that would make her look like a tantalizing confection. A sweet.

His sweet.

He pressed his lips to her shoulder and then, over her shift, he worked his way back to the swell of her breasts. Her fretfully impatient whimper made him smile against the thin fabric.

She tugged at his nightshirt. "Shall I remove this?"

"Well"—he chuckled softly—"aren't you a confounding combination of bold and polite?"

"Womanly nerves?" She leaned into him, placing her hand over the open part of his shirt.

"You are not at all of a nervous disposition." Her light scent unmanned him, as if he were a youth unschooled in carnal experience. Slowly, he palmed her breasts. "Womanly however..."

She tugged up his nightshirt. He leaned to the side, helping her work the garment over his head. She couldn't possibly see much more than shadows, but her sigh was pure gratification.

"Very nice. Just as I imagined."

"Imagined?"

"You aren't the only one who can paint pictures with your mind." She placed her hand on the center of his chest and pushed him back against the raised part of the chair.

"What's this? he asked, though he offered no resistance.

"I'm choosing bold, rather than polite." She further pinned him down by climbing onto his lap. "And I have recently learned, on excellent authority, that a *méridienne* is made for repose."

"Is it, now? How fortunate I happen to have one," he observed. "Are you warm enough to remove your shift?"

"Yes," she replied with a smile in her voice. "And I'll remain quite warm as long as you stay beneath me."

"Am I to stay beneath you?"

She answered in a sound that was an affirmative. Then, she pulled the garment over her head. Unclothed at last, she wrapped her arms around his neck with a motion so fluid, so full of sensual promise, he lost the ability to comment. There would be time for words later. Time for explanations. For rationalizations and reasons.

Now was the time for experience. For embracing the moment.

Embracing the darkness.

She tucked her legs around his thighs. He growled beneath the consummate torture of her naked weight. He should have been shocked, but breathless anticipation obliterated all dismay.

She draped herself over his chest with a sigh that emanated from deep within her body. The sound undid him. He crushed her to him and claimed her mouth. Rather than yielding, she ignited. Her hands found his hair, gripping painfully.

He didn't care.

He was, once again, fully alive.

Cherishing the sting, he kissed her face with an intensity that matched the blood rushing through his veins.

She paused to suck in a desperate breath. "What are you doing to me, Godric?"

"What am *I* doing to *you*?" She was a comet, a celestial event stunning in brilliance—and one, he hoped, that would return again and again. "You—*you* have cast cosmic sorcery on me."

"Yes," she sighed into his mouth. "Yes, I think I have. I *have* cast a spell. And you are helpless now. You must pleasure me."

She positioned his cock between her legs and, without taking his cock inside, used her body to caress his length. Thrill shot through his groin. He couldn't move—not without dislodging her, so he gave himself over to long, slick moments of halted breath torture.

She was the only thing he wanted. And he was willing to do anything to have her, even follow where she led...and lay utterly at her mercy while she used him for her pleasure.

Keeping his cock outside her body, she ground down again and again, until she found her release with barely any help from him. Her body shook slightly, then, she collapsed against his chest and sighed.

"My duke...at midnight."

Well, then. She'd shown him she knew what to do with a tool.

And she wasn't finished.

She cupped his face, tracing the line of his chin, down his throat, as if she were learning his shape by feel. She leaned in to capture his lips; her breasts crushed against his chest.

Delicious weight.

Lush, feminine scent.

Heady seduction.

"Minx," he whispered.

"Complaining, *duke*? You sound"—she kissed him deeply— "as if," she took a breath, "you are complaining."

"Not in the least. Complaining is *your* office."

She tightened her thighs.

"If that was meant as a punishment, you utterly failed in the task."

"Not punishment." She traced his lower lip with her tongue. "I think I'll have the whole of you, now.

"Are you ready for me?"

"Do you have to ask?"

He raised himself up on his elbow as he slid a hand up her thigh. Then, he buried his finger in the soft tangle of curls. She was more than ready. She was completely wet. As he let his fingers play, she clasped him to her breast. He suckled as he stroked.

"Too much," she breathed.

He wasn't deceived.

She had found some satisfaction, but she hadn't fully relaxed. Not yet. But—he slid his palm against her mound— she would. And when she did, *then* he would enter her.

She made deep, needy sounds entirely without sensibility. Each time his fingers slipped inside her breath hitched higher.

"Yes." He bit lightly on her nipple. "*Yes.*"

"What are you—? I already—! I *can't.*"

"Let go," he commanded, holding her arse firmly while rocking his hand.

She arched against him with a gasping whimper and then she broke into a shiver that quaked through every limb.

"What the devil?" She murmured. *"Twice?"*

He smiled into the darkness, vowing to test that limit, too—in the future. For now, he positioned himself above her opening. As he slid inside her welcoming body, her languid limbs suggested she'd lost sense.

No matter.

He grasped her by the thighs and moved her as *he* wished. And soon enough she found the rhythm. He found, not just pleasure, but quintessential pleasure. Pure, blissful need—thrusting upward as she rode him.

He was just aware enough to withdraw in time.

He crushed her to him, holding her tight as waves of pleasure passed out of his body. She rested her face in his neck. Over and over, she whispered, "Godric."

As their heavy breath mingled, he doubted he'd ever have enough.

"Hera," he sighed.

And one day soon, *my darling*.

Chapter Nine

Hera awoke with an unfamiliar lightness of spirit, as if she were a child anticipating a special treat. Still possessed of the starry-eyed afterglow of the prior night, she decided a fall from society could hold some advantages, after all. Significant doors had closed to her, but others stood wide open.

And, through one of them, she'd found pleasure like she'd never known.

She'd made up her mind to raise her daughter among people of a more open mind.

Artists, perhaps. Poets. Thinkers out of the ordinary way. People who were more concerned with discovery than with the binding of free souls for the benefit of a few.

Free souls.

She liked that idea...

Only, Hurtheven was a duke—the very definition of a world battened down with rules and expectations and hierarchy, the world of conventional society. The unwelcome thought was a sharp reminder to keep a firm rein.

The fancies of a free future she'd been spinning could never include him.

The clock struck nine. She abandoned the sobering thought, threw back her bedcovering, and then rushed to prepare for the day ahead.

Still tucking her hair beneath her cap as she ascended the stairs, she followed the sounds of two rapturous children. When she entered the nursery, two discordant explanations for their joy simultaneously assaulted her ears.

"There now," Mrs. Small laughed. "Let Mrs. Montrose catch her breath and then you can tell her what the duke has planned—one at a time."

"Me, first," Fee said.

"*I'm* the eldest," Delmare insisted.

Hera squelched the argument. "Let me guess—you're to go on the picnic Uncle Heven had planned for yesterday?"

"Yes," Fee sulked.

"No, silly," Delmare rejoined. "Not *just* a picnic—an *excursion*. I'm to ride the pony."

"Well!" Hera exclaimed, attempting to sound suitably impressed. "Won't you look the perfect little gentleman!"

Fee brightened again. "And *I'm* to ride with Uncle Heven."

"Because he doesn't trust you on the pony," Delmare said.

Fee stuck out her tongue, then, after catching Hera's scowl, she pretended as if she only meant to lick her upper lip.

"And what is the destination?" Hera asked.

"We're going," Fee replied, "to take the path along Uncle Heven's stream to a pretty little spot where daisies grow..."

Hera immediately heard "pretty little spot" in the voice of wonder Hurtheven used with the children and smiled.

"...*So* many daisies," Fee continued. "Daisies *must* be more interesting than that other flower."

"Other flower?" Hera prompted.

"The one from the place my doll came from."

"Edelweiss." She didn't want to think of the doll. "Daisies are certainly more plentiful," she added, diplomatically.

She and Mrs. Small combined their talents to bundle Felicia into a coat and sturdy shoes. By the time Delmare, too, had been properly prepared, Hera insisted that the older woman rest while she took them down to meet the duke at the stables.

Hera blinked into the warm, bright sunlight and shook her head bracingly as they crossed the bailey. Daylight Hurtheven, she reminded herself sternly, was not hers.

And yet, even when all she could see of him was the outline of his shadow inside the stable, her heart skipped a beat. And in that same moment, he turned away from his head groom and raised his hand in greeting.

Why, when she locked gazes with him, did the world around them disappear?

"I trust you all slept well." he said, with a light slap of a riding crop against his hand and an evident twinkle in his eye.

The children sung their yeses. Hera nodded, stifling a yawn.

"Come along," he held out his hand to Felicia, although his gaze rested warmly on her own. "Your nursemaid is tired. She's well earned her rest."

Felicia scowled. "Mrs. Montrose can't be *tired*. It's morning!"

Hurtheven crouched down. "But I wager you gave her trouble about that coat, didn't you?"

Fee ignored the question, holding tight to Hera's hand. "Can Mrs. Montrose come with us? *Please*?"

"Oh yes!" Delmare joined in. "You must come, ma'am."

Hera glanced between them, bemused and a little touched. "Now why would you want me to come with you when you could have Uncle Heven all to yourselves?"

"Because if you come, too, we will have more fun," Fee explained.

"Does Mrs. Montrose ride?" Hurtheven asked.

"Yes," Fee answered in unison with Delmare.

Did she ride? She bit back a retort.

After the intimacies of the prior night, his ignorance of this very basic part of her life seemed unthinkable, and yet, how was he to know what her life had been before?

"There was a long period of time I did not ride, but when the duchess discovered my skill, she encouraged me to go out with the children. However," she addressed the children, "I did not pack a habit and one cannot assume Hevenhyll's stables have a mount and a saddle appropriate for me."

"There is!" Delmare insisted. "Mum keeps a saddle here."

"It appears the children have settled your fate amongst themselves." Hurtheven sighed, longsuffering. "However, if you do not *wish* to join us..."

His tone held an unspoken challenge.

She turned her gaze toward the duke. A gleam had entered his eyes, which she suspected, meant mischief. "I believe my duty is to do as *His Grace* wishes."

"*So* accommodating..." the duke murmured.

Fee giggled.

"...and with so many surprising talents, too."

She'd been right. *Mischief.* She mimicked his brow raise. "Again, I have no habit."

"Please come," begged Fee. "I *particularly* want to show you Uncle Heven's stream."

"*Particularly!*" Hurtheven widened his eyes, as if this were a very persuasive point.

"Yes," Fee replied. "And the acres and acres of daises. You love daises."

"I do," she agreed. "*Acres*, is it?"

"Oh, yes! The *whole mountain* belongs to Uncle Heven."

"Why, that certainly *must* recommend him," she answered dryly. "*Imagine.* A whole mountain. All to yourself."

The duke laughed. "I see I must content myself with your approbation of my library, as you're clearly not impressed with my mountain, my castle, or my title. Not to mention my consequence."

"Gracious! Is that all you have to recommend you?" Hera interrupted.

Neither she, nor the duke missed the groom's sharp intake of breath. She sent him a speaking, pleading glance.

Please do not provoke me any further.

He inclined his head. "Mrs. Montrose, I would be honored if you would accept my formal invitation to picnic with myself," he placed a hand on each child's head, "this little hoyden, and this young rascal."

She shouldn't. What if he were to provoke her again?

But neither could she decline, not while three sets of brows were raised in such a hopeful manner.

Against her better judgement, she acquiesced.

The groom prepared an additional mount, and they set

out together on one of the well-tended bridle paths. Soon, however, the groom had gone on ahead with Delmare, while she, followed by Hurtheven with Felicia, had fallen behind.

"Your nursemaid is quiet," the duke said to Fee.

"Very," she agreed.

"She's regretting having displayed her penchant for rudeness in your presence."

Fee giggled. "Penchant."

"*Penchant,*" the duke adopted Hera's accent, "means a strong tendency." He returned to his own. "Am I correct, Mrs. Montrose?"

"Your definition is correct," she replied with a quick glance over her shoulder. "Although I object to the character."

"Mrs. Montrose is never rude," Fee supplied loyally.

"Without fault, is she?" the duke asked.

"*No one* is without fault," Hera replied.

The duke pulled up beside her. "*Certainly not you,* she leaves unspoken. And yet, the temptation lingers. Well, Mrs. Montrose. Indulge yourself. My faults, if you please. You've been longing to make them plain since the moment we met."

She glanced askance and met his laughing eyes. Was he *flirting?*

"Arrogant will do," she said primly. "And entitled."

"Now, the rules of fair play dictate I must be given a chance to answer the charge."

She lifted a brow. "*Can* you?"

"Well, to the second, of course I'm entitled, I'm the very definition of the word. You can hardly blame me for that."

"And the first?"

He cleared his throat. "Perhaps I had better list my assets, instead."

"Fee already did."

"I did?" Fee asked.

"Acres of daises, in season," she replied. "And one, *whole* mountain."

He laughed. "That, of course, but I was referring to assets of character."

She moved her gaze askance. "What sterling qualities do you deign to possess?"

"I'm loyal. I'm generous. I'm known as someone who can solve any problem no matter what the obstacle..."

She glanced heavenward and then shook her head.

"...I've also been known to be frank. A quality you, too, possess."

"One can be too frank," she said wryly. "I suppose you're now about to tell me that whatever you do, you do extraordinarily?"

"Certainly." He flashed an even-toothed grin.

They'd nearly caught up to Delmare and the groom at the point where the pathway narrowed. The duke slowed, allowing her to slide in between Delmare and himself.

While Hera *did* ride, she'd done so infrequently in the past few years. And, although the mare the duke's groom had chosen for her was beautiful, biddable, and calm, she was conscious of the desire to show herself to her best advantage.

Why, though?

His gaze on her back?

Without the benefit of a habit's full skirt and a proper train, she must look affright. Her shift was generous, but not *so* generous to satisfactorily cover her ankles.

If he *was* studying her from behind, she was certain to come up wanting.

Not that she expected a man of Hurtheven's experience

to be overcome by the sight of a woman's ankle. Especially after what he'd seen last night. The thought was *too* absurd.

Unwittingly, she laughed.

"A delightful sound," Hurtheven said. "You should laugh more often."

"Mrs. Montrose laughs a great deal," Fee confided. "When she first came, she hardly smiled at all. I like her much better, now."

Too much to hope he'd missed the implication...

"Do *you* like Mrs. Montrose?" Fee asked.

Hera's breath caught.

"Fee—don't be a meddler!" Delmare exclaimed.

"I don't see why you should scold, Del. *You* said Uncle Heven showed Mrs. Montrose a decided partiality."

"It's not polite to repeat a private conversation," Hera said, cheeks burning.

What *must* the groom be thinking?

"Why shouldn't I be partial to someone who takes such good care of my favorite godchildren?"

"Favorite?" Fee asked.

"There's Thaddeus, too, of course," the duke replied.

"He's not a child," Fee replied. "That means we're the favorite."

"He isn't a child any longer," the duke responded. "Is he?"

She was grateful he'd changed the course of the conversation, and suspected he'd done so to save her from further mortification. But, when they arrived in a clearing, and the groom assisted her to dismount, she could not, in good conscience, meet his gaze.

She'd difficulty correctly identifying her emotion.

She was tired. Flustered. Confused.

Why he'd taken to teasing her was obvious enough from

the look in his eyes. After days of fraught denial, he'd finally satiated his need, and now he was quite pleased with his prowess.

Men. There was a little boy in every one of them.

Then again—she watched Fee spread out her skirt and twirl amid the daises, face lifted to the skies—she wasn't much different.

Fee laughed as she caught her breath, looking very much like Hera felt when she had Hurtheven's attention. But they had both better take care. Even Karl had never given a reason for speculation to rise in his children or his household staff.

"There!" Fee pointed over Hera's shoulder.

She turned around and her breath caught in her throat; the sight was so lovely.

From this aspect, the view that had been hidden behind a copse of trees, revealed itself in full splendor. The hills were layered with mists that lent an almost ethereal nature to the whole scene.

She'd thought she was partial to the sea, or at least to mighty rivers, but this—this had its own majesty.

"There," Hurtheven repeated with a wink. "Mine."

But he wasn't looking at the mountain. He was looking straight at her.

He shouldn't treat her with such familiarity, even if his warm regard made her heart skip.

She sent him a haughty expression. "*You* said it was a mountain."

"I beg your pardon!" he said with mock horror. "It *is* a mountain."

"No." She shook her head. "*That* is a hill. A large hill, I'll grant you..."

"Hill?! A hill!" Fee bounded between them. "She says that looks like a *hill*."

"Well," Delmare put in. "It doesn't look dramatic like the mountains in Scotland."

The duke turned toward the view and placed his hands on his hips. "*That*, I'll have everyone know, is a perfectly good, English mountain."

"To be fair, there isn't a *jagged* peak," Delmare noted. "And there isn't any snow."

"Hills are rolling, pleasant. Mountains have menace. That"—he pointed to the hill—"has menace."

"Well, ma'am?" Delmare asked. "Is it a mountain?"

"I suspect that's a question for a cartographer." If she let the teasing go on any longer, she'd never be able to face the groom. "But the view"—her gaze involuntarily flicked to the duke—"is beautiful."

She turned away from his grin, occupying herself with removing Fee's stockings so she might dangle her feet in the stream. She steadily ignored Delmare and the duke as the latter lead the former along the water, speaking to him in low tones.

Troubled, she took a place on the blanket the groom had spread out for their use and reclined on her elbow, keeping a careful eye on Fee. Soon enough, the duke's shadow fell across her legs.

She squinted up at him, accusation in her eyes.

He took a place on the blanket. "You look as if you have something on your mind."

"Your marked attention will subject us to gossip."

"Allow me to put your mind at rest," he replied. "My staff would never tell tales, least of all about me..."

She sent him a dubious expression.

"...But I will do my best to rein in my enthusiasm in the future."

"Enthusiasm."

"I enjoy you, Hera," he said, voice low. "Your conversation. Your presence. Your look of flustered forbearance when I tease you...among other things I won't, at present, enumerate."

She looked away.

It was one of the nicest things anyone had said to her in a very long time. Worse still, she felt the same. She turned back to reply in kind, but he'd already stretched out, and fanned his arms behind his head, giving the appearance of sleep.

With a troubled heart, she returned her attention to the playing children.

She hoped she would hear from the duchess soon.

If he persisted in this level of charm, eventually she was going to succumb to her feelings...and fall fully and hopelessly in love.

* * *

After Hera had chastised the duke, rather than curbing his flirting, he chose instead to expand his exuberance, including everyone in a joie de vivre that proved universally infectious.

And painfully endearing.

By dinner, Hera'd had enough. Citing the need to write the duchess, she retreated, first to her room, and then, once the letter had been written, through the secret panel.

After last night, the armory shouldn't have felt strange. Yet, it did. Without the distraction of windows—never mind the duke—the walls became the only focus. Besides being adorned with various gruesome implements of death, a pattern repeated every fifth stone.

His family seal, she realized.

Lions, of course.

Between the weapons, shields and chainmail, and the proof of patriarchal power etched into stone, any woman would have felt out of place in this room, herself especially.

Though her father had been a country squire, she'd no notion of her mother's family, and she doubted either had a recorded history as long as the duke's. She was a woman out of place. And, in this room, out of time as well.

Then again, wasn't that what midnight was for?

A time of transformation? A time to become someone else. A time of magic.

She would pretend she belonged, that she was the kind of woman who took the attentions of a duke as her due. She held her chin at just a certain angle and put a lofty look in her eye.

"Mrs. Montrose."

How long had he been standing there? She eyed him rather sheepishly. "Your Grace."

"You're early." He strode inside the room. "I will assume you are as eager as I am."

She gazed up into his twinkling eyes and hadn't the heart to scold him. For the first time since they'd met, he seemed genuinely happy. Could she really be the cause of this transformation?

He held out his arms.

She did not hesitate, but rather melted into his embrace. Linking her arms around his waist, she rested against his chest. His brocaded dressing gown was soft against her cheek.

"Were I to miss the witching hour," she replied, "the transformation would be incomplete."

Together, they listened to the final reverberation of the clock striking twelve.

He whispered against her hair, "Are you transformed?"

A shiver ran down her body. "Yes." Boldly, she lifted her face and then reached up to cup his neck. "Within these walls, I am a woman who takes what she wants."

His impossibly big hands rested heavy on her hips. Rather than let the feeling overwhelm her, she snaked her other hand around his neck and brought his head down toward her own.

The touch of his lips was like a wizard's wand, sending a glittering warmth and an expanding sense of belonging and ease rushing downward through her body. Being held by him just so felt right. How effortless confidence was when so securely sheltered.

"I have been thinking about this all day," he said.

"I gathered as much."

"Am I to receive another scold?"

"Mmmm." She pressed his cheek to hers. "One was enough. Right now, I'd rather you describe what has been on your mind."

His mouth quirked—a funny feeling against her skin.

"You. In that bed."

"What? So pithy? Surely you can do better."

"Why waste time on words, when I have the real thing?" He took hold of her hand, and then turned in the direction of the canopied monstrosity.

"Are we to make use of *that*?" She asked as he pulled her along behind him. "A *méridienne*, I've heard, is solely for feminine—"

He'd swung around and crushed her to him, abruptly

interrupting her sentence. With a rough meeting of their mouths, he literally stole the word from her lips.

Presently, however, the kiss transformed into one tenderly long, deep, and thorough. When he finally lifted his head, she'd forgotten that she'd been mocking him.

"You were saying?" he asked.

"*Was* I?" she responded, dazed.

"I'll have to remember that trick." He grinned. "Not that I'm likely to forget. You were about to say, "Why, yes, Godric, I *yearn* to join you in the bed you've so beautifully and cleverly made.""

She hadn't been certain that he approved of her using his given name, but Godric had slipped out of him quite naturally. She was content.

When she called him Godric, he was her very own.

"I *yearn* to join you in the bed you've made?" She smiled up at him. "Why yes, I believe you're right. How obliging of me. I've been obliging quite frequently of late. Don't you think? *Did* you make up the bed?"

"Indeed, I did," he said, not without pride. "Procuring clean, fresh bed linens without arousing the curiosity of one's staff is a thorny problem. You've no notion!"

No, she supposed she hadn't. She was touched by his consideration. "How did you—"

He kissed her again. "Never you mind." He stepped backwards, pulling her along. "Your office, at present, is to be impressed."

"I am positively dazzled, I promise. Your audience appreciates your talent."

"While yours"—the back of his legs hit the edge of the bed—"feels it's time for a change of costume."

Without waiting for a response, he yanked the string of her dressing gown. She raised her brows inquiringly, almost in challenge, as she lifted the garment from her shoulder and then let the fabric pool in a heap on the floor.

She whooped as he swept her off her feet—oh, yes, he'd reliably respond to any challenge—but she hadn't a moment to enjoy being held as if she were of trivial weight before he deposited her in the center of the mattress.

"There." He climbed abed on his knees.

She could think of no appropriate response. Nor, apparently, did he require one, as he was busy divesting himself of his own clothes. She tucked an elbow behind her head. With half-closed lids, she observed.

Where Karl had been wiry, he was broad. But she refused any further comparison and focused only on the man that mattered—the duke in the bed.

His hips were rather a work of art, and the rounded curve of his ass simply begged caressing. A smattering of short, soft curls made a sort of expanded hourglass shape—covering his upper chest and then reducing to a thin trickle, a pathway down toward his already stiffened shaft.

Yes. There were advantages to not dousing the lights.

He rested a fist on one hip "Am I to do all the work?"

"Poor duke..." She pouted sympathetically.

"Off with the shift, wench."

She laughed as she lifted herself onto one elbow. "I prefer to watch *your* exertions."

She made minimum effort to assist him as he worked her shift beneath her bum, allowing him to manipulate her limbs as if she was one of Felicia's dolls. Finally, he lifted the garment over her head and tossed it aside with a triumphant grunt.

"Exhausted?" she queried with pity.

"Mmm." His gaze fixed to her breasts. "I have my reward."

She regarded him, bemused.

Sometimes, Karl's lascivious stare had caused her discomfort, making her feel as if she and her body were separate objects, the latter good only for his use. But Godric tilted his head, and touched her gently, reverently, as his eyes soaked in—absorbing her with desire, but also with something akin to amazement, as if she were a gift.

She was unashamed.

"Godric," she lifted herself to her elbows once again.

"Lay back, love," he replied.

And when she did, he arranged her hair.

"Just," he murmured as he carefully manipulated each strand, "thus." He sighed, admiring his handiwork. "Comfortable?"

"So comfortable, I could fall asleep."

"Could you, really?" He smiled, wolfish, and straddled her, one knee at each of her hips. He took his member into his palm. "I've a mind, then, to use my own hands."

She grinned. *"Beast."*

"La Bête et la Belle."

"Am I beautiful?"

"Objectively, yes." He lowered himself until his chest hair tickled her stiffened nipples. "And, to me, unparalleled." He slipped a hand between her legs. "Irresistible."

She closed her eyes, giving up to the sensation of his radiant heat and the hand, stroking her in the very place where she throbbed. She inhaled sharply as he dipped a finger in her cleft.

"You don't *feel* tired…you feel wet."

What a strange sensation his hair was creating—the lightest of stimulation that cut a blade of need down through her core, making his hand…inadequate. The two vastly different frictions forced a soft whimper through her lips.

"Please," she whispered, eyes closed, cheeks heated.

He answered with his body, sliding down between her parted legs. With a hard, thorough thrust, he was inside. She met him with angled hips, struggling to take him deeper within.

By measures he gave her his weight, driving into her so that each thrust touched her in the place of her want, a lack that soon reached a fevered need, drawing helpless, animal sounds from deep in her throat.

She opened her eyes.

Just above her, his face was raw with naked thirst and furious strain, his temples wet with labor. She jerked each time he slid inside her, completely taken, almost painfully full.

Then, with his most forceful push, he remained still. Crouched over her body he grunted and then buried his head in her hair. She held him close. Her release breaking in rivulets of euphoric bliss, cool and tingling.

Immediately, he withdrew, spending his seed against her belly with a sound that she felt in his body.

After a moment of shock and wonder, he collapsed at her side, threading his fingers through her limp hand.

She made no move to clean herself, but stared, unseeing, at the elaborate carvings on the inside of the top of the bed.

"Well," she sighed, "now we've come together in bed just as you described the night in the library."

"I wondered if you'd realize."

"Not at first," she replied. "But the notion vaguely dawned on me sometime between my *helpless whimpers*."

He placed the back of his free hand over his eyes. "I blush to remember."

"You? Blush?" She gurgled with laughter. "Well? Did I meet your expectations?"

"My expectations were squawking fledglings, then you swooped down and claimed the entire nest." He rolled onto his side and released her hand to trace a line down her face. "I was crass."

"Yes. You meant, I think, to mortify me."

"Never." The bedclothes rustled as he retrieved his dressing gown and then procured from its pocket a handkerchief. Tenderly, he blotted away every trace of his lust. "I only hoped to excite you."

She placed a finger beneath his chin and turned up his face. "You did…"

Such dark eyes. Richly fertile, muddied earth. She could become easily mired. She was *already* mired. Bound to him in a world of their own making. Eden in a castle armory.

"…Paint another."

He lifted a brow. "Don't encourage me."

"*Without shame* you said."

"Without shame," he repeated. "Doubtless, I can come up with something that will curl your toes. At present, however, I must recover."

She smiled. "I look forward, then, to your future efforts.

He tossed aside the soiled linen and laid back down, folding her against his chest.

"I wonder," she mused, absently tracing his collarbone, "if shame is the reason men need some women to be angels and others, whores…"

His body tensed in response to the word.

"...If," she continued, "a *woman's* nature is at fault, then men can absolve themselves of blame."

"I don't think of you as either."

"Either?"

"An angel, or...that other word."

Could he not even say it? "Our contract says otherwise."

"Hang the contract." Anger roughened his voice. "Hera...I apologized for my anger that night. I never meant things to progress in that manner."

"I know," she said. "I understood, though not at first, that I had insulted your sense of honor."

He sighed. "But do you know *why*?"

Could it be because he really had wished to ask her to marry him?

The conversation had slipped into dangerous territory. She reset its course. "You didn't seem surprised when I told you I wasn't...untouched." She edged away from what she feared would be a confession. And she was too undone, too hopelessly open, to rebuff him as she must.

He frowned. "I don't suppose I *was* surprised."

"Did I *look* like a fallen woman?"

He bubbled his lips as if perplexed. "Not particularly. But you did call yourself *Mrs.* Montrose."

"You never believed I was wed," she retorted. "Nor did you think I was telling the truth about my name."

"Actually, I *hoped* you hadn't been wed—but I knew very little about you." He shifted. "Why do I feel as if there is ice beneath my feet? Very, very *thin* ice."

She exhaled, snuggling closer to his side. "You're right. Let's not spoil this moment." Perhaps she had sounded peevish. "I didn't mean to say that your lack of surprise was a fault, per se."

"*Per se?*"

"I don't expect you'd understand."

He lifted her hand from his chest and threaded his fingers through hers. "Why don't you explain?"

"I will try." She exhaled slowly, thoughtfully. "A young lady is *supposed* to safeguard her virginity at all costs."

"So I have heard."

"And I did not."

"So I gathered."

"Your lack of surprise suggested you had *assumed* I did not. Which makes me wonder what kind of woman you thought I was."

"I'm almost never surprised by the things people reveal." He curled toward her so that they faced one another, pillowed head to pillowed head. "You, however, are proving a constant marvel."

"To be surprised," she noted, "you must have had certain expectations. I take it they were low?"

"I don't think in the dichotomy you've described. I never have. Do you always expect the worst of people?" He looked as uncomfortable as she'd ever seen him look. "I don't for instance, think that women can only be painted in one of two colors...although I have known men who did think that way."

"Thank you for admitting that, at least."

"I don't *like* the idea of you having had a lover, any more than I suppose you'd like the idea of any of mine."

Any of. Meaning multiple.

But of course. He wasn't a young man. She mimicked his voice. "...I gather from our exchange that you aren't completely without," she paused, "experience."

He chuckled. "You delight in throwing back my words."

She did. "What made you so perceptive?"

217

He shrugged. "I lost my parents young. I was, I suppose, confused by the behavior of the people around me…"

She imagined him, a young, small boy in this vast castle meant to be a home. A pervasive feeling of loneliness swept through her, and she rested her head against his shoulder.

"…I was told to pay attention and people would always reveal."

"Who imparted such wisdom?" she asked.

He chuckled softly. "If you must know, it was my nurse."

"Wise Mrs. Small."

A distant rumble beyond the walls interrupted their conversation.

Hurtheven sat up quickly, his eyes suddenly and strangely fixed. He was silent and still as several moments passed. Then came another explosion of sound.

"A storm is upon us," she observed.

"It's not close," he said, eyes still on the passageway that led to the panel. "Not yet."

* * *

Not close, but closing in. He felt his inner need stir. Why he so often went out into storms, he could not explain, but he had been doing so—though *only* when he was at Hevenhyll —ever since he'd recovered from the accident.

He didn't have a rational reason to go out in the rain.

"Godric?"

Startled out of his storm-charged reverie, he instinctively turned toward the sound of his name, taking in the vision that was Hera. Fire colored curls in decadent disarray. Pale colored skin, mottled by the remnants of satiated lust. *Hera.* His lover.

His love.

Inside the depths of her wide, blue eyes lurked concern. A slight crease marred the space between her eyes. To her, he supposed, his reaction to the sound of the advancing strikes would seem unusual, possibly even frightening.

Only she didn't look scared. She looked curious.

And he—thunder rumbled in the distance—could not help but be restless.

He should be out there. Out there in the rain.

He found a kind of release as the pellets fell around him and he dared the deadly white streaks to try for him again. Only a storm without had ever been able to fully silence the constant storm within.

And he'd give anything for that inner silence.

He grabbed her hand. "Come outside with me."

"Outside?" She jerked back. "You're mad."

"No." This was urgent. "Well, yes. A little. It's just something I *must* do."

Her concern turned to horror, and then, when the next rumble had him reaching for his dressing gown, to resolve.

"I'll go," she said, already shrugging into her shift. "If I cannot keep you from going."

He kept her hand in his firm grip as he led her through the corridor. Instead of going out the way he'd come, he opened the panel that led to her room.

"You'll need a cloak," he said.

"And you?"

"I'll be warm enough," he replied.

He bundled her into her cloak and, together, they crept onto the landing. Deftly, he made his way through the dark. The tower contained a spiral stair ending in a rarely used egress. They made their way down, him leading and her, close behind.

He released her to lift the board that served as a bolt, and before he could set the wood down, she had already opened the door.

A flash rent the sky, blanching her features just before she stepped into the rain.

"Wait!" he whispered harshly.

She did not heed him.

In the next flash, he saw she was still moving, face pointed up toward the sky. He was conscious of a sensation, a jolt like he'd had in the garden, the first time their eyes had met.

What *was* he doing? What had he asked her to do?

He faced the storm. *He* dared the capricious skies. But until this moment, he had not truly understood that he had been taunting death to make himself feel alive.

A loud rumble ended in an earthshattering crack. White light lit up the night, the briefest of visions brighter than day.

"Beautiful," she breathed.

No. Not beautiful. *Lethal.*

God Almighty. His breath came fast and heavy. Bringing her out here had been as reckless as his father's choice to go out in the storm.

Worse, really.

His heartbeat thumped in his ears. He leapt forth and seized her as the lightning struck so close, the old door rattled, and the rumble shook them both to the bone.

He swept her up, cloak and all into his arms and dashed back inside, kicking the door closed with his foot.

"Put me down," she whispered fiercely.

He didn't listen. Nor did he continue to hear the fury the weather gods were unleashing outside. Instead, he held her with iron arms waiting for his pulse to slow.

"You asked me to come," she said.

"Yes," was all he could reply.

He couldn't count the number of times he'd gone out this very door, advancing into the rain just as she had, believing he was daring the storm, and, by placing himself in danger, testing his strength and resolve.

Holy Hell.

He trembled within and tightened his already secure grip.

"Godric," she said softly. "You're hurting me."

He gentled his hold and then, very slowly and carefully, set her on the ground. Silently, he guided her back up the stairs. After they slipped inside her chamber, he held her closely for a fraught moment.

He didn't need to challenge the storm to feel alive anymore.

All he needed was her.

He kissed her brow—too wildly charged to express anything in words.

"Thank you for showing me the storm."

Thank him!

Raindrops made her eye lashes cling together. Her eyes were radiant and wide. He could have wept with self-recrimination. Or, roared with relief. Instead, he wiped a trail of damp from her face.

"Goodnight, Hera." If he'd felt less, he could have said more.

As it was, he could only stand there stupidly staring.

She cupped his cheek. "Goodnight, my"—she stopped herself—"friend."

He dropped his hand from her shoulder, running his light hold down her arm until he reached her wrist. He held to her palm even as she turned away and ambled toward her bed. When her fingers slipped from his, he felt bereft.

"I will douse the lights," she said softly. "You're drenched, Godric. You must change before you catch cold."

Change. Yes. He must.

He already had, in fact. Though he could not seem to find a way to tell her so.

"Until tomorrow," she said as she disappeared through the panel.

He let himself out and then closed the door. With his wet head resting against the doorjamb, he remained still until he heard the soft click that told him she'd reentered her bedchamber. He listened to the sounds she made as she prepared for bed.

His heart was full to overflowing—threatening, in fact, to bubble up and leak from his eyes. He'd thought feeling had returned the moment he laid eyes on Pen.

But this—this was something else. Awareness of Hera lived inside every part of his body. What he felt for her was a force he'd never be able to control, no matter how many rules he attempted to apply.

When the sounds ceased, he felt his way back to his room and then quietly let himself in. All this time, he'd thought himself daring.

He'd been wrong.

He'd been reckless and raging at the skies—fighting against his need for the greatest thing he'd lost and the one thing his heart truly desired—to, once again, have something to lose.

To once again, have someone to love.

And he knew without a doubt he'd found her.

Chapter Ten

Hera stretched out her legs, carefully arranged her skirts in a modest fashion, and then rested her back against the low stone wall. Across the field, Hurtheven, Felicia and Delmare were setting up to fly a kite. He had brought himself to the children's level by resting on bended knee and was gesturing to the kite frame's binding while both children nodded in unison.

A now-familiar spasm compressed her chest—a pain, she'd discovered in the past fortnight, particular to watching Godric with the children. A pain which, at heart, was an impossible, unspoken wish for herself...and for Annis.

He'd attentive parental instincts and a rare capacity to care.

If—*oh, only if*—he'd been Mr. Smith.

Foolish to wish things other than they were, however. The past two weeks had been an illusion—a dream state, that, through an improbable sequence, had been briefly and beautifully brought to life. Animated. Electrically charged, she might even say.

What ran between them certainly felt like a charge.

A charge that must be as brief as one of those bright flashes that had lit up the inner bailey the night of the storm. That night, he'd come close to speaking of his feelings. She'd rebuffed him then, and since, he'd relied heavily on gestures.

Words she could have deflected. Evidence of his goodness was harder to resist.

She hadn't much longer to savor this ephemeral dream. Surely by now, the duchess had discovered who hired the Runner. And the date of the hospital directors' decision was approaching fast.

"Are you watching?" Fee demanded.

"Yes!" she called back in return.

Hurtheven held the kite aloft and let the silk suspended across the frame catch the wind. His grin couldn't have looked more boyish than Delmare's. Soon, the colorful contraption rose up into the air. The late afternoon breeze infused with the children's incoherent sounds of delight.

"Well done!" She clapped loudly, gaze fixed on his upturned face and the wind rifling through his thick, dark locks.

The kite twisted to the left, then to the right and then—*No!*—dove precipitously toward the ground. And yet, somehow, Godric was there, just in time and in the right position to prevent the frame from plunging into the ground.

A lull followed as they set up a second attempt. This time, when the kite caught the breeze, Delmare held a steadier, more practiced hand on the roll of twine. Other dives followed, of course, but the children managed to keep the kite aloft.

Mostly.

Once they had mastered the technique, Hurtheven

blocked the sunlight from his eyes with a raised arm and strode toward her, his face beaming happiness and pride.

Another pain squeezed her heart.

"They've learned more quickly than I did." He settled down beside her.

"Perhaps they had a better teacher."

"Yet another compliment?"

"I shall have to take care," she replied, "else they become commonplace."

"Impossible!" He bent his knee as his eyes followed the children, making sure they did not want any further help. Once satisfied they did not need him, he fixed her with a twinkling gaze. "You could compliment me all day, every day, for the rest of my life, and I would still hoard every morsel of commendation as a pearl of great price."

She sent him a disapproving scowl. "You must not have attended your gospels with the same studiousness as you attended kitemaking lessons. There can be only *one* pearl of great price."

"Yes, I know." He covered her hand with his own. "And I *would* sell all I have for its possession..."

He shouldn't speak to her so. The allegory was quite blasphemous. Not to mention painful.

"...These past few weeks—"

She cut him off with a forced, light-hearted tone. "Have been heavenly, have they not? When I write my memoirs, I will call this chapter *A Curious Idyll*. I thought of that phrase once before, now the words feel even more apt."

"A curious idyll?" He glanced askance. "I thought we were—"

"Oh, you don't need to worry," she interrupted, maintaining her carefree manner. "My memoires wouldn't mention you by name, of course."

"Hera—"

She yelped as the kite whooshed down, nearly knocking her on her side.

"Pull!" Hurtheven commanded.

But Felicia hadn't the strength. The kite came crashing down not five feet from where they'd been sitting. The children ran towards the heap on the ground, eyes wide with dismay. Hurtheven, of course, was immediately on his feet.

"You've ruined it!" Delmare yelled.

Fee's lip quivered ominously.

"It's not ruined," Hurtheven consoled. "But I don't have what I need to fix it here. Come now, Fee—no tears. Kites dive and fall and crack all the time. Failing is a necessary part of learning."

"She *let* it fall!" Delmare complained.

"Did you not do the same the first time you held the string?" Hurtheven asked. "She is younger than you are, and not as strong."

"It *is* my fault!" Fee's voice cracked.

"Yes," Hera said. "But Uncle Heven will fix the kite and you will try again, and, next time, the kite will stay up even longer."

"Will you be able to fix it?" Fee asked hopefully.

"Certainly!" he replied with confidence. "I'll just need to build a new frame."

"That's like making a whole new kite!" Delmare complained.

He tousled Delmare's hair. "The work will go faster if you help me. Would you like that?"

'Would I?!" Delmare replied as if the question demonstrated supreme ignorance.

"Can I help too?" Fee asked hopefully.

"Yes. In fact, let's head back to the house and start the

repairs right now. Now,"—he helped Hera to her feet—"be good children and carry the kite between you, while I give Mrs. Montrose my arm."

She sent him a disapproving scowl, while secretly loving the way he always found some excuse to touch her. She placed her hand against his sleeve as the children ran on ahead, broken kite flapping between them.

Not wanting him to pick up the conversation from where he'd left off, she searched for a distraction.

"Did you make the kite specifically for Delmare and Felicia?"

"Like myself, the kite is older than it looks..."

His sidelong wink made her smile.

"...Chev, Ash, and I were about fourteen when we first constructed the frame. We'd decided we wanted to recreate Benjamin Franklin's key and kite experiment."

"You flew a kite during a storm?" she asked, surprised.

"Yes, as a matter of fact. And we managed to collect a charge in a Leyden jar by following the instructions Franklin printed." He smiled at the memory. "My godfather was furious. He said we could've killed ourselves."

"Yes! If you had used only one set of twine, or if you hadn't managed to keep the second set dry."

"Or, if the lightning had directly hit the kite."

She inhaled sharply. "I hadn't thought...but *of course*." She shivered, glad that his exploits had not caused him harm. Those of his adult years, however... "Some dangers,"—she sighed—"aren't readily apparent until one has truly entered the thick of things, are they?"

They walked on in silence until they'd drawn close to the outer ramparts.

"Were you speaking metaphorically?" he finally asked.

"Or have you, of late, entered into an... *experiment* whose dangers were not readily apparent?"

Up ahead, the children passed through the gate before disappearing into the bailey.

"*I* have been, from the start, well-aware of the dangers." Why did he have to radiate so much heat? "I fear, however, *you* have forgotten them."

He greeted the gatekeeper as they passed through, but before they reached the castle's inner courtyard, he stopped walking.

"Dangers abound, I know. Love will not fail, though our courage might."

Love.

He'd said *love.*

The word landed like a cannonball in her heart, hollowing out every other feeling.

Love. What would she be if she denied that truth? Because love was the true meaning of the dissonant note of pain ringing in her ears. *Breathe.* Her heart hammered. *Breathe.* Her throat dried. *Breathe.*

Then, from the courtyard beyond, Fee let out an unholy squeal.

Without a further word, she and the duke broke into a run, circling around the bend in long, unison strides. The kite had been abandoned in the middle of the gravel and both children were running as fast as they could toward a standing carriage.

The silhouetted figures of the dukes of Ashbey and Ithwick stood just outside the post chaise's open door and the Duchess of Ashbey crouched down beside the steps with her arms already outstretched.

"Damnation," Hurtheven cursed as he slowed his pace.

Hera's breath came heavy and hard. She placed a

palm against her breast, willing her heart to slow. Between the run, the gauntlet he'd just thrown, her sudden fear for the children, and the surprise of seeing the newcomers, she hardly knew how to parse her emotion.

So, she donned the armor of her profession, tucked up her hair, and strode toward her employers with a fixed, bright smile on her face.

Hurtheven angled toward the coach, too. When he reached the door, he lent his hand to Penelope as she exited. "Forgive the lack of welcome," he spoke to Penelope, but included the rest with a brisque nod. "I was not expecting you."

"We wrote to you the day we set out." The Duchess of Ashbey fixed a significant gaze on Hera. "But, using postilions, we must have neatly beat the mail."

Torn between the hope of good news, and the dread of discovery, Hera cast her eyes down to the gravel.

Never play at piquet, my dear—the duke had once warned.

Something, she was sure, would give her away. Which of her secrets and to whom she would unintentionally reveal them was simply a matter of time.

"Mrs. Montrose," Ashbey greeted, "I trust everyone has behaved, including this reprobate?"

Hera was helpless to prevent blood from creeping up beneath the skin of her neck and into her cheeks. "Certainly."

"We..." Hurtheven cleared his throat. "...That is to say, the children and I... Well, we're all delighted to see you, aren't we, Mrs. Montrose?"

We! Hera dared not give him a scolding glance. "Shall I go inform Mrs. Whitby?"

"I daresay their arrival has been noticed," Hurtheven said under his breath.

"Come"—Delmare tugged on his mother's hand—"I *have* to show you my frog."

Not to be outdone, Fee took hold of her father. "And I have to show *you* mine."

"You *both* have frogs?" Ashbey asked.

"She does not," Delmare replied.

"I *do*," Fee insisted.

"I trust we will have time to...discuss the children, Mrs. Montrose?" the Duchess of Ashbey asked.

"Dinner has already been set for an hour hence," Hurtheven intervened. "Cook, I'm sure, will be able to expand the menu. After, you ladies will have all the time as you wish."

"Later, then." The duchess smiled reassuringly.

As the duke, the duchess, and their children disappeared into the hall, Hera read all she could into that smile. Surely, the cheerful expression meant the duchess had no *bad* news to impart. Hera turned to Penelope with a questioning expression.

"All is well," Penelope answered. "Much better than expected, actually."

Hurtheven snorted. "Of course, all is well. Did you doubt?"

"I'd never doubt you," Penelope laughed—just a touch too brightly.

Hera purposefully changed the subject. "I cannot *imagine* the explanation Fee will devise to excuse the absence of her own frog."

"Don't be too sure she won't find one before they reach the nursery," Hurtheven replied. "The world has a way of supporting those with unquestioning faith in themselves."

"And you've some experience with self-assurance, haven't you?" Ithwick clapped a hand on Hurtheven's shoulder. "You wouldn't be our Zeus if you did not."

"Zeus?" Hera repeated faintly.

"The name we've given him," Ithwick answered. "Did he not tell you?"

Was *that* why he'd been so startled by *her* name? *Good Lord.*

"Off with you both," Hurtheven said, coloring slightly. "I'm sure you wish to shake off the dust—and Mrs. Montrose and I have a kite to collect."

Hera waited for the duke and duchess to enter the castle. She turned to him and with lowered voice, said, "Zeus?"

He cleared his throat. "A longstanding joke. From childhood. Nothing to do with you."

"Ah," she replied, not feeling any better about the coincidence. "Their arrival, I suppose, will put an end to our midnights?"

His expression blanked. "Is that your wish?"

No. She glanced at the open doors. "There is a greater risk we'll be caught."

"There is," he agreed. "But I'm not willing to give this up."

Neither was she, though she must. A haunting gloom passed through her spirit. In fact, depending on what news the duchess had to impart, this next meeting could be their very last one.

She swallowed roughly. "Midnight, it is."

* * *

Hurtheven rolled the stem of his wine glass between his fingers. From his vantage at the head of his dining table, he could observe every one of his guests as Delmare—with occasional interjections from Fee—regaled them with the tale of the lion at the inn.

And he could studiously avoid meeting the gaze of the one seated directly across from him—*Ashbey*.

He'd no doubt Ash had, on arrival, immediately and correctly assessed the situation between himself and Hera. However, by Hurtheven's encouragement and design, the sartorial preparations for the evening meal—among other demands for Ash's attention—had left Ash without the opportunity to give Hurtheven a private excoriation.

Hurtheven could not yet answer Ash's inevitable question. Hera had cut Hurtheven off on every occasion he'd attempted to revisit the prospect of their marriage.

His gaze settled on the lady whom he still hoped to make his duchess. Her posture was one of a woman on pins and needles awaiting some dire revelation. She angled toward Delmare, listening intently to the boy's version of the events, her features clouded with apprehension carefully masked as interest.

He hated having to be her secret. Were he to have his way, she'd have nothing to hide from his friends. She belonged here. Hell, she belonged across from him, at the other end of the table.

Rather than ducking away from Ash, he'd much rather be facing the vision of Hera's sparkling eyes, her smoothly coiled hair, and the expanse of pale skin below her throat that, tonight, showed a hint of cleavage before disappearing into a becoming lavender muslin dress.

For the past two weeks he'd been doing his best to *show* her how good they were together. From time to time, he caught a glimmer that suggested she shared his dreams, but that glimmer had not yet turned to consistent glow.

She *still* refused to believe.

Now, he'd run out of time to prove he was sincere through actions alone.

He must speak to her tonight. With any luck, their next meeting would mark the end of this "farce" and the beginning of a true betrothal. Having decided, he turned his attention back to the conversation just as Delmare completed his story.

"Well!" Pen exclaimed. "What a magnificent tale!"

"Yes," Chev agreed. "With much to be commended in all of you."

Hurtheven lifted a shoulder in a careless shrug, as if, without much effort, he'd bested a lion on multiple occasions.

Alicia shivered. "I will never, *ever* be able to thank you enough, my dear Mrs. Montrose. I *know* what you risked. I will be forever in your debt."

"No," Hera replied quietly. "It is I who am in yours."

Alicia's tremulous smile suggested Hera had risked more than just her life. But what more had anyone to hazard than their very existence? And what of Hera's answering gaze—equally heavy with obligation?

Had they left something significant unspoken?

But no—he frowned—Ash's glower simply had him seeing things in *everyone's* expressions, whether real or not.

"Delmare," Fee added, "said Uncle Heven was just like Heracles. He vang...I mean *vanquished* a lion, too, you know."

"Vanquished is a very good word, Fee," Alicia commended.

"You see?" Chev spoke to his wife. "I told you

Hurtheven would have to face Herculean Labors before he'd see the light."

"You did." Pen lost her fight to suppress a smile. "And I believe"—she glanced between Hurtheven and Hera—"he *has* seen the light."

"Light?" Hurtheven's frown deepened. *What light?*

"Oh, just idle talk." Pen waved her hand. Then, she turned to Hera. "You must have all been exhausted by your ordeal."

"Mrs. Montrose fainted," Fee explained. "And so, Uncle Heven—only he was Uncle Papa then—made us all spend the night."

"Did you...*Uncle Papa?*" Ash asked darkly.

Hurtheven cleared his throat. "A rather infamous occurrence—a lion in a courtyard. I thought it best to further disguise our identities by inventing a closer relationship."

"But what about the penny?" Felicia asked.

"Hardly relevant to the story," Hera interjected. She turned to Ash. "You would have been so proud of your children, Your Grace."

Ash's gaze softened considerably. "I *am* very proud of my children. And like my wife, very grateful to you."

Hurtheven noted that he had not been included.

Chev leaned back in his chair. "There are, in fact, other interesting parallels between Hurtheven's many feats and the Labors of Heracles. I'd scarcely be surprised if he told us he'd introduced man-eating birds on the estate."

"Weren't the *mares* man-eating?" Penelope asked.

"As I recall," Alicia winced, "the labors involved a few different kinds of man-eating beasts."

Pen cocked her head. "And doesn't your estate boast a herd of deer, Hurtheven?"

"Don't forget the boar," Chev noted. "Doubtless he has a few pigs. And cattle! Plenty of mares, too."

"Alas." Hurtheven lifted a brow. "I'm fresh out of Hydra, I'm afraid."

"But surely, you've snakes! They'd do for Hydra," Alicia said triumphantly. "And I know you have an apple orchard, so the golden apples are taken care of, too!"

"Perhaps," Pen said with a twinkle, "he's been laboring all along."

Ash snorted. "I doubt Hurtheven has lowered himself enough to muck out his stables."

"In fact"—Hurtheven arched a brow—"a dam on the estate recently failed. I happen to be planning a new dam that will divert the river. One of the happy effects will be the clearing of a bit of marsh favored by the cows."

"As usual," Ash replied, "you've an answer for everything."

"What's that leave?" Alicia queried.

"The last labor was a visit to Hades," Ash said, sounding as if he wished to supply the means for that visit.

"You've forgotten The Belt of Hippolyte."

All heads swiveled to Hera.

"Ah yes," Alicia replied. "The belt Heracles took from the Amazon Queen."

"Gave," Hera corrected. "She *gave* him the belt."

"And then she was killed by a mob, wasn't she?" Alicia asked.

"In some versions," Hera replied. "In others, Heracles kills her himself."

Hera's grave expression reminded Hurtheven of her reaction to the statue of that, particular labor in his library. *An excellent warning to women...concede nothing, else you be stripped of the whole.*

Pen visibly shivered. "*Such* horrible tales! So full of violence."

"They're only metaphors," Hurtheven consoled. "Some good, some, like that one, clearly wanting."

"I thought you *admired* Heracles," Hera said almost accusingly.

"I did—I do." He ventured a tentative smile. "But not even a hero can be entirely without fault. A better man would have cherished Hippolyte's gift and defended the giver."

Hera continued to hold his gaze, and he thought he'd seen a brief flash of longing within her eyes.

But longing for what?

He'd willingly—no, *gratefully*—share with her everything he had. He'd thought he'd made that much clear. *Repeatedly*.

"Well, I prefer Wordsworth's metaphors," Pen said. "Besides, unlike Heracles, Hurtheven hasn't anything to atone for!"

Ash made an ominous sound.

Alicia glanced curiously at her husband—and then between Chev and Hurtheven. "As amusing as these reflections have been," she said, "I think it's high time we leave the men to their port."

"Yes, let's," Pen replied.

"Come, children, say good night," Alicia urged. "Auntie Pen, Mrs. Montrose, and I will take you up to the nursery together."

After the usual protests, followed by a hearty round of farewells, the men were left alone.

Uneasily, Hurtheven turned to Ash. "We *all* have things for which we must atone."

"I *will* hold you to your promise," Ash replied.

"I would expect nothing less. In fact, I was on the verge of proposing marriage just before you arrived. But the situation is a delicate one."

"A delicate one," Ash repeated. "Has she even told you about—"

"A proposal!" Chev interrupted. "That is *wonderful*—in the truest sense. As in, I am left in utter wonder! I wish you both happy, my friend."

"Of course, *you* do." Ash stood up and glowered menacingly. "Once Hurtheven's married, presumably, he'll no longer be dangling after your wife."

Hurtheven shoved back his chair. "What is *wrong* with you, Ash?"

"If you're too arrogant to realize that she hasn't—"

"Sit down, both of you." Chev interrupted again.

Ash pursed his lips but complied. Then, after a wary glance between them, Hurtheven returned to his seat, too.

Chev wiped his mouth. "Ash, mentioning Hurtheven's attachment to Pen was uncalled for. All that has long since passed, as you know. Besides, Pen was merely a safe object for his distant idolatry..."

Hurtheven frowned.

"...Anyone can see he's devoted in a different way to Mrs. Montrose. He *said* he intends to propose." Chev glanced significantly at Ash. "The lady, I believe, should have the final say. It is not for us to *interfere*."

"Indeed not!" Hurtheven exclaimed. "I *love* her, Ash. I believe she loves me."

"Love," Ash repeated. His hard expression softened slightly.

"Yes, love!" He didn't care who knew.

"*If* she has earned your trust," Ash replied slowly, "*then* I will wish you happy, too."

Ash kept his silence as Chev poured a round of port. With a guarded expression, Ash even joined in Chev's toast. Hurtheven drank deeply. God only knew what had gotten into his friend, but, for the present, Ash appeared to have reined in his ire.

Hurtheven's mind drifted back to Hera, ravishing in lavender. Finally, he understood Ash and Chev's occasional impatience to be alone with their wives. Only a few more hours...

"You *should* marry, Hurtheven," Chev said. "It's high time you became someone else's problem. Don't you agree, Ash?"

* * *

Hera froze outside the door to the dining hall.

She hadn't meant to eavesdrop. She'd only returned below stairs because she'd forgotten her shawl. She decided she needn't retrieve the garment after all, and slowly backed away. All she'd distinctly heard was the Duke of Ithwick saying, *'You should marry, Hurtheven'*.

But those words had been enough.

Godric would, of course, marry.

She'd seen his list. She'd known the prospect of his nuptials to be an inevitability. Her reaction, then, had been a surprise. A creeping sense of dread, followed by her heart's violent protestation. Even worse, her mind had instantly reordered the phrase.

'You should marry Hurtheven'...without the implied comma.

This afternoon, when Godric had uttered the word love, she'd finally understood the depth of what she felt for her duke. Heavens! *How* she wanted him to be *hers*.

She *was* in love. And she wasn't even sure when this catastrophe had happened. What was sure was a sudden, passionately covetous feeling toward the duke.

When he married, as he must, would she become like her namesake—through love, driven to bitter destruction?

She turned swiftly on her heel and fled up the stairs. She did not stop until she'd closeted herself safely in her room.

She didn't know how long she'd stood there staring at the floor, her mind completely blank, when she heard a light knock.

"Please come in," she said hesitantly.

"I thought I'd heard you come back." The Duchess of Ashbey slipped inside. "Pen's upstairs reading to the children. I was a useless second. So, I thought I'd come down to look in on you." She smiled kindly. "We've not had a moment alone."

"No." What was *wrong* with her? Her mind should have been focused entirely on Annis and what the duchess had learned of the Runner. "I have, of course, been anxious to know if...if..." Her voice wavered.

Did her preoccupation with her feelings for the duke mean she would make a terrible mother? She held a tightly closed fist against her lips.

"What's happened?" the duchess exclaimed.

"Nothing," she sniffed. "Nothing that will not shortly be undone, anyway."

"Are you upset with Hurtheven?" The duchess searched her gaze. "No, no, my dear! I didn't mean to make you feel worse. You've no need to look so distressed. I only noticed an...affinity."

"He—He is in no danger from me, if that is your

concern." *Oh God.* She *must* prevent tears. "I wouldn't presume."

"If he isn't in danger from you—which I don't believe—I'd wish he would be!" the duchess exclaimed.

"You cannot be serious!"

The duchess took a deep breath. "Interesting choice of word, *presume.*"

"Meaning"—Hera reverted to her governess tone—"look higher than my station."

"Yes, I understood your meaning," the duchess said gently. "After all these years, I can still remember how deeply I dreaded the question, 'who does she think she is?' when I considered marrying Ash."

The duchess's eyes were all that was kind.

"Did anyone ask you such a thing?" Hera asked.

"Not directly, but I heard the whispered words. Words, in my experience, spoken out of jealousy. Or fear." She frowned. "*Both* perhaps. Jealousy because I dared to reach for something someone else decided should be beyond my touch. Fear because, if the rules of hierarchy can be so easily broken, what can be left to protect those in power?"

"*You* were born a gentlewoman," Hera reminded.

"You are, are you not, the daughter of a baron?"

"Yes, but..."

The duchess raised her brows. "But?"

"*Annis.*"

"Have you told Hurtheven about Annis?"

Hera shook her head *no.*

"I cannot," the duchess said carefully, "speak for the duke. But I would encourage you to confide in him. I expect he'd surprise you—as he often does us all."

"Please," Hera protested, "I know you mean well but..."

"But your heart is breaking."

Hera nodded.

The duchess wrapped her arm around Hera's shoulder. "Well, I have said my part and encouraged you to trust him." The duchess sighed. "Please tell me you'll at least consider my advice."

"I will," Hera promised. "Will—will the knowledge that he and I..." She shrugged balefully. "Will this affair affect your character reference?"

The duchess jerked back as if completely surprised. "Why should it? I am to report on the care of my children. For which I have not a single complaint."

"But you are also to reassure them I have," she sobbed, "*reformed.*"

"*Reformed.*" The duchesses face pinched. "As far as I'm concerned, your character is sterling. Perfection is unachievable, no matter what the moralists would have us all believe."

"You cannot mean that."

"I should know." The duchess sat down beside her on the bed. "I performed the part of the perfect, long-suffering lady while my first husband fell madly in love with the world's most famous actress."

Hera sniffed. "Even *I've* heard of the affair between Captain Stone and the countess." She frowned. "Don't you mean infamous?"

"No, actually. The countess was—and *is*—exceptionally charming. Admirable in many ways..."

"How *could* you not hate the woman?"

The duchess shrugged. "...She catapulted her way through society from the lowest to the highest. There were plenty of men who were willing to take advantage of her until she found the one man who loved her truly. Unfortunately, he happened to be my husband."

241

"But did they not take advantage of you?

"Certainly. Though I doubt either spared a thought for me at all. Anyone witnessing what was between them would testify to the sincerity of their affection. In truth, I was not jealous. But I *was* deeply envious. I'd never loved Octavius in quite that way, but I wanted what they had. I wanted someone to look at me with wonder in their eyes."

"And now you have found that person."

"Yes." She hesitated. "I'm not saying there shouldn't be *any* moral standards. *Of course*, we should all strive to be kind. And faithful. And just. I'm only observing that...well, the heart doesn't always listen to reason. And the truth is complicated." She patted Hera's knee. "The duke looks at you with that same kind of wonder, you know."

Hera closed her eyes. He *did*.

But once he learned the truth—would that wonder last?

"I will consider your counsel." She wiped her eyes. "But now, please tell me what happened in my absence? Have you found out if the Runner was sent by Karl?"

"I've wonderful news! The Runner was *not* sent by Karl."

Not Karl? "I don't understand."

"We wanted to tell you as soon as we arrived, but Ash reminded us not to assume you'd taken Hurtheven into your confidence."

"*Ash?*"

"I think," the duchess replied carefully, "I had better begin from the start. The Runner came to question us just after you left—and despite Ash's threats, he refused to divulge the purpose of his visit or provide the name of his employer. But he did give Ash the direction of the law office where he was to send his report. Ash refused to allow me to hunt down the office without his assistance, so we—Chev, Ash, Pen, and I—decided to travel to London together."

"I know," the duchess continued, "you did not wish me to reveal the whole to my husband. And, in truth, I was not the one who did. The Runner's report traced you as far as the foundling hospital—Ash guessed the rest. My dear Miss Bythesea, I have something rather shocking to reveal to you. Something that happily changes *everything*."

Chapter Eleven

At dinner, the Duchess of Ashbey—Alicia, on her renewed insistence—had suggested *she* would be forever in *Hera's* debt. Even then, Hera felt quite the opposite to be true. Now, after what Alicia had just revealed, Hera was certain she'd the greater obligation.

She'd never be able to repay the duchess for all she'd done.

On visiting the address the Runner provided, Ashbey and Chev combined their talents to persuade the solicitor to furnish both the Runner's report and the reason the office had been asked to find Hera. Eventually, the solicitor revealed he'd been charged by the executor of a Mrs. Francis Grant—Hera's grandmother—to find her daughter's daughter.

While that lady's husband lived, he'd refused to acknowledge they'd ever had a child, let alone a granddaughter. But on his death, Mrs. Grant named Hera Bythesea—or, if Miss Bythesea was no longer living, any of her issue—as sole beneficiary of her will.

Hera had never known her grandmother, of course.

Nor had she known much about the family that had refused to see her mother after they learned she was with child. The solicitor had not felt revealing the exact amount bequeathed to Hera in his power, but had said the number would, when the estate was fully settled, be a sizable enough sum to be considered an independence. Additionally, Hera's inheritance was to include a London boarding house her grandmother had run.

Which meant the directors would be satisfied Hera could provide for Annis. All barriers had been removed. When the board met less than a week hence, Hera would be reunited with Annis.

After Hera profusely thanked the duchess, both for her aid and for her discretion, the duchess left the room. Hera sat in silence, slowly digesting the information she'd received as if each piece was a morsel taken from an extravagant meal.

An independence was hers...and without reliance on that blasted contract. She and Annis would soon have a London home of their own. What was more, Alicia truly believed that Hurtheven would accept Annis.

Dare Hera trust all these things to be true?

And how odd that her fortune could change so dramatically in such a short time! What a different life she could be leading if she had known of her grandmother's sentiments and intentions.

But Hera couldn't lament the past—not with Annis as her future—nor could she truly mourn a woman she'd never known.

All she could do was decide how she wished to proceed.

Mrs. Small could take charge of the children while they were here, and, by the time the Ashbey family returned to Wisterley, Mrs. Chatten expected to be free to resume her duties. Hera no longer had a reason for staying at Heven-hyll. In fact, the duchess was willing to travel back to London with her tomorrow to ensure everything went smoothly at the hearing.

Which left Hurtheven.

Godric.

Had the duchess been correct? Dare she tell him the whole?

If he loved her *as she loved him,* surely what he'd said just this afternoon must prevail. Love would not fail them. But how could she know?

How could she be sure?

He told her he never intentionally revealed his secrets. She seen evidence of at least one—the pain he carried. Did he have other secrets that could weigh upon their future life together? Could she trust him not just with her heart but with her child?

The unanswered questions left her feeling heady, vulnerable.

She had to see him. Maybe then, she could be sure.

She crept out into the corridor to check the long clock on the landing. An hour yet to midnight. Then she heard footsteps simultaneously on both sets of staircases. Tentatively, she placed her hand against the wall and peeked around the corner to see who was coming up from the hall.

Godric...and he was wearing *such* an expression of anticipation, as if he were bathed in light. His entire body was glowing in response to the person descending to meet him.

His eyes glinted. A smile curled his lips. He'd even a slight spring in his step. She almost didn't recognize him. She followed his gaze to Penelope.

"You," Hurtheven sighed.

As he passed by, Hera plastered herself against the wall, heart thumping.

"Hurtheven. *Dear*, Hurtheven," Penelope's lowered voice was rich with poignant intimacy. "How...how very lovely. Truly. I'm so happy to see..." Penelope's voice cracked. She touched a finger to her lips.

"Ah, Pen." He spoke in a softened tone Hera had never heard him use. "I should have known you would be able to read me at once."

Hera forced herself to look again. From her angle, she couldn't see his face, but she could see Penelope's. In the duchess's eyes was a look of infinite tenderness.

"Of course, I can." Penelope moved her hand to his cheek.

He tilted his head into the cradle of her palm. Hera went rigid as if she'd been caught in a sudden gust of icy air.

"You know you've always been very dear to me," Pen quietly intoned. "You were a friend when I had none. A surrogate father to Thaddeus when he was most in need."

Hurtheven chuckled softly...*ruefully*. "And yet," he replied, "you refused me when I asked for your hand..."

Refused him. A cold blade of jealousy pierced Hera's chest. He'd asked *Penelope* to *wed*?

"I refuse to marry you because I knew you deserved someone who loved you with all of her heart." Penelope's smile was born of decades of friendship. "I love you...but not like that."

"I know." He tucked a whisp of hair behind the duchess's ear. "I understand."

What a vision they made together. *Blonde.* She recognized a fragment of his list. In fact, but for petite, the duchess was a perfect fit for all Hurtheven's qualifications!

How had she not seen that before?

"I'm so glad you finally understand." Penelope embraced him.

Hurtheven hummed a discordant, wounded tone. "I..." He held her close, resting his cheek against her hair. "I haven't secured what I truly want."

"No?" Penelope queried. She exhaled. "Well, you'll forge a path. You always do."

Another rueful laugh. "I will do my best." After a moment, he again sighed deeply and said, "Your husband, I believe, anxiously awaits."

"Good night, my dear friend."

As she withdrew, Penelope passed Hera on the landing, coming so close her light scent lingered in the air. Hera's stomach turned over.

She'd often wondered why the duke—who clearly had so much to offer—had remained unmarried all these years.

Now, she had her answer.

Perhaps she would have seen the truth from the beginning, if only she hadn't misinterpreted him at every turn— just as she had misinterpreted the reason for the Runner's visit. Hurtheven wasn't closed and unreachable. He didn't distrust women.

He loved one above all others.

And that woman was married to one of his two closest friends.

To be so near to the one you love and yet forever separated.... Well, she understood exactly how much pain he felt.

Absurd, this chain of longing—Hurtheven watching the duchess disappear down the corridor, herself, gazing after Hurtheven. She couldn't bear another moment, and yet she could not look away.

Love and longing, polished to perfection over time. She didn't know if she should laugh or weep.

Suddenly, Hurtheven glanced in her direction. He did not seem surprised to see her there. He looked pensive...almost weary. As if all emotion had just been wrung from him.

"You love her." The words were out before she'd a chance to muffle them.

"Yes." Something flashed in his eyes—pain? Anger? The flicker had been too quick to define.

"I see."

"I don't think you do." He advanced. "I love them *both*. Pen and Chev." He paused. "Just as I love Ash and Alicia. Although Pen did, at one time, spark a deeper feeling."

Had he just asked her to distrust her own ears? Her *eyes*? She'd seen him lean into Penelope's embrace! "It is none of my concern."

"Hera." His voice had softened again.

She hated the way her neck prickled. "You asked her to marry you."

"I did...a long time ago. She was alone. Vulnerable. Chev's cousin had just had him declared dead and Ithwick Castle had been overrun by potential suitors." He sighed. "I made a mistake."

"You had no way of knowing her husband was alive."

"*She* did. She trusted."

So, not just love. *Guilt*.

"Chev and I have been close for as long as I can remember. Chev wasn't his father's heir, then. But he came from a ducal household. When we became friends, I think that I felt...understood for the first time in my life."

"Ashbey was a ducal heir."

"Chev and I were friends first. Ash was never... Well, he

wasn't an easy person to get to know. Everyone knew Ash's father was mad. He was mercilessly teased. Chev appointed us both Ash's defenders. From that point, the three of us became sworn brothers. But what's at the heart of our friendship is trust."

He searched her gaze.

"Tonight," he said, "Ash asked me, in a manner of speaking, if I had earned your trust. Have I?"

Now, it was her turn to feel exposed.

Hurtheven had known from the start she was hiding something. She'd been on the verge of telling him everything tonight. But now...

She thought of the look he'd had on his face when he was climbing up the stairs. He'd been *elated* to see Penelope. Then, he had held her close and said he hadn't secured what he truly wanted.

Penelope.

Her chest contracted.

She could only ever be second best.

She'd always been second best—when she was thought of at all.

Born of a second marriage and never accepted by her brother, but instead, treated like his servant. Given a Prince's attention...but only when he was sure no one else would notice. And, until the duchess had stepped in, she hadn't even been capable of being first in her own daughter's life. *Giving up* Annis had been the only way she could protect her daughter.

Hurtheven was honor to his core, but she could not place her life—and the life of her child—into the hands of a man who loved another.

She, too, deserved someone who would love her with all of their heart.

"I think," she replied haltingly, "you are the most trustworthy, loyal man I have ever known."

He smiled, for once, accepting her response without question.

"Midnight?" he whispered.

"Midnight," she answered.

She turned back toward her room.

She'd prevented him from speaking of his hopes because she'd been afraid he wouldn't want her after he learned of Annis. She'd been worried about him getting too attached. Now, she knew he'd never been completely hers at all.

At least she had one more midnight before she had to let him go.

* * *

He should have escorted Hera directly from the landing into the armory. She'd needed reassurance. But the household had still been astir. And he'd promised to do everything in his power to preserve her reputation. He had to undress, dismiss his valet, and wait for the appointed time.

He glanced at his pocket watch. Five more minutes.

Quietly, he removed his dressing gown from the cupboard, and then, standing in front of his long mirror, slipped his arms within. He stood to the side, critically inspecting his profile. He straightened the seam and then smoothed the fabric—a surprising bit of vanity.

Why *had* he done that? Why had he—without intending to do so—needed to perfect his appearance?

Why? Because he wanted to look his best, of course. And, if he were honest, he not only wanted to look his best. He wanted to *be* his best.

251

He wanted to be worthy.

He scowled. Of course, he was *worthy*. He was a bloody duke. And she was Hera to his Zeus. ...Only, he no longer wanted to be Zeus, god of all he surveyed.

He just wanted to be with her.

He wanted to make her smile. He wanted to pleasure her by every means he could imagine. He wanted to and he *would*.

He loved her as he had never loved before.

Chev's words came to him then. *Pen was merely a safe object for his distant idolatry...*

Had Chev been right?

Had Pen been easy to love only because he could never truly touch her heart? If so, was Hera, too, just a creation of his mind?

No.

He held in reverence Hera's shining, spiral hair. Her tender touch. The inward, marvelous curve, hip to waist, as she stretched out beside him. But what he truly needed came from within her heart. A quality manifest in the careful, intent way she watched him when she thought he wasn't looking, and the artless fascination she radiated when she gazed deep into his eyes.

Mostly, however, he loved her because of the way she'd unlocked everything he'd boxed up deep inside. The way she made him want again to be childlike—open and free.

At the sound of the first chime, he slipped out of his bedchamber. By the tenth, he was already in the armory.

She stood, back to him, gazing at the bed. Her dressing gown flowed in goddess-like folds to the ground. He threaded his arms around her waist, and she leaned back against his chest with a sigh.

She was no figment.

She was a flower, and she was opening to him in trust. Or, if not to him, to the moment, to their agreement.

Tell her.

Tell her how all his accumulated wealth melted to nothing whenever she was near. Tell her how, in her presence, the pain he carried within him dissipated. Tell her for the first time in his life, his waking thought wasn't of the beam of electricity that had shot down from a dark night sky to steal his family, his happiness, and his security.

Instead, he said, "Anything can be taken away at any moment."

She turned in his arms and lifted her face. Questions lurked behind her eyes.

Tell her!

He couldn't. He tried, but, well, words that could capture that night, words that could explain the deep, thick fear-laden internal bog he carried around inside of him that was intimately connected to how much he needed her to love him...those words did not exist.

Instead, he simply whispered, "Marry me. You've never definitively answered, though I've already asked. Multiple times, I might add."

Her gaze shuttered. "I am not the kind of woman you'd marry."

"If that were true, I would not have asked you."

"You're just enthralled." She stepped out of his arms. "When this is over, you'll find a proper little thing who will hang on the wisdom of your vast experience—"

"Hang?"

"—and thus harden beyond redemption every one of your worst flaws."

He ignored the impulse to return her verbal punch.

Eyes on the horizon. "Why do you do that? Why do you push me away?"

She was silent for some time. "How *do* you think of me, Godric?"

"As someone that could, I suspect, show me the meaning of love."

"You *know* how to love."

She sounded almost...*bitter?* He couldn't be sure. She had turned away from him again and did not look back.

"You love the children," she added in a lighter tone.

"Yes. But *this* is different. I've never"—his voice involuntarily cracked—"wanted someone...who has also wanted me."

"Women have *eyes, duke.*"

Back to *duke*, were they? He tried again. "I'm not just speaking of lust...I'm speaking of the way you make me feel."

"How?" She glanced over her shoulder. "How do I make you feel?"

Oh, hell.

He remembered this experience—slowly fading hope. He'd felt similarly just before Penelope rejected his proposal. But a difference existed between what he'd felt then and what he was feeling now.

He attempted to describe the difference.

"I'm standing on a precipice, Hera. If, given just the right encouragement, I could dive down into a deeper understanding of everything I've thought I already understood. *You* are the precipice *and* the encouragement."

Longing flickered again in her eyes. And just as quickly, it extinguished. "I've seen your list of requirements. I don't meet one."

He frowned. "My list?"

She raised her brows.

His requirements...? *Oh, God.* Not *those* blasted requirements. "How *the devil?*"

"You—or one of the others—dropped the paper."

He ran his hands through his hair. "Whatever points I came up with were made in *your* mirror image. I was running away from what I'd felt for you—almost instantly—in the garden. And what was then merely possibility is now a raging fire."

She didn't believe him, he could tell.

Her eyes narrowed. "*Intelligent* was on your list."

"Intelligent without the pretensions of a bluestocking, if I remember correctly."

She lifted her chin. "How do you know I *don't* have bluestocking aspirations?"

"I wouldn't care if you had! Anyway, it doesn't matter. I've just formulated a new list."

She glanced heavenward.

"Aren't you going to ask me what qualifications I've chosen?"

"No."

"There's only one." He advanced. "And my *one* requirement is that my future wife *must* be Miss Hera Bythesea."

She briefly closed her eyes. "What if I had a list, too?"

Pride made him perverse. "I imagine I could fulfill any of your prerequisites." With an increasing sense of desperation, he tried for a jest. "What more could you wish than rich, handsome, and virile?"

Her eyes flew to his. "Virile? How would you know?"

He threw out his hands. "One hopes."

"Have you illegitimate children?"

"No!"

"Oh, thank goodness." She sank onto the bed. "I

shouldn't be here." She threaded her hands into her hair. "I don't know how we got here."

He sat down beside her. "I've never before sincerely wished I possessed Zeus-like qualities. If I had, maybe I could convince you to be my Hera."

"Do you know how Zeus won my namesake? He made himself a helpless little bird. She took him in, nursed him because he was broken and in need, and she fell in love. Then, his infidelities transformed all Hera's compassionate care into vengeful, jealous cruelty."

He blinked. "Hera was, by natural disposition, a jealous woman."

"Goddess," she corrected. "And by natural disposition? I think not. She was jealous by *influence*. By Zeus's false image and his selfish use of her compassion."

"I will *never* make myself helpless," he vowed. "Or misuse your compassion. Or give you reason to be jealous."

She stared at him, wide-eyed, accusing. "How can you, who perceive so much, understand so little."

"I'm not sure what you mean."

"You've *already done* as Zeus did. You've made yourself that wounded bird by simply *being*. Having caught a glimpse of you—the *real* you—and that, only the smallest glimpse you *involuntarily* allowed...how am I *ever* to settle for anything less?"

"You don't have to."

"Perhaps not..." She turned to him. Something urgent burned in her eyes. Something almost wild. "Tell me something about you *no one* knows."

There was only one thing about him no one knew—an experience rather than a fact. And, often, the experience *did* render him helpless.

He heard the sound. The screeching wheels. The desperate cracking.

His arms tingled as if his blood was dripping out from the bottom of his fingertips. Suddenly, all the arguments he'd made in his favor felt hollow.

His father, too, had been a duke—and had he been able to protect his duchess?

No. His reckless choice had cost him her life and his own. And who, two weeks past, had encouraged Hera out into that storm—when, at any moment, a strike could have taken *her* life?

He was danger personified.

Like his father, curst by the gods for his hubris.

So, he looked into her eyes, and he lied. "I would. But I have no secrets to share."

* * *

If she hadn't left that stupid penny wrapped up in a handkerchief and tucked inside her bedside drawer, she would have hurled the metal chip at his head.

She *knew* he'd suffered. She'd *seen* the still-living suffering within his eyes. And she'd witnessed that terrible wreck of the carriage. Yet, he'd gazed at her with complete sincerity and *lied*...just after he'd asked her to marry him!

Did he even understand what that would mean for her? How she'd have to give up her separate existence—legally, physically, and spiritually—and become one with his own. He'd asked everything of her when he'd long loved another and then would not even confide in her his greatest pain.

She would have taken a chance. She'd would have told him about Annis, and, if he'd agreed to take them both, put at risk her heart and her being to give him her hand. She'd have been willing...if he'd have first given her *his* trust.

Perhaps selfishly, she'd wanted something of him that didn't belong to Chev or Ash or Alicia...and certainly not to Penelope. Even if he already confided his past to any or all of them—and she did not believe he had—she would have settled for him telling her the simple truth.

But he'd *lied*.

Worse still, she'd ached with him when she'd seen the torment that had briefly flashed across his features. In that moment, *she'd* grown old and smarting. Now, she felt vastly alone—a visceral premonition of how she'd feel if she were to live with the unrecognized shadows he carried about inside of him.

She could not.

And so, she would have to leave him tomorrow.

He was so—she ran the back of her hand down his cheek—beautiful.

Too beautiful.

Yes, he'd been called by some, a devil. She understood why. His very presence formed a tide, a natural, irresistible pull. And yet there were hundreds whose lives depended on this man. Maybe even thousands.

"You're at the very top of society. Your name is legend. Your line will carry on into infinity."

"Without you, the line will die out with me."

"No. It won't." He would do what was right.

He would find a proper wife to sire a proper heir.

The flare of hope in his eyes caused her a stab of guilt. But if she told him the truth—if she told him she meant to leave him tomorrow—he'd protest.

Tears crowded in her throat. She swallowed them

down. She would not allow him to guess her intention. He mustn't know this was the last time they'd come together.

The last time.

"Why are you looking at me like that?" he asked.

"Like I want to savor you?" She smiled to hide her lip tremble. "Because I do."

He tilted his head, suspicious.

She pushed her fingers into his hair. "Sometimes I just can't believe you're real."

There it was again. The shadow across his features. Not only pain, but self-reproach. Why the latter?

Because he truly loved, not her, but Penelope?

She scratched beneath his chin. He smiled, warm and sensual, in response. She couldn't help but mirror his upturned lips...just before he fitted them over her own. The kiss was soft and sweet and tender. Full of words unspoken, emotion constrained. She sunk into the thick, murky mess, bathing in his heat in his tenderness.

What was it about strong men who were gentle with those in their care?

She held to his shoulders, near drowning in shattered hope.

Then, his intensity changed. He gripped her arms to the point of pain. She delighted in his power and, at the same time, had an overwhelming urge to subdue his strength, as if in overpowering him, she could prove to herself she would survive him.

She encircled his wrists and removed his hands from her person. Holding his arms at his side, she walked him back to the bed, and then pushed him down until they were both tangled atop the mattress.

Curiosity shone in his eyes. Curiosity and desire.

"I want to take you." She spoke in a gravelly voice. "Take *from* you."

Where had that come from?

Yet, She'd spoken true. Her desire was edged with grief and want and pain, and if he would not voluntarily give her his secrets, she could, at least leave her mark on his mind.

A memory hot and fierce.

She shifted her position until she was poised above him, staring down. She rested a hand on his chest, directly over his heart.

"Would you let me? I wonder."

"I'm at your mercy." He made no move. Instead, he stared deeply into her eyes. "Susceptible in more ways than you'll ever know."

"Good." She made her voice light. If only that were true.

But she couldn't challenge the falsehood. Already she was in too deep. She could feel the web between them spinning, every second added another sticky thread. Her mind was already thick with them.

"What would you have me do?" he asked.

"It's what I'd have you be." *Hers.* Her heart skipped. "I think that tonight we should play."

His mouth quirked. "Don't we always?"

"Shh!" She scowled.

He pressed his lips together, but a ghost of a smiled lingered.

What *did* she want? She focused on the hard, pink seam of his mouth, slightly turned up at each end. What *could* she extract from this, the last, most bittersweet of their unions?

"I want you to pleasure me..." A hot rush sped through her body. "...with your tongue."

Karl had asked to pleasure her in this way and have her pleasure him in the same. She'd refused, revolted. With Godric, on the other hand, she wasn't at all repulsed.

Slowly, she inched backwards, lifted herself over his feet, and then, with her back against the footboard, languidly stretched out her legs. As she eased into a comfortable position, he raised himself onto his elbows, silently watching her all the while.

For a moment, he lay still. His eyes weren't at all conquered, only intent. And, perhaps, just a little entranced.

She lifted her hair and then dropped the mass of locks around her shoulders. Curls cascaded downwards in frothy red waves. A sound rumbled forth from his chest—a sound she felt between her legs. She let her knees drop to each side and then motioned for him to come closer.

His shoulder muscles flexed as he turned onto his stomach. Then, he snaked along the bedcovering until he disappeared beneath the fabric she'd scrunched up as far as she could.

She felt his ear against her flesh as his hair tickled her inner thighs, then his breath heated her in intimate places, and she threw her head back and closed her eyes. She nested in a place of pure sensation, a tight bud of tension beneath his breath ferning up in spirals of clawing need deep inside her gut.

He shoved his hands beneath the curve of her ass, and she slipped down, and tilted her hips upwards toward his mouth. Then, his soft lips framed her, and his tongue darted out. Her pleasure came serrated like a knife, points of near-pain, followed by hollows of intense bliss.

She released her shift and smoothed her hands up her torso, eventually coming to hold her own breasts. To intensify her pleasure, she flicked her thumbs across her aching nipples. She would touch herself this way when the memory of him was all she would have left.

The three points of pleasure drew ragged breaths from her chest, and then, she lost control. The quivering began in her legs, and soon encompassed her all. Comets, planets, stars all rushing outward against the darkness of her closed eyelids.

She whimpered through her release, jaggedly whispering his name.

Then, it was over. Her head lolled against the wood; her strength lost in the swampy, satiated feeling.

Slowly, he lifted his face. "Satisfied?

She blinked him into focus, listening to the rush of his hard, fast breath. His cheeks were flushed, his mouth, parted, and his lips, indecently wet. She etched every part of the moment—sound, sight, feel, and musky, sweet scent— to memory, then, she veered forward, adding her own tangy taste.

She parted her lips over his, kissing him silent. Because she wasn't fully satisfied in the least. She could never be. Not unless he was fully, devotedly hers, not for the length of a contract, but for the duration of his life.

She urged him first to his knees, and then, onto his back. Again, she encircled his wrists, this time, holding his hands to one side as she straddled his legs. Holding his gaze, she traced the throbbing vein in his cock with the tip of her fingernail.

His manhood involuntarily jerked.

"Looks painful."

He groaned. "Not sure pain is exactly the right word."

"Irritation, then?" She slid her thumb over the ball of

moisture gathering on the tip. "Ache?" She licked the pad dry and then closed her lips around her finger.

"Hera." He wheezed her name as he struggled against her hold.

She pinned him back down. "No."

She studied his manhood. Would his cock even fit in her mouth? Certainly not all at once. Then again...

She made the attempt.

"*Hera...*"

His member twitched as she let him go to reply. "*Shh!*"

He hissed as she again wrapped him with her lips. She lapped her tongue over the tip as she mimicked the motion he made when he thrust inside of her—slowly up, and then quickly down.

Was she performing the deed correctly?

Was there such a thing, in this case, as *correct*? Cock sucking was not the sort of thing a governess studied, after all. Fleetingly, she wondered if this was something brothels had to teach. Did penis tutors exist?

Her gurgled laugher made him grunt.

He broke free of her hold, gripped her chin, and forcibly raised her face. She licked and then sucked her bottom lip.

"I've never done that before," she confessed. "Was I all wrong?"

"Not"—he briefly closed his eyes—"at all. But I want...No, I *need* to be inside you. May I?"

"Yes," she replied, before using the filthiest word she'd ever read as an invitation.

He made a feral sound, tossed her on her back and, with one, hard thrust was fully sheathed. Now, he'd taken her, too.

Damnation.

She bit his shoulder.

He cried out but didn't stop. She stared at the angry red mark as her body jerked. Poor duke. She hadn't really meant to hurt him. *Much*. Softly, she covered her mark with her mouth. Then, she closed her eyes and gave herself up to the ride.

She was too raw—and his thrusts too frenzied—for her to find a second release. Besides, a little death was not what she wanted—she wanted to fully witness his. She gripped his ass as he panted into her neck.

She repeated the filthy word and added a command.

He threw back his head with an untamed, though muted roar. His belly went taut, his buttocks constricted. Her hands fused of their own accord, holding him in place. Too late, she felt his hot seed spreading into her core.

"Hera," he whispered brokenly. "I meant to...I would have..."

"I know," she replied, slowly stroking his hair.

"Would you welcome my child?" he asked.

Sweat had dampened the short, curls just above his ears.

"Yes," she replied. Why had she taken such a risk? She knew the consequence better than most.

"We'll marry soon," he self-consoled, and rested his head against her breast.

No, they would not.

The arrangements had already been made. By the time he awoke tomorrow, she would be gone.

Chapter Twelve

Hurtheven dove for the door like a wild man, but Ash, Penelope, and Chev resolutely blocked his path. Ash's mouth was still moving, but the rushing sound in Hurtheven's skull, fully silenced him.

Pen's soft voice cut through the noise. "She's gone. And you cannot follow."

Like hell he couldn't. Again, he lunged forward, and again, he was restrained by Ash's iron arm and Chev, who flanked his other side, boxing him in.

"Would you *listen* for once in your life?" Ash gritted.

"She's getting farther away. I'll lose her if I don't go!"

"If you try and stop her," Pen reasoned, "you will lose her for good."

"Obviously, he already has!"

Penelope silenced Ash with a look. Then, she turned her gaze back to Hurtheven. "She's given us leave to explain her actions. I intend to do so presently *if* you'll promise to be still."

"I can't simply let her leave..."

Penelope's pitying look felt like a splash of ice water.

"...What if the carriage is overtaken by highwaymen?" he asked, he thought, reasonably.

Ash rolled his eyes. "She's traveling by postchaise in daylight with armed servants and my wife. Do you think I'd permit Alicia to travel in a manner that would invite harm?"

He frowned. "*Alicia?*" He only just realized she was not present.

"We've already told you Alicia is with her." Pen sighed. "Twice."

"You mean *tried* to tell him," Ash corrected.

"Dig down, my friend." Chev's steadying voice sounded in Hurtheven's ear. "Find calm and settle. We are, of course, on your side."

Were they?

They did not feel like allies. He rather felt imprisoned. Worst still, his dearest friends were the ones standing between him and his goal.

He looked into Chev's chillingly blue gaze, reading understanding but also resolve. He might be able to overpower his friends, but not without risking wounds—physical and otherwise.

He closed his eyes.

Storm winds howled. Rain echoed all around. A wheel on a broken axel squeaked as it turned. And, deep within, a child's helpless howl.

"She's gone," he repeated weakly.

"She's gone," Chev replied. "But perhaps"—he exchanged a brief glance with Pen—"not permanently lost to you."

Ash groaned in disbelief. Hurtheven ignored him, focusing on Chev's steady gaze.

Not. Permanently. Lost.

There was something he could do, then. Chev—and, he

turned his head, Pen, dear Pen—would help him. He slackened in Ash's grip.

Chev stepped back. "Let him go, Ash."

Ash did not immediately comply.

"Let him go," Chev repeated.

"Very well." Ash released him. "But if he's off like a flash of thunder—"

"Lightning." Hurtheven rubbed his arm, slowly coming back into himself. "Like a flash of lightning. And I would be...if I was sure I could bring her back. At present, it appears I must yield to your greater understanding."

"Finally!" Chev exhaled. "Now, why don't you sit down?"

"Fetch some brandy, would you, my love?" Pen requested. "Or some stronger spirit, if there is one."

Chev snorted. "At Hevenhyll? What else would there be?"

Cabinets and glass clinked behind him. He turned his attention to Pen. "What did Miss Bythesea give you leave to explain?"

"She gave you her real name," Ash commented in surprise.

Hurtheven sent Ash a withering gaze.

"How much has she revealed?" Pen asked.

Everything. Or so he'd thought. "I cannot say, can I? ...If I don't know the whole." He ran his hand through his hair. "I was under the impression she had agreed to wed me last night."

"Last night," Ash repeated grimly. "I wager you've been bedding her longer than that."

"You're not being helpful, Ash." Chev returned with a drink.

"I *told* him to take care. He *never* listens."

"You told me to offer for her, should she and I make a carnal arrangement. Well, I *did* offer for her. Which is more than you did after *you* fuc—"

"My *wife* is present," Chev interrupted.

Hurtheven muttered an apology to Pen. Then he turned back to Ash. "You said you weren't in her confidence."

"I wasn't. And I didn't know then..." He glanced askance at Pen. "...As much as I know now."

"How much of her past did she reveal to you?" Pen asked.

"She told me she'd had an affair," Hurtheven replied.

Ash folded his arms. "That's all?"

Pen laid a silencing hand on Ash's shoulder.

Hurtheven grimaced. "Just let Ash tell me what I missed. He's dying to make me feel small."

Ash lifted a brow.

"If you can't stop yourself from glowering, would you just take yourself off?" Hurtheven demanded. "I asked her to marry me—and not because you demanded I do so, but because I love—" He shifted in his seat, moving a suspicious, defensive gaze between all three of his friends. "Because I *love* her, and I *wanted* to propose. Just tell me where to find her, would you? I will handle the rest."

Ash shook his head. "Your arrogance has saved me on more than one occasion. Saved Chev, too. Your absolute conviction that you can bend the world to your will earns you plenty of hate, but believe it or not, until today, I've always seen it as your greatest strength."

"Then *tell me* what I have done wrong!" he gritted. "Tell me so I can follow her and make things right."

Pen knelt. "She doesn't want you to follow her." She placed a hand on his knee. "If you do, you will damage her reputation and almost certainly harm her chances of getting what she truly desires."

"Hang gossips!" He frowned. "Did you say, 'what she *truly* desires'?"

Pen took a deep breath. "She has a child, Hurtheven. A child she was forced to leave with a foundling hospital. But, with Alicia's character reference, she hopes they will soon be reunited. She begged us to prevent you from interfering, because if there is *any* suggestion, she has not reformed..."

"A child?" He interrupted, amazed.

She had a *child*? And she had begged *them* to keep *him* from *interfering*?

Ever since he'd set eyes on her, a part of him had known she was *the one*. Had she felt the same? She couldn't have. She'd never trusted him at all.

"Why didn't she ask me to intervene?" he said. "No board of directors would reject *my* plea."

Ash snorted.

"I'm afraid they could and would," Chev replied. "Any suggestion that they are not keeping to their mission would put their mission—and the hundreds of innocents dependent on that mission—at risk."

Were his hands truly tied, then? Frantic for a way out, his mind circled back.

"*When* did you know?" he demanded of Ash.

"Chev and I learned for certain last week...although I have suspected since the start. When she first came to Wisterley, there were...signs she'd recently given birth. Physical signs. *That's* why I so vehemently warned you to leave her alone. I didn't know her circumstances and thought you could, unintentionally, do her grave harm."

Ah. So that's what had been behind Ash's strange behavior.

269

Hurtheven turned to Pen. "And you?"

"I've known since the morning after the garden party."

"Why...?" His voice cracked, preventing him from finishing his question. He wasn't even sure what he'd meant to ask.

Why had she told Pen and not him?

Why hadn't she trusted him?

Why had she left without a word—allowing him to be humiliated in this way? A deep, visceral shame flared in his gut. A blush licked like a flame up his neck. Horrified, he crushed the base of his palms against his burning eyes.

"Leave us," Pen ordered. "Let me talk to him alone."

"If you think it's best," Chev responded.

"I do."

Hurtheven kept his eyes on the floor as the door clicked closed. His shoulders jerked with a suppressed sob. "God *damn* it, Pen. She told *you*. Not me. Why?"

"I suspect," Pen said carefully, "she had her reasons. You had not won her confidence."

He gritted his teeth. "You could have warned me."

"When you found Chev," she reminded him, "you did not at first, reveal to me that he was alive. Why? Because it was *his* secret. *He* had to make up his own mind to come home."

She was right. Which made him angry.

"You'd known Hera for *three days*."

"And you've known her for three weeks," Pen retorted. "Think. She must have given you *some* hint."

He dragged his mind through a haze of individual memories as if tripping along a sewn seam, searching for a single, dropped stitch. Then, with a sinking feeling, he found one.

Inwardly, he cursed. "She *did* tell me. She asked me to

be the guardian of her child, and when I answered *only if there is a child,* she insisted on the phrase *any child.* Not an explicit confession, but—"

"Hurtheven," Pen said disapprovingly, "just what kind a discussion were you having?"

He swallowed. "We were negotiating."

"Negotiating?" Pen folded her arms.

"A contract...for her, ah, services."

Pen gasped. Then, she stood up in a huff.

"I *always* intended to offer for her," he defended. "In fact, I had already offered for her at that point. *She* suggested the contract."

"And that makes treating her like a doxy *better*?" She placed her hands on her hips. "You're hurting. And so, I will give you wide berth. But you should be angry—with *yourself.*"

"I bared my heart to her." Although he hadn't, had he? He inhaled sharply.

Last night, when she'd asked about his past, he'd lied.

"Apparently, you did not make her feel safe enough to bare her own!"

"Safe," he scoffed. "No one is ever *safe.*" A man can only be safe on the inside. Where he can't be—he closed his eyes, feeling wet against his lashes—*touched.* "I asked her to marry me multiple times. I practically begged."

Pen shook her head. "You have *no idea* what it is to be a woman. Her innocence was lost to circumstance, and, with it, the life that she was raised to have. And you...you perpetuated that wrong. *A contract.* I cannot *believe* you! I love you like a brother, Hurtheven, but frankly, I understand her decision."

"What," he gritted, "does that mean?"

"I certainly cannot explain—not when you aren't even

271

trying to understand. You're the sun. The whole solar system revolves around you. How could you possibly understand what it is to be earth?"

Pen turned on her heel, strode to the door, and then yanked it open. "You take him, Chev. *I* cannot make him hear. Thick headed fool that he is."

Chev hooked his finger beneath Pen's chin. "But is it truly love?"

Pen glanced back. "Yes." She exhaled. "The cut is deep."

"Leave him to me, then."

Pen nodded. And then she left.

Chev said nothing. Instead, he drew up a chair and sat quietly at Hurtheven's side. Chev's presence was a steadying force. Every challenge Hurtheven had ever faced paled when compared with all Chev had survived.

Chev radiated strength. Hurtheven halted the impulse to turn to his friend and weep in frustration and despair against his shoulder.

Instead, he asked, "How did you do it?"

"Do what?"

He turned his head. "I *know* what you've been through."

A shadow passed over Chev's features.

"Not that my current grief—"

"Grief is grief," Chev interrupted. "Let's not waste our breath weighing whose burden is heavier to bear."

"What am I to do?"

"Only you can find that answer." Chev rested his hand on Hurtheven's shoulder. "When I was at my worst—when what was inside of me had proven insufficient to the challenges I faced—all I had left was a belief in something stronger than my pain."

Hurtheven frowned. "I'm afraid I am not following."

"Let me use a metaphor, then. Remember when Odysseus tied himself to the mast?"

"Of course."

"The siren song, in this case, is a combination of grief and pain with the power to drown you. You thought you had your ears safely stuffed. You've just learned they aren't. And now, you've got to keep yourself fixed to a mast until the song has finished."

"Pen's love was your mast."

Chev nodded. "Pen's love. And—to a not lesser, but different extent—yours, Ash's, and Thaddeus's, too. The future I could have if I made it through."

"How do I reach someone who does not wish to be found?"

"She only said she did not wish to be *followed*, not *found*. Once she has secured her child, the matter might change."

Tentative hope rained down as prickles that spread across his skin.

"Perhaps," Chev continued, "a better metaphor in this case is *your* favored myth...the final labor."

"The descent into hades?"

"And back. The journey every earlier labor had trained Heracles to make. Make your own myth, my friend. I know you can."

Could he?

"She told me I was the most trustworthy man she'd ever known. And yet she didn't tell me her secret."

"So, give her *your* trust. Show her how much you need her. She is afraid. Show her you will not only accept, but embrace, her child. You would, wouldn't you?"

"Of course I would!"

He would do *anything*. And yet, he might not succeed.

He'd wished for love. If he'd known what he'd wished for would entail this—the complete upending of his world—he would never have wished it.

Only, that was a lie, too.

The last time he'd faced overwhelming odds against him, had not been by choice, but, quite literally, by accident.

Surviving horrible destruction—being changed, utterly...destroyed by knowledge of the fragility of breath, and yet having to carry on, to inhale, to return to the mundane with that new reality always pulsing, a part of his heartbeat, now.

He'd thought to mend the part of him that was Pen's.

He'd got what he wished.

And he was worse off than he'd started.

To procure a wife and an heir had felt like a simple matter of making a list. To find a love and build a life too precious to risk its loss...?

It might well destroy him.

But who was he if he did not find the courage to try?

Internally, he repeated the words he'd said to Hera. *Love will not fail.*

Nor would he.

"Will you call back the others?"

Chev smiled slowly. "Ash! Pen!"

They entered.

"Hurtheven, I think, has something to say."

Hurtheven exchanged a glance with Chev. Then, he faced his friends. "I need your help."

"What was that?" Ash put a hand to his ear. "I didn't quite understand."

"Oh, stop it," Pen scolded. She smiled radiantly and

then held out her hand. "Of course, we'll help you—in any way you require."

* * *

So far, the two-day journey to London had been fraught. Hera had done a good deal of hidden-as-best-she-could weeping, only to have Alicia encourage her to give way to her sentiments, assuring her that airing them would purge them.

Hera knew better.

The pain she was experiencing was pain that would never heal. At best, she must learn to live with the constant ache.

However, she'd found in Alicia, a sympathetic ear. The duchess did not question nor criticize her decision, although she made it clear that she did not agree with Hera's portrait of Hurtheven.

"You had to think of Annis first, dearest," Alicia said. "As a mother, I can fully understand. However, you cannot anticipate all the possibilities that you'll find open to you. Hurtheven may surprise you yet."

Hera touched her crumpled handkerchief to her nose to hide her doubt.

The only way Hurtheven would see her again is if they'd created a child last night. And even then, she was not sure, under the circumstances, he would renew his offer to wed.

She'd been a coward for asking the others to tell him the whole. She'd wanted to spare herself the scene. And she'd thought it best that the news be delivered by his friends.

Now, she wished she had found the courage. She wished she'd forced him to voice his ultimate rejection.

Perhaps the pain of it would have made this other pain more bearable.

"Thank you for your many kindnesses." Hera leaned back against the cushions, taking in the view outside. "You needn't have come. I'm sure you will miss the children."

"I already miss them! But"—she chuckled to herself— "I'm sure you noted how thrilled they were to have another week at Hevenhyll before returning with their father to Wisterley. I will see them soon enough. And you must promise to visit."

"I will." When there would be no danger of seeing Hurtheven.

"And now, you must turn your mind to your most urgent tasks—reacquainting yourself with your child and settling into your new life." She gently and kindly redirected Hera's attention.

And so, they talked of other things, mostly pertaining to the rearing of a young child. If the directors made a definitive decision, she'd have Annis safely at home just before her first birthday.

"Tell me again about the boardinghouse?" Hera asked.

"From the outside, it appears to be just as it was built, the home of a family of means. But internally, the inner sleeping apartments have been transformed into suites of rooms. Each with a bedchamber, a dressing room, and a parlor. Meals are shared in the main dining hall. And residents, I'm told, often gather in the downstairs parlor at night."

Cautiously, Hera allowed herself to dream.

Her grandmother—Mrs. Grant—had owned and lived in the house Alicia described. She'd been the granddaughter of a country squire—her father, his youngest son. She'd married a wealthy merchant, and they'd had one child,

Hera's mother. Hera's grandfather, the merchant, had been the moralist who cast out his child.

Hera's grandmother had not been of the same mind.

After Mr. Grant's death, Mrs. Grant had turned their home into a boarding house for unwed mothers and widows. She'd written to Hera's father.

Hera would never know what, if, or how her father had replied.

Imagine! A grandmother who would have taken her in, only a mile's walk from where Hera had resided with her brother. They might have passed each other in the market or stood in line awaiting a fresh cup of milk!

In any event, her grandmother had willed Hera the whole, with the caveat that the home retain its current purpose. What was left over would be just enough for Hera to support herself and her daughter in a modest fashion.

She and Annis, they would be safe.

The sum bequeathed wasn't anywhere near what Hurtheven had written in the contract, but Hera did not intend to demand that right.

In fact, at the moment, she couldn't bear the thought of being in contact with him at all.

* * *

After a gruelingly suspenseful hearing—made only somewhat less potentially hazardous by Hera's changed circumstance—and the full repayment of all expenses the foundling hospital had spent on Annis's care, Hera was able to legally reclaim her daughter.

Soon, they were happily settled in their new apartments. With a competent housekeeper in charge of the day-to-day running of the boardinghouse, Hera was able to fully focus on her child.

Annis, at first, was a serious little thing...shy and quiet and reticent. Hardly surprising, given her early circumstances. Hour by hour, however, the tension was draining out of her little body, though she still kept a tight grip on any part of Hera she could grab.

But she did venture an occasional smile.

Hera was content. Each time she gazed into her child's wide, blue eyes; her bruised heart surged with love. They *would* heal.

They would heal together, just the two of them.

Hera had stifled a tear when her courses came. She hadn't wanted a pregnancy to force either her or the duke's hand, although she hadn't realized until that moment that a part of her had been holding out hope...

She sighed, brushed Annis cheek with her knuckle. The baby gurgled at the sound of a knock on the door.

"Shall I answer?" Hera asked.

Annis drooled in reply.

Hera kissed the child's head before opening the door.

"Ma'am." A housemaid bobbed a curtsy. "You've a visitor." The young woman's eyes were wide. "A *duchess*."

Odd. She'd parted ways with Alicia, the Duchess of Ashbey, more than a week ago...just after the successful hearing.

"I will go down presently. Would you mind watching Annis?"

The maid brightened. "Not at all! She's never any trouble." She smiled down at the child. "Are you?"

Annis bubbled her lips and *coo*ed.

When Hera entered the parlor, she wasn't greeted by

the Duchess of Ashbey's petite form, but by the willowy figure of Penelope, Duchess of Ithwick.

"Your Grace." She curtsied.

"Penelope, please." Penelope crossed the room and took both Hera's hands into her own. "I trust everything has been arranged to your satisfaction?"

"Oh, yes! We are—Annis and I—quite content."

Penelope lowered her chin and gazed deeply into Hera's eyes. "*Are* you?"

Hera withdrew her hands. "Won't you sit down?"

They took chairs opposite the fire. The clock ticked away an uncomfortable silence. How long was the appropriate length of a morning call? A quarter hour. Surely she could survive fifteen minutes without mentioning—

"I've come here today on a very specific errand," Penelope interrupted her thoughts. "A mutual friend asked me to plead his case."

Hera inhaled sharply.

"I'm far too direct," Pen said sympathetically, "I know. I wasn't raised to soften the truth. And, in this case, I see no reason to temporize, nor is there any cause for explanations if you are dead set against the renewal of his acquaintance."

Feeling overrun by a verbal carriage, Hera could only blink.

"*Would* you consider giving Hurtheven another chance?" Penelope pressed.

She'd wanted to give him a chance, but he'd *lied*.

She looked away, stopping the words from spilling forth. Whatever the duke had or had not shared with her, she did not wish to discuss the subject with anyone else—especially not the woman he loved.

She frowned. Of all people to send! She glanced back angrily. "He is in love with *you*."

Penelope's jaw dropped. She quickly recovered. "He *thought* he was," she said slowly, "at one time. But that was a long time ago. And, in my opinion, not at all the same kind of attachment he shares with you."

"But I *heard* you acknowledge his affection..."

The duchess frowned. "Impossible!"

"...the night before I left. He was coming up the stairs, you were coming down from the nursery."

"Ah." Penelope lifted her brows. "While I cannot recall the specifics of our exchange, I believe you must have misread the situation."

"I *saw* him. I saw the way he was looking up at you..."

"Oh, Hera." Penelope shook her head. "He was looking up at the shadow of a woman coming down from the nursery. What *I* distinctly remember is the way his face fell when he realized it was me—not you—descending the stairs..."

Could that be true?

"...I had suspected his affections were fixed at dinner, but when I saw his expression, I knew for certain he'd finally fallen in love. What's more, he realized I knew. Whatever words we exchanged were in that vein..."

Hera covered her mouth. That radiant look of expectation had been for *her*?

She didn't believe.

She couldn't.

"...I was, at once, relieved—I cannot express *how* relieved. For years, I've prayed he would find someone to love. Someone who could love him back with equal fervor. But I could never quite imagine him finding among his acquaintance the kind of person who could see past the bravado to the heart within. You are that person. What you heard was me, expressing my relief, and wishing you both happiness."

"But I saw his list—"

"The list, my husband assures me, was the result of teasing. The boys are merciless with one another, you know."

"The *boys*?"

She shrugged. "They were still boys when I met them. Three sixteen-year-old boys who thought disrupting a public assembly a lark." She smiled at the memory. "To hear Chev tell the tale, two of them fell instantly in love with me, but only his was true love."

"Why didn't you fall for Hurtheven?"

Pen chuckled. "Spoken like a woman who cannot fathom that everyone does not see the brilliance of her shining star. I didn't choose Hurtheven because I didn't even *see* Hurtheven." Her gaze unfocused. She smiled. "When Chev is in the room, I *still* don't see anyone else. Don't get me wrong, I do love Hurtheven. As I've told you before, he was a rock in my time of trouble. I just don't love him, well, the way *you* love him."

Hera stiffened. "I've never said I loved him."

Pen gave her a pitying glance.

"Oh, very well," she conceded. "I do."

Penelope grinned in triumph. "Will you give him a second chance?"

She chewed her lip. Loving him and trusting him were a far cry from one another. "How did he react when you told him about Annis?"

"He was *devastated* that you left...I've never seen him so distraught. Chev and Ash had to combine their strength to hold him back from chasing after you."

Devastated?

"And when I told him about Annis, he was, at first,

angry you had not confided in him, but his anger turned quickly inward. He knows he has only himself to blame. *Believe* me—he knows."

She'd been blaming him, too. The idea of him dwelling in self-recrimination, however, gave her pain. "And is he recovering?"

"What do you think the answer to that question is?"

Hera didn't immediately reply.

"Perhaps," Penelope continued, "I had better put it this way—he has recovered as well as you have, which is, I think, not at all."

Hera lifted her chin. "He hasn't written."

"Until Alicia returned, none of us knew if the hearing had been successful. He did not want to mar your chances."

She glanced up. "He could have written since."

"He sent me. I rather think he didn't trust his eloquence to be as convincing."

"Hurtheven," Hera said in disbelief, "didn't trust his own eloquence?"

"Shocking, I know." Penelope nodded. "His arrogance has completely disappeared, at least in this, his most important calling."

"And have you delivered his message?"

"Now, let me see.... I believe his exact instructions were to ask permission for him to pay court—a courtship, of course, that will include your daughter."

Hera's hand had unwittingly crept up to rest against her heart. She could hardly believe what she heard.

"If you'd like my opinion, I think you should marry Hurtheven." Pen unknowingly echoed her interpretation of Ash's words to the duke.

You should marry, Hurtheven.

You should marry Hurtheven.

Hera gave a short, involuntary laugh. "I didn't know how much trouble could be caused by a preposition and a comma."

Pen wrinkled her brow. "Pardon?"

"Never mind." Hera pressed her hand against her cheek. "For now, tell him this—I would be honored to present him to Annis."

Chapter Thirteen

"Well, son." Sir Lawton handed Hurtheven a set of keys, stretching his arm over the expanse of his large desk inside the home office. "I don't know what you think you will find in the house we leased to Prince Karl while he was in London—nor do I understand your reason for being inquisitive, but now that his death has been confirmed, you are welcome to look."

Hurtheven nodded. The keys jangled as he slipped them into his pocket. "Are you sure nothing about his death was suspicious at all?"

Sir Lawton lifted a brow. "You knew him better—Karl had plenty of enemies. But, at present, it looks like a case of footpads."

His godfather wasn't an expressive man, but there was something in the way the man's eyes shifted that made Hurtheven believe he hadn't been told the whole.

No matter.

Prince Karl could no longer hurt Hera or her child, and

that was all that mattered to him. ...but it wouldn't be all that mattered to Hera.

"And what has the home office learned of his children?" Hurtheven asked.

Sir Lawton glanced up sharply. "Did you meet his children when you were in Vienna?"

"No," Hurtheven replied carefully. "But I've...an interest."

"They were, to the best of my knowledge, given over to their mother's family," Sir Lawton replied. "The family resides in Switzerland, just outside Geneva."

They were safe.

His former guardian templed his fingers in a way Hurtheven knew well. Sir Lawton then waited for Hurtheven to reveal the purpose of his inquiries.

Suddenly, Hurtheven was again a young boy.

Unsure of how much he should reveal, given that he had not yet spoken with Hera, he held his silence. Instead, he reached out and straightened the ink tray on Lawton's desk.

"I trust Ithwick and Ashbey are well?" Lawton asked, finally.

"Thriving," Hurtheven answered. "I spent a good deal of time with Ashbey's children of late."

"And"—Lawton cleared his throat—"with their governess?"

Hurtheven frowned.

"You may stop going through your mental list of those in your employ, searching for disloyalty. *You* asked me to discover all I could about Karl's current whereabouts, and the time he spent in London. You must have known *I* would be interested in the reason."

Given the light that had entered the older man's eyes,

Hurtheven decided that lying to him would be useless as well as dishonorable.

"Not governess." He held his guardian's gaze. "Nurse-maid, in this case. She served as nursemaid to Ash's children. Now, she is their *former* nursemaid. And, should things proceed as I anticipate, she will be my wife. I will not be as often at the disposal of the home office."

"I see."

He suspected Lawton did *see*. "Nothing is yet settled, however."

"In your hands, I trust any troubles will be taken care of. There will, I believe, be a..."

Hurtheven lifted his brows.

"...*minor* scandal."

"One I expect to survive."

"I suppose this is better than requiring my services to, say, arrange to avoid a court martial, bring a man back from the dead, or cover up a war hero's familial negligence?"

Hurtheven had, over the course of the prior decade, made each of those requests on behalf of either Chev, or Ash.

"I've asked you nothing for myself," he said stiffly. "Ever. Nor do I intend to do so."

Had Lawton's eyes softened?

Hurtheven sighed. "*If* all goes well, I will also be taking a bastard child as my ward."

"Ah." The fingers templed again. "The child of the governess-in-this-case-nursemaid...Karl's child."

Hurtheven's cheek went taut. "The *gentlewoman*. And, once the matter is settled, I will consider the child mine."

Lawton gazed out the window, for a long silent moment. His gaze hazed, as if in memory...or in calculation.

Hurtheven would not be moved. Not even by this man—to whom he owed his survival, his education, and his pride.

Lawton sighed. "At least it's not the pig farmer's daughter."

Hurtheven bristled.

Lawton waved his hand. "I mean no insult. The Duchess of Ithwick has been a credit to the name. For your part, I had wished for a better alliance. But..."

"But?"

"...your father would have counseled you to follow your heart, and so I will do the same. Will I like her, do you think?"

"Do you plan to publicly countenance the match?" Hurtheven asked, surprised.

"*If* you succeed in convincing her." Lawton chuckled. "Her standards might be too high to accept a rascal like yourself." His expression gentled. "Hurtheven, my boy, when have I ever given you reason to suppose I would not lend you my support in anything that mattered to you?"

Hurtheven shifted uncomfortably in the chair. "Never."

"It is *you* who have insisted on solitude."

"I know," he acknowledged finally. "And I have my just desserts. She won't take me by halves."

Lawton's smile slowly spread. "Well, then, son, you had better find a way to give her the whole."

"It's what I intend," he said.

They shared a drink together, then...a toast to his success. Soon, he was on his way. As the boardinghouse came into view, his confidence completely left him. He had no idea how—or if—he was going to succeed.

* * *

The downstairs parlor of the boardinghouse—*Hera's* boardinghouse—was modestly furnished, although the paneling and the mantle suggested the dwelling had once had grander pretentions.

His gaze traveled through the room, unintentionally identifying each article of furniture. Hera's chair. Hera's table. Hera's rug. Hurtheven was conscious of a feeling of discomfort—of taking up space in a place he neither belonged, nor could command.

He shoved one hand into his pocket and, with the other, gripped a chair.

He—who prided himself on his perception—had never truly experienced the humbling nature of existing under someone else's roof. Even when Hurtheven had been a boy, Sir Lawton had taken up residence at Hevenhyll, though matters of business necessitated his frequent absences. There had never been a question of the Duke of Hurtheven —no matter how young Godric had been when he'd subsumed the title—leaving his domain.

The final labor.

Although this, of course, was not the descent into hell. That would come later. What had he told her once? That love would not fail, but courage might. He'd no idea how prescient his words.

When she entered, he was glad he'd taken hold of the chair. Two weeks, that was all they'd shared at Hevenhyll. And yet, his body reacted not dissimilarly than when, after a seven-year absence, he'd found the presumed-dead Chev very much alive in a smuggler's cottage on the coast.

The back of his knees weakened. His mouth lost moisture. He braced his shoulders and leaned on the chair for support.

"Your Grace." She curtsied.

Curtsied. The gulf between them yawned wider than ever.

"Mrs—" He realized he didn't know which name she'd chosen to use.

"Montrose," she finished.

"Hera," he said weakly.

She closed the door behind her and then drank him in with wary eyes. "Won't you have a seat?"

He'd prepared a speech. He'd forgotten every word. His hands had grown damp. His heart thrummed faster than a hummingbird's wings. What would he do if she denied him?

"Are you...and your daughter...comfortable here?" he asked.

"In the boarding house, yes," she replied. "Other mothers live here. Some widows, some...not. We look after one another's children. Annis is, at present, gone with one of them to the park. But if you'd come back tomorrow..."

"I am anxious to meet Annis, and conscious of the honor—"

Her brows scrunched skeptically together.

"—but I also wish to satisfy myself that *you* are well."

"I am..." She dropped her gaze. "...content."

Was she content? Was she trying to tell him she no longer needed, nor wanted him? "The neighborhood seems—"

"I realize it's not in the *first* stare of fashion," she interrupted. "But do not suggest it is *bad.*" She pursed her lips and a tell-tale flush of anger flared within her cheeks. "Oh, certainly, it is not as gleaming as Mayfair, but neither do the people who live here have armies of servants at their disposal. It is *not* inherently bad, it is simply *neglected.*"

He blinked. "I—I wasn't about to cast aspersions."

"I apologize." Her shoulders slumped as if a wind had shifted course, deflating her anger. "I am, perhaps, overly alert to criticism."

"I am quite familiar with the state, as you know." He smiled wryly. "I only wish to be assured that you...you *and* your daughter...are safe."

She did not return his smile. "You have no obligation to either of us. That last night..." She bit her lip. "There is no consequence."

His heart sank. His purpose, however, remained strong. "We have an agreement. A contract, in fact—"

"That's over," she interrupted again.

"I pledged you my word as a matter of honor," he reminded quietly. "I promised to serve as guardian to any child of yours."

"Please, Hurtheven."

Please, what? "You have a right to rage at me, and I, a responsibility to absorb the blows, but if you think I am going to voluntarily walk away to spare you the embarrassment of telling me explicitly to leave you alone, you are mistaken."

She swallowed roughly. "I should not have left the explanation to others."

"And I should not have assumed you'd be happy to wed me. I—I thought your refusal modesty on your part. If I had known the truth—"

"You would have simply accepted me and my bastard child?"

"Again, I agreed to serve as guardian, did I not?"

Her expression blanked. "You did not know then that I conceived Annis before I knew you."

"I wish you had told me." He palmed his hands together in a prayerful, pleading manner. "Hera...keep me at arm's length if you must but allow me to perform this service. The Chancery, I believe, regularly handles such matters."

"You would do that...because of the contract?"

"I would do that, because I love you. I want to marry you. But, if you can tell me honestly that you do not love me, I will content myself with performing the service I've already pledged."

She turned away. "If we marry, there'd be a scandal."

"And?"

"You don't know what you're asking. *You* cannot know what scandal truly means. You have never had the circumstances of your life—your failures, your poor judgment—laid out before a panel of people predisposed to think ill of you. If you had, you would no longer simply dismiss opinion as something easily ignored."

He could not imagine how painful the hearing had been for her. He took a step toward her. She flinched. *Very well.* He folded his hands behind his back, and, since he could not hold her, he tightly gripped his fingers.

"I doubt there is anyone alive who has never faltered in their character. The foibles we allow for in our friends we call," he paused for emphasis, "intolerable arrogance in others."

"I'm sorry I called you arrogant."

"You were not wrong. I *am* arrogant. I have—by deliberate cultivation as well as by the privilege of my birth—an *almost* unshakable confidence. But what I *do not* do...what I would *never* do is assume other's lives are of less value than my own."

"Odd for an aristocrat. Even odder for a duke."

"Thank the army of servants who raised me, then."

She stared down at the hand-woven carpet beneath her

feet, her face averted from his scrutiny. "I could not bear you coming to shame in the same way I have."

"And I," he retorted, "cannot bear to be parted from you."

"We are at an impasse, then."

"A standstill, more like. We will move as soon as we wish to move."

She raised her gaze. "You are...difficult to deny."

He half-smiled. "I know."

She sniffed. "What do you want from me?"

Everything. "Two things, for now—your permission to pursue guardianship and the chance to court you."

"And if I decline?"

"You may, of course, decline either point, but if you do so, you must swear you are refusing me because your heart is not engaged—and not for *my* own good. I treated you as if I knew better what was best for you than you knew for yourself. Don't do me the same bad turn."

She sighed. "Thank you for acknowledging as much."

"However, before you make your decision, I have another wrong I must confess." He grasped for a way to broach the difficult subject. "I should have told you my intentions first—if I had you might have even told me the truth then. And, from this day forward, I promise I will."

"What did you do?" she asked with alarm.

"While you were still at Hevenhyll, I asked my godfather—through the home office—to locate Prince Karl."

"No!"

He winced. "It could have gone badly, I now understand. And I profoundly apologize. I will not make decisions on your behalf in the future. But the result is this, he cannot harm you any longer. He is dead."

"Dead," she echoed, wide-eyed.

"He was set upon on route home from Vienna. He did not survive. And you need not be concerned for his children. They are with their mother's family in Switzerland."

She felt her way to the settee as if blind to her surroundings. Then she sat. Her faraway expression fixed on something that was not presently in the room. Something he could neither see nor share.

He took the seat beside her. "May I," he swallowed, "hold your hand?"

She looked down at the appendage in question as if surprised to see her own fingers. She flexed them, tightened them into a fist, and then finally, slowly, placed her loose fist into his open palm.

He held her one hand in both of his own and then tentatively threaded their fingers together. "I *am* sorry," he said. "Whatever you felt for him, I am certain his death has come as a shock."

"A shock." She wet her lips. "Yes."

"I *thought*," he said haltingly, "under the circumstances, you might wish to revisit the house."

"The house?"

"The house he let while living in London. I have the keys. But if you do not wish to return..."

He felt the blood in his cheeks.

What had he been thinking? He'd kept the literally wrecked pieces of his past—but had revisiting them ever eased the pain? *No.* Why would she wish to revisit the place where she'd suffered so much?

"...I thought taking you there might be a way to reckon with the past. A terrible idea, on reflection. An impertinent presumption."

"No." She placed her free hand on top of his. "I—I

believe I *would* like to return. If, that is"—she raised her face—"you would come with me."

Dawning hope felt like a raw abrasion. "Of course."

* * *

The wheels of Hurtheven's carriage rumbled over London's cobblestone streets carrying Hera back into the heart of her past. Karl's former townhome had, at first, represented a place she could begin anew, a place she could earn her way and become, if not self-sufficient, at least independent of a brother who had never asked for, nor relished, her presence in his house.

Her life certainly had taken a turn under those eaves.

Karl. Dead.

The idea was bewildering. How could someone who had exerted so much influence in her life be, simply, gone?

Hera searched her heart for some greater feeling than relief—something that could capture the complexity of what she felt for the father of her child. The most gracious emotion she could define, however, was pity. Pity that he'd never have the chance to become a man who made *himself* proud.

His death was a waste of life. A waste of power and vigor.

Her heart was...

Bruised? Aching?

She wasn't sure. But facing the literal architecture of her past would help her find some measure of peace. How had Hurtheven understood she'd have this need? Because he'd kept the evidence of his own worse nightmare?

She glanced askance.

Hurtheven's head was turned toward the street. She

could not see his face, only the black curls hugging his collar, a stark contrast to the snowy white lawn of his shirt. She had armored herself against him when he'd first appeared, ready to do as she thought she must and send him on his way once again. Of course, that armor had failed.

She was glad for his presence. Glad he'd anticipated this need. Even if she had still not fully forgiven him for approaching his godfather with matters that were her concern and her concern alone.

Strange to be thought of in such a way.

Sitting next to a man whose silent, solid presence was a comfort beyond words. The burdens of life seemed lighter when he was near.

"Arranging for me to visit the house was"—she paused— "thoughtful of you."

He turned. His expression was unreadable.

"I'm a little afraid," she added.

"You'll be fine." He placed his gloved hand over her own. "And should you need me, I will be by your side."

Once they'd entered the house, she wasn't interested in the grand parlors, the gilded ballroom, or the long, state dining table, its chairs now draped in holland covers—none of those places had formed the most significant of her experiences in this house.

The servants' stair, however, she remembered well.

She led him through high-ceilinged, empty rooms. until they found the dark concealed passage where their footsteps no longer echoed on marble but clicked against worn wood.

Up, up they climbed until they'd reached the highest floor. Then she wove through the narrow corridor to just the right door. She let go, and he transferred his palm to the small of her back. The single point of warm solace gave her strength.

Cautiously, she stepped inside.

The air crowded around her. She inhaled damp heaviness into her lungs.

The room had no windows, but above them winked a patch of sky. She'd expected to feel sad, perhaps even angry. But the prickle in her neck, the heaviness in her heart was more akin to resignation.

She'd been telling herself she'd had a choice the night Karl had first entered this room. She knew now that the answer was less simple.

The house had been Karl's. The position she held, Karl's.

Yes, she'd lifted the covers and welcomed him into that little bed because she'd resolved to do so, but also because the alternative to these four walls had been too vast, too unknown, and too frightening to bear.

Could Hurtheven see? Could he appreciate what she'd experienced in this place?

She turned to face him. He was looking up into the skylight. Muted rays fell onto his shoulders making sharp shallows that rendered his face severe. His jaw flexed.

He'd stopped breathing.

Surprising tears gathered in her eyes. "This room felt safe." She refused to let them fall. "Until it did not."

His face was dark, his expression grim. He glanced back up at that square of light, then over to the bed, and then back into her eyes.

Fleetingly, she remembered how she'd felt when she'd seen the carriage wreck. Well, this was *her* wreck. The secret she carried.

The pain she'd expected never to share.

"It's hard to breathe in here," he said softly.

"I know."

"I didn't understand."

"I know that as well." She turned back toward the bed. "The walls constrict not just the body, but the soul."

She attempted to recall the times she'd found pleasure with Karl, but reality stripped her excuses. Beneath them she finally found her anger, although Hurtheven was the one to give that fury voice.

"I want to burn this place to the ground," he said.

"Me, too," she agreed. She faced him again. "I appreciate the sentiment. But there are thousands and thousands of these rooms. There are rooms like this in your very house."

He pressed his lips together. Then, he nodded. "I recognize something I hadn't before."

He did. She could see it in his eyes. The shock. The sadness. He'd linked her pain to his own. He would never know completely what it was to have no good choices and no means of self-support, but he would try. He was, right now, doing his best.

"I didn't fully appreciate the power I held over you," he said. "Accepting your suggestion of a contract was ghastly."

"I think you were rather pleased with the idea of saving me."

He winced. "You might be right. Only, you didn't need saving, did you? You'd survived so much already on your own."

"I don't need you to *solve* me or save me."

What she needed was a friend. A person she could trust with her secrets and who would trust her with his own.

"Hurtheven, had you ever drawn up that sort of contract before?"

He shook his head no.

"You *never* kept a mistress?"

"I've had lovers. But a mistress? No."

"Because of Penelope?"

"Not just," he replied. "I hadn't room for any long-term intimate connection. I was too busy searching for some dramatic challenge that would make everything else disappear. I both longed for—and feared—another strike that would change everything."

He fingered the slip of hair at her throat.

"Then, I saw you. You had on a hideous green dress. A coarse apron. An unappealing cap with a drooping fringe. You'd tucked up your skirts, ready to plunge into the hedge, only, being the chivalrous man I am, I saved you the trouble."

Her gaze softened.

"You were right. I loved Penelope. I loved her so deeply that my life changed. But I've never felt like this—like I've lived thousands and thousands of lifetimes, and that the point of every one of them was to find you."

"You truly wish to wed me, and intend to accept Annis into your home?"

He nodded.

"I'm not a suitable duchess."

"I won't tell you I don't care what other people think—I do. Everyone should..."

She frowned.

"...But only if those 'others' are trusted, respected friends who know you well and who are motivated by a desire for your happiness."

"Ashbey. Ithwick."

He nodded. "And Alicia. And Pen. And my godfather."

"Your godfather?"

"Yes—the man who served as my testamentary guardian. And, before you suggest that he will protest. I have already told him that I intend to marry you, and I intend to claim our child. That is, if you love me."

"*Our* child?"

"In my heart, already, and for the world—she will be nothing less."

Ah, Godric. He'd laid before her almost everything she wanted. But she couldn't trust him with her life, with Annis. Not yet.

"I brought you up here to show you my greatest pain...even though you've never trusted me with your own. How can I tell you I love you...how can I be sure you love me...until you share your own secrets with me?"

Chapter Fourteen

Hurtheven stared down at the soft fawn leather exquisitely fitted around Hera's fingers. She hadn't worn gloves like this before. They were part of the life she'd created without him. She didn't need him any longer.

And yet, she'd asked him to accompany her here.

He hadn't expected her to invite him into the heart of her pain.

He could see the smallness of the world she'd had to live in. The lack of hope. In this room, she'd had nowhere to turn and nothing that could save her but the strength within her own mind.

He *did* understand, but he could see her doubt. If he didn't find a way to show her, he might lose her. This was a pivotal moment. So why were his eyes fixed to her hand?

He raised his gaze to hers.

In shock, he realized that this descent into hades was not about finding a way for her to face her worst pain but was, rather, meeting her challenge to revisit his own. She knew what he hid. Somehow, she knew. But she needed him to tell her. She needed him to explain.

He'd wanted to share the nightmare with her before but how could he? The memory was *sound*—not words. Squealing wheels. Endless rain. Helplessness beyond expression of any kind.

A noise came from his throat. An odd sort of squeak that made him shudder.

Breathe.

What existed between them, what bound them together was love, and love wasn't softness and light and beauty. Love was risk and vulnerability. Everything could change in a moment.

In a flash.

He'd seen life itself snuffed for the first time in a coach, but many times since. To keep others safe was his chosen calling. And to do so, he'd thought he had to keep this particular memory boxed.

But to allow himself to be loved was to resurrect the part of the little boy that had died that night in the carriage. To resurrect the part of himself that had shrunk to near nothing because of that boy's raw terror.

"You asked me to tell you something even my closest friends don't know."

"I did," she answered slowly.

"As lovers we *should* share..." His voice cracked. He cleared his throat. "What I mean is, your inclination to ask was a natural one. My refusal was cowardice."

"You are anything but a coward," she whispered.

A carriage wheel squeaked. Inside the suffocating room it was raining. And dark. And cold. He swallowed through a throat raw from yelling.

"Godric"—her hand was warm against his neck—"I've seen the carriage."

"How?"

"The children—it doesn't matter. But I've seen it, do you understand? You don't have to explain."

"*I can't*," his voice cracked. "Not because I don't trust you. Not because I don't want to explain. I *can't* because I don't remember. Not in words or even in pictures. We were jostling along. My parents were laughing. And then...nothing..."

She lifted herself to her toes and touched her forehead to his.

"...No." His voice cracked. "Not nothing. My own, terrified screams. Sometimes, I move outside of myself, and I hear them still..."

She wrapped her arms around him.

"...Now, you're the only one who knows."

Inside he was hollow, the emptiness that had overwhelmed him the first time she asked him to reveal himself had opened a crack at the very center of his soul. Now that he had told her, the fissure widened. He was helpless again. He couldn't even hold her back.

She moved him...somewhere. Because his legs didn't need his strength any longer. He must be sitting. Was he sitting? He didn't care.

"They left you," he heard.

"Yes," he choked.

"In an instant."

The words were brutal truth, but the voice who spoke them was soft, almost soothing.

"Grieve, now," the voice insisted. "It's time—*oh Godric* —far past time for you to grieve."

She sounded as if she were in deep distress. She *must* be

disturbed because she was crying. He felt the wetness on his cheek. But when he would have brushed away the damp, he discovered the tears were his own.

He blinked at his hand.

What? His fingers were moving. Trembling. Then, his shoulders jerked as well. His body would not heed the inner command to be still.

Some horrible sound was ripping from the empty place inside—pried, unwilling, from the deep. A horrible, ugly moan. A sound containing all his loss.

But no. Not all.

Because more terrible sobs followed, each coming faster than the last. They rode him until every part of him felt bruised and broken.

And then, something landed in his lap. Hot, pliant straps wound about his thighs and his shoulders, and he found himself securely bundled against something soft and warm, vibrating with his name.

And that something bound him together as the storm around him roiled.

Godric. I'm sorry. I'm so sorry. Godric. They loved you. They wouldn't have left if they'd had a choice. Godric. Godric. Godric.

And then, the words that gave the disembodied voice a name.

"Godric, *I* love you. You're *not* alone anymore. Do you understand? I love you and, and, as much as in my power, I will never leave you again."

Hera.

The sobs receded, leaving him gasping for air.

"Hera." He didn't recognize his own voice.

"Yes," She pulled back, hands clasping his face. "Did you hear me? Did you understand?"

Hear her. *Yes.* Yes, he had. She'd said she loved him.

"I'll tell you what I tell myself," she said. "You only feel like you're going to break apart. You won't. I won't let you."

"You left me," he said stupidly. Plaintively. He could not think of anything else to say.

"Only because I thought...well, I didn't understand. But I do now. I *swear* I do."

Was she *straddling* him?

Her face was white and worried. And her eyes, shining with tears of her own. She'd just sworn to something. *Understanding me.*

"I understand," she repeated.

"I know." A spark flared within like stricken flint. His arms, no longer limp as a marionette's, encircled her waist. His hand slowly inched up her back, proving she was present. And real. And unharmed. His fingers reached her shoulder, and he clasped her hard. "I know."

"Oh, thank heaven," she turned her face against his shoulder.

How had he thought love a lightning strike—something swift and destructive?

Love was standing inside the brightest, most shocking, life-ending stream of energy, spreading one's arms, and saying—with total faith in something larger and incomprehensible than one's self—*I'm here.* I'm ready.

He had power.

He had charm and presence and a pleasing appearance. He'd sought out and cultivated the closest of friendships. As for how the rest of the world related to him, well, he was either beloved by people who craved his notice or derided by those who envied his fortune, his appeal, or both.

But no one had ever looked into his eyes and said, simply, "you."

Not out of desire, but out of recognition.

He hadn't realized. His whole life, he'd been waiting to be seen.

He'd been waiting for his match.

He'd been waiting for her.

He listened for the sound of the rain. For the squeaking wheel. There was only silence. Silence. And the beat of Hera's heart.

"Hera," he whispered. "My darling."

* * *

"I wanted to tell you that last night at Hevenhyll, but I couldn't find the words..." Hurtheven sighed. "And I suppose I didn't want you to see me as helpless."

Hera brushed his hair away from his face, her fingers shaking with relief. He'd come back. He'd come back to her.

"I don't see you as helpless," she said. "I never could."

"I never told anyone I'd any memory of the night at all," he continued. "The people of Hevenhyll—they needed me to be strong."

"And you were. You are. They love you."

"I love you," he replied.

"And, I you."

They held each other in silence until his breath evened and his temperature cooled. Then, he withdrew a handkerchief and wiped her face before tending to his own.

"More than you bargained for, I wager."

"Never," she replied. "But let us leave this place."

He nodded. "Let's."

They held tightly to one another's hand as they retraced their steps through the house. And, when they reemerged into the light of day, they emerged together.

She stilled on the stairway. "May I have a moment alone?"

"Of course," he replied.

With a backward glance that was both sympathy and support, he meandered back toward the carriage. She sent him a reassuring smile and then faced the house.

"Goodbye, Karl," she whispered. "You were little more than a selfish scoundrel, but I thank you for Annis. She's going to have a beautiful life." She glanced over her shoulder. "And a fine father."

She exhaled her regrets, turned toward her future feeling lighter than she had in weeks. Hurtheven handed her back into his carriage.

"You know, *duke*," she teased. "I can almost believe you have changed."

"I *have* changed."

"People don't."

"*I* am not people."

She chuckled half-heartedly. "Perhaps not totally changed."

"Would you want me to?"

"Godric," she said under her breath. "What am I to do with you?"

His expression turned serious. "Give me a chance? Is that fair?"

"Fair," she breathed. "Do you care?"

"Very much so. I want a wife—an ally, an accomplice, and even, dare I hope, a friend."

She lowered her lashes. "And a lover?"

"Yes, of course." He touched her cheek. "Though we'll have none of that until marriage."

"*None* of that?"

"Well," he smiled crookedly. "*Nearly* none."

He leaned over and kissed her lightly on the lips. She hummed in response. "I've missed you." She kissed him back. "And this..."

She angled her body and took him into a deeper embrace.

"I can feel that," she murmured.

He chuckled. "It's just a tool. And only one of many..."

She snorted.

"In all seriousness...you've a life—a home." He searched her eyes. "I will love you for all of my lifetime, but, if you prefer to remain independent..."

Oh—she tilted her head—*what a valiant effort at humility*. She was touched. Truly moved. But she did not believe him in the least.

"Really, Godric! And here I was hoping to find you building willow cabins at my gate."

His mouth quirked, "I might, to borrow further from the quote, 'Halloo your name to the reverberate hills,' or,"—his eyes twinkled—"across my mountain."

"Ohhh!" She laughed. "I'd forgotten about your *mountain*."

"I *did* list my mountain as an asset."

"You *did*, didn't you?" She sighed. "How pleasant it would be to have a mountain of my very own!" She glanced askance. "Unfortunately, you're far too honorable for bribery."

"Not in the least. In your case, I'm perfectly willing to bribe. I will write up a contract..."

"Don't you *dare*," she warned. But she was smiling. "I think Annis and I must take you for our own—if only to protect the rest of our sex."

"Hera...are you certain?"

"Well, first, you must get Annis's approval."

"Is she bribable, too?"

She drummed her fingers thoughtfully. "She *does* have a penchant for being rocked."

"Then I will rock her as much as she wishes. I'm very good with children, you know."

"I've heard that about you." She patted his cheek. "But aren't you getting ahead of yourself? You haven't yet asked *me* the question, have you?"

He glanced rather doubtfully at the floor. "Difficult to go down on one knee in a carriage."

"Too arrogant? I under—"

He whipped around and knelt on the carriage floor.

"Hurtheven! You'll muddy your pantaloons."

"I daresay I already have." He grinned up at her. "Miss Hera Tyhee Bythesea, will you do me a great honor, and allow me to be your husband, a father to Annis and, of course, any and all of your future children?"

"On approval of Miss Annis, I will *gladly* consent to be your wife."

She squealed as he pulled her off the bench and they both tumbled in a tangle onto the floor. "Pending the approval of Miss Annis, of course, when do you wish to wed?"

She frowned. "I'm not even sure what parish should post the banns!"

"Silly things, banns." He reached into his pocket and pulled out a sheet of paper.

"Godric! You bought a special license?"

"Yes."

"And if I had refused?"

"My purchase would have gone to waste—and the poor Archbishop of Canterbury, or his secretary, would have researched for naught."

Now, she was certain he'd wanted to marry her all along. "I might cry."

"I seem to have left my handkerchief behind. You may use my shirt if you wish. It's already been hopelessly creased."

"I rather like you disheveled."

"Then I shall do my best to be so more often." He frowned. "I'm sorry, however. This isn't the most romantic of proposals."

"Oh yes," she sniffed. "Yes, it is."

The carriage slowed. "Oh dear! Do I look affright, too?"

"You, as always are a picture of perfection..."

"Lies." She shook her head.

"And all I wish to be is presentable enough to meet your daughter."

She ran her fingers through his hair. "*There*. Now, you are presentable enough to meet *our* daughter."

Together, they climbed the stairs and then entered her apartment. She told him to wait while she collected Annis.

She thanked the other mother and, with a happy sigh, cuddled her baby close.

In the corridor, she pressed her face to the little blond head of curls. Annis smelled of soap and baby and the freshness of new life. "I've someone I'd like you to meet, my love. Do you think you'd like to meet him, too?"

Annis simply blinked.

When they entered, he was standing at the mantle, hands clasped behind his back. His gaze softened. Hera beckoned him to come forward and he approached cautiously.

"Hello, little one," he cooed.

Annis glanced at the duke, then to Hera and back again.

She clutched a strand of her mother's hair tightly in her little fist.

"Gentle," he said softly. "That's one of my favorite things about your mother, too."

Annis replied in unintelligible babble.

His brow wrinkled. "Is that so?"

Happier, more insistent babble followed.

"Well! I hadn't considered that particular perspective."

Annis hiccupped.

"Indeed?" he replied. "If you think so, then I must agree. I promise to think through things more clearly next time."

He held out his hand. After a moment, Annis transferred her grip from Hera's hair to his finger.

"I thought as much!" He winked at Hera. "I'm irresistible, you know." He turned his attention back to the child. "May I hold you, Miss Annis?"

Annis swung toward him and then she reached out to him as if she'd known him all her life. Something in Hera grew whole that hadn't been whole before.

"Well Miss Annis..." Which wasn't entirely correct. "What say you? Do I have permission to wed your mama?"

Annis reached up and grabbed a fistful of his hair. Then, she yelped.

"I think we can take that as a yes," Hera replied.

"Then, it's settled."

The baby gurgled and rested her head on his shoulder as he placed a light kiss on her mother's brow.

* * *

Not long thereafter, the Chancery Court approved Hurtheven's guardianship of one Miss Annis Montrose.

On that same, bright summer morning the Duke of Hurtheven wed his duchess in the hall of his friend Ashbey's London townhome. The wedding was presided over by a slightly scandalized vicar—who internally vowed never to admit to *anyone* that the bride and groom had not, in his opinion, dressed for the solemnity of the occasion.

The groom's cravat looked as if the fine silk had been piteously and mercilessly crushed by some sort of rabid creature. The bride's bonnet, while fetching, had what appeared to have teeth marks on the rim. To top things off, for reasons he did not inquire, the groom insisted on holding a young, very vocal child throughout the ceremony, a child whom he had introduced simply as Miss Annis.

But who was he to argue?

The vicar would always hold the distinction of having conducted a wedding with *three* dukes present, two duchesses and a duchess-to-be, one handsome heir on the verge of manhood, another heir with young eyes full of mischief, and one little lady who ordered everyone about and refused to answer to any honorific but the rather undignified *Fee.*

When the ceremony concluded, the vicar gratefully took his leave, blessing the sweet, sweet sound of silence once happily ensconced in his own home.

Meanwhile, the remaining guests made merry.

"Now that you are my aunt," Delmare told the bride, "I have decided to forgive you for leaving us to Mrs. Chatten."

"That is very gracious of you," Hera replied. "I appreciate your condescension."

"And since you no longer need a brother now that you have a husband..."

"I should think not!" interjected Hurtheven.

"...I shall settle"—Delmare sent his Uncle Heven a scowl—"for being your nephew."

"And," Felicia announced, "we don't have to *pretend* the two of you are wed because you really, truly are!"

"Really, truly," Hera repeated, with a warm gaze for her husband.

"No need to pretend at all." Hurtheven slipped his arm around Hera's waist. "We are a family."

"We are all," Penelope added, "a family."

Annis punctuated this observation with a gurgle and a drool.

"Ugh." Delmare wrinkled his nose. "Babies are dis-*gust*-ting."

"Are not!" Fee said, with great offense.

Annis appeared to agree. She squealed and bared her single tooth at Delmare.

"Coo," Fee addressed the baby. "I just had my birthday, you know. You *do* give the best presents, Uncle Heven. My favorite present of all is my new aunt...and cousin." She held out her arms to Annis. "Let's go play with my dollies."

Annis approved of this plan with a sharp yelp and a hearty clap.

Hurtheven knelt and gently passed the child to Felicia. Despite being only three feet tall, Fee happily carried the child from the room, with promises of delights to follow.

"Well, Del," Thaddeus said, "We single men must stick together—else we'll find ourselves leg shackled, too."

"Leg-shackled?" Delmare harrumphed. "Is that how one refers to the looks you share with Lady—"

Thaddeus threw his arm around Delmare's shoulder and covered his mouth.

Delmare pulled back Thaddeus's hand. "I was just joking. I know the rules—friends close, secrets closer."

Hurtheven cleared his throat. "I've recently amended my rules. With the right friends, you needn't have secrets at all."

"Bah," Delmare replied.

"How about your adage?" Ash said. "About trouble always coming down to a woman?"

"Hurtheven!" Hera exclaimed.

"Still true." He winked at his wife. "All the trouble, and most of the solutions as well."

Thaddeus groaned. "I think it's time we leave these children to themselves, hey, Del?"

"They've been *such* a disappointment of late," Del murmured as they headed out into the garden.

As Alicia embraced Hera, Pen embraced Hurtheven.

"Ask me again if I'm happy," he said to Penelope.

"*Are* you happy?" she asked with a smile.

"More than I thought possible."

"Brings a tear to the eye, that does." Chev mockingly wiped his face.

Pen released Hurtheven and then took Hera by the hand. "Welcome, Hera! You've finally made our numbers even. And, do you know what? I have just had the most marvelous idea! A secret society. A sisterhood..."

Chev groaned. "*Now* see what you've done?"

"I see..." Hurtheven paused. "I see I've made us complete."

He'd made *himself* complete.

"I *said* you had a soft heart under all that bluster," Alicia crowed triumphantly.

Ash held a hand to his ear. "What was that?"

"She is right," Hurtheven replied with a jaunty lift of his chin. "In fact, I've the softest heart of us all."

"And," Ash added wryly, "the humblest?"

"Rogue," Hurtheven retorted.

Ashbey grinned. "Coxcomb."

"He does have the softest heart," Hera defended, looking up at him. "And I can hardly believe he's now *my* duke...not just for a few stolen hours, but every day, until the end of our days."

THE END

Author's Note

First, a request & a few recommendations:

If this book touched you, please consider recommending it to a friend or posting about it on your preferred social media platform. I've found my favorite books by recommendation.

Off the top of my head, some recommendations by writer friends & acquaintances I've received & adored over the years: from Megan Frampton, Loretta Chase's *Lord of Scoundrels* and PB Ryan's four Nell Sweeney Mysteries; from Gaelen Foley, Laura Kinsale's *Flowers from the Storm*; from Jess Russell, Fiona Davis's *The Address*; from Amanda McCabe, Kate Saunders's *Secrets of Wishtide*. In turn, I'd recommend Megan's *Duke's Guide to Correct Behavior*, Gaelen's *Lord of Fire* & *Lord of Ice*, Jess's *Mad for the Marquess*, and Amanda's *One Naughty Night*. Really, anything by all the authors above.

Two other romances I remember highly recommending are Carolyn Jewel's *Scandal* (deeply emotional with an innovative then-and-now structure) and Eileen Dreyer's *Never a Gentleman* (which made me cry in public on a plane!).

The above list is by no means exhaustive—they are only the books and recommendations that came to my mind first.

Next...about *all* those dukes.

"Are you still writing Regencies? You know there were only a handful of non-royal dukes and none who were attractive and single during the Regency, don't you?"

An acquaintance posed those questions to me just as I was about to release *His Duchess at Eventide*.

My answer? Yes, I knew this.

Yes, I am aware a series with three, handsome, dukes who flout societal conventions and aren't afraid to express their affection to one another or to their wives, is historically improbable. I hope, however, readers have found the characters in the series *emotionally* realistic. I do my best to portray historically accurate settings and use historically accurate language.

Historical romance is my favorite jam. Give me an arrogant protagonist who has everything in the world they could possibly need and then let me cheer as their counterpart brings them to their KNEES armed only with the power of love.

I believe in the power of love. I've experienced the power of love. And I want jam. I want *everyone* to be able to enjoy *multiple* flavors of jam, especially their favorite.

So, yes, I am still writing Regencies...and I will continue to write Regencies, even as I explore stories in other time periods and genres.

I hope I've done justice to Hurtheven's story, though finishing this series took me far longer than I expected. The process taught me that I cannot permanently give up writing any more than I can voluntarily give up breathing. The process of writing is how I learn, grow, and find meaning. The reader and writer communities are my lifeline.

And one more historical note

Founded in 1739, the stated purpose and mission of The Foundling Hospital (formally the Hospital for the Maintenance and Education of Exposed and Deserted Young Children) underwent a change in the early 1800s as public sentiment concerning unwed mothers shifted. Even before that time, not every foundling was accepted—the mother's circumstances mattered. I was able to find a few cases of mothers who were able to reclaim their children after having given them up, and those mothers had to both prove they had reformed as well as be able pay any expenses the hospital incurred while their child was under the hospital's care. *'Unfortunate Objects': Lone Mothers in Eighteenth-Century London* by Tanya Evans was an invaluable reference.

Lastly...

A special thank you to my critique partners, authors Bliss Bennett, Jess Russell, and Gail Eastwood. To developmental editor extraordinaire, Lindsey Faber. To Inara Scott for her mad BCC skills. To Leeyanne Moore for being the world's best accountability partner. To Addison Fox (and Jess again) for the regular, cathartic, writerly & rollicking girls nights in. And to talented author Louisa Cornell for both Copy Edits and for giving a Regency Fiction Writer's (Then the Beau Monde) presentation that included a slide from 1816 depicting the lion that had escaped from a traveling menagerie attacking the night mail service from London to Exeter. Louisa's presentation was the very first spark of Hurtheven's story, and accounts of that event informed the scenes that appear in this book. To Terry, Becca and Susan at Write Better Faster, for excellent advice. To PJ for her FB comment that said she hadn't forgotten about Hurtheven. To Debbie, Alison, Dee, and Dwight, for support when I was faltering. To all my sisters and nieces and nephews—we may be far-flung, but I couldn't feel closer to you all, and I depend on our Sunday messenger meet ups. To Richard Pearson for going through my entire catalog last year and demanding more, making me think it might be time to try again—I can't tell you what that meant to me. To Richard LaCapra, for listening and making suggestions as I hashed out the plot for the 100th time on our road trip last summer and for, of course, being my real-life hero.

And to you for purchasing & reading this book.

Until next time, sending my love & gratitude.

Wendy La Capra

Books by Wendy LaCapra

Available Now

Excerpts available for all books on Wendy's Website

The Mythic Duke Series

Her Duke at Daybreak

His Duchess at Eventide

Her Duke at Midnight

The Lords of Chance Series

Scandal in Spades

Heart's Desire

Diamond in the Rogue

Free Novella Connected to Lords of Chance – Mrs. Sartin's Secretary

The Furies Series

Lady Vice

Lady Scandal

Duchess Decadence

About Wendy

Historical Romance author Wendy LaCapra writes award-winning books reviewers describe as 'heart-pounding, entrancing', 'lusciously romantic and sparkling with wit.' As a teen, Wendy discovered spine-tingling gothics in her local public library, inspiring her to craft her own seductive tales full of secrets and scandal. She lives with her husband in a quirky, historic building in NYC and loves a girls' night in. For new release, sale alerts and other news, sign up at http://bit.ly/GetWendyNews

https://www.wendylacapra.com

facebook.com/WendyLaCapraAuthor

instagram.com/wendylacapra

goodreads.com/WendyLaCapra

bookbub.com/authors/wendy-lacapra

amazon.com/author/wendylacapra